Swift

R J ANDERSON

ORCHARD

ORCHARD BOOKS
338 Euston Road, London NW1 3BH
Orchard Books Australia
Level 17/207 Kent Street, Sydney, NSW 2000

First published in the UK in 2012 by Orchard Books

ISBN 978 1 40831 263 6

Text © R J Anderson 2012

A CIP catalogue record for this book is available from the British Library.

3 5 7 9 10 8 6 4 2

Printed in Great Britain

Orchard Books is a division of Hachette Children's Books,
an Hachette UK company.

www.hachette.co.uk

In memory of my grandmother,
Ivy-Mae Menadue Michell,
whose legacy of love and saffron cake
still endures

prologue

'You could always make it *look* as though you had wings,' said Jenny, her voice echoing off the granite walls of the treasure cavern. 'A little glamour, just for tonight—'

Ivy let the delicate wing-chain slide through her fingers, spilling it back into the chest. 'I'm not that good with illusions. Cicely can cast better glamours than me, and she's five years old.' She shut the lid with a snap. 'Anyway, why bother? I'm not going to fool anyone.'

Jenny looked pained, but did not argue. Already she was growing into a beauty, with the sturdy bones and warm complexion that all piskeys admired. Her wings were no less striking, all grey-white ripples above and a blush of pink beneath. She didn't need jewellery to make herself look fine.

Ivy, on the other hand, had inherited her mother's pale skin and small, spindly frame. No matter what she wore, Jenny would always outshine her. But Ivy didn't care about that. She wouldn't mind if she were ugly as a spriggan, if only she'd been born with wings like Jenny's.

Or indeed, any wings at all.

Suppressing her envy, Ivy blew the dust off another chest and heaved up the lid. 'What are these? Pipes?' But no, they were too shiny for that. Unusually large armbands, perhaps.

'That's armour,' said Jenny in hushed tones. 'It must be a hundred years old.'

Ivy had heard of the ancient battles between the piskeys and their enemies, but she'd never seen armour before. Daring, she slid her arm into one of the guards and held it up to the light. But of course it looked silly on her; it had been meant for a warrior, not a skinny girl-child. She dropped it back into the chest.

'Girls, it's almost time.' The soft voice came from Marigold, Ivy's mother. There were shadows beneath her eyes, and the wan glow of her skin barely lit the archway in which she stood. She'd been working too hard again, no doubt, helping the other women prepare for the feast to come. 'You'll have to hurry.'

'I'm done,' said Jenny, touching the topaz pendant at her throat. 'I was just helping Ivy a bit.' She nudged the younger girl affectionately. 'I'll see you later.'

Marigold stepped aside to let Jenny pass, then moved to Ivy. 'What's the matter?' she asked. 'I thought you'd like to pick out something special to wear to your first Lighting. Do you want me to help?'

Her mother meant well, Ivy knew. But her tastes ran to the pink and glittery, and that wouldn't suit Ivy at all. 'No, it's all right,' she said. 'I'll find something next time.'

She expected Marigold to lead the way out, but instead her mother lingered, fingering Ivy's black curls. 'You've grown so much these past few months,' she murmured. 'My little woman. Are you frightened, to go above?'

'Not really,' said Ivy, truthfully. She had made Jenny tell her everything she could remember about her first two Lightings, so she would know what to expect and no one could trick or scare her. It was her only defence against her brother Mica and the other piskey-boys, who would be trying all night to catch her in their pranks.

'Not afraid of anything?' asked her mother. 'Not even the—' Her voice caught. 'The spriggans?'

No wonder people said Ivy's mother was flighty. She was always worrying these days, even when there was nothing to fear. 'They won't come,' said Ivy. 'Not with Aunt Betony there to protect us.' Betony, her father's sister, had recently been crowned as the new Joan the Wad – the most powerful, important piskey in the Delve. It was her task to surround the Lighting with the same wards and glamours she used to protect the mine from intruders, and Betony never did anything carelessly.

Ivy picked up the trailing end of Marigold's flowered shawl and draped it back over her shoulder. 'We can go now,' she said. 'I'm ready.'

As Ivy followed her mother through the tunnels towards the surface, she was glad for the lights of her fellow piskeys heading in the same direction. Not that she was afraid of losing her way even in the dark, for Ivy knew most of the Delve's twists and turnings by now. But the tunnels were magnificent, and it would have been a shame not to see them.

Every passage carved by the piskey miners – or knockers – was unique, from the polished granite of Long Way where Ivy's family lived, to the delicate mosaics of plants and animals on the walls of Upper Rise, where she and the other children sat for lessons. But Ivy's favourite tunnel was the one they were walking through now, lined with tiles of deep blue china clay. Her father had told her once that it was the colour of the sky, and when no one was watching her, Ivy would run through it with her arms outstretched and pretend that she was flying.

Which was what Jenny and the other girls would soon be doing – spreading their wings and launching themselves up the crude but useful shaft that the humans had dug out long ago, before the mine was abandoned and the piskeys moved in. The Great Shaft was the quickest route out of the mine, and if it weren't for Ivy, Marigold would surely have flown to the Lighting that way herself. But now the two of them could only plod through the tunnels to the surface, like the men.

Humiliation curdled in Ivy's stomach. What crime had she or her parents committed, that she'd been born wingless? Her magic might not be as strong as some piskeys', but it was good enough: she could make herself tall as a human or tiny as a mole, even turn herself invisible if she didn't mind a bit of a headache afterwards. But something had gone wrong with Ivy's making while she was still unborn, and she'd come out with nothing but a pair of bony nubs between her shoulders where her wings should be. And neither Yarrow's healing potions nor the Joan's most powerful spells, it seemed, could change that.

Though not long ago, Ivy's mother had said something about her own wings not being right when she was young… or had that been a dream? Ivy had been struggling all day to remember, but every time she tried her head began to swim.

Perhaps she was just tired. After all, she'd been looking forward to the Lighting so much, she'd hardly slept last night.

'We're almost there,' whispered Marigold, taking Ivy's hand. After the twisting bends of the Narrows and a climb up the Hunter's Stair, they had reached the Earthenbore, a tunnel of packed clay baked to hardness by the power of the Joan herself. Ivy had never been this close to the surface before, and her pulse quickened as she followed the other piskeys into the passage.

At the first junction they turned right and began to climb again, the tunnel narrowing and the floor rising steeply as they neared the exit. The air smelled earthy, sweet with heather and bracken and the scent of blossoming gorse – plants that until now Ivy had only ever seen cut and tied in bundles. What would it be like to walk among them, to see them living and growing all around her? It was hard to imagine, but in a moment she wouldn't have to. She would know.

'Look at her big eyes,' snickered one of the younger piskey-boys, nudging his companion, and Ivy stiffened. Just like Keeve to tease her at a time like this. He'd be calling her *Creeping Ivy* next.

'Ivy's always got big eyes,' said the taller boy, elbowing him back. 'Shut your mouth.' He glanced at Ivy and gave her a shy half-smile before ducking out the archway into the night.

And that was just like Mattock, always looking out for the younger ones. She thought of her little sister Cicely, tucked into her bed with a sleeping-spell that would keep her there until morning. Last year Ivy had been just as oblivious to the celebrations taking place above her head, but it was her time now. She would not cling to her mother, like a baby; she would step out boldly, as the others were doing. Ivy pulled her hand free of Marigold's, plunged forward…

And with a crackle of undergrowth and a last wild thump of her heart, Ivy was outside.

As she stepped out onto the surface of the world, the

scrubby grass crunched beneath her feet, and a dry rustling filled her ears as the breeze – the first she had ever felt – stirred the gorse and bracken that surrounded the tunnel entrance. Underground the air was still, but here it danced around her, teasing and tugging her from every side. She turned a slow circle, trying to accustom herself to the strangeness of it, as her hair tangled about her face and her skirts swirled against her knees. Then she looked up – and her mouth dropped open in awe.

Jenny had tried to describe the sky to her, and she'd heard the droll-teller mention it in his stories. But what words could capture the grandeur of a roof that stretched out forever, too high for even the mightiest giant of legend to touch? It should have terrified Ivy to stand beneath that vast purple darkness, with the innumerable stars burning white-hot above her and the moon like a crucible of molten silver. But it only made her feel quiet and very, very small.

Then there was the landscape, just visible beyond the patches of waving bracken and bristling tufts of gorse that walled her in. It had no walls to contain it, only a few tangled hedges interspersed with the occasional tree. And those white, square shapes away to her right…could they be human dwellings? Even at piskey size – about the height of a grown human's knee, or so the droll-teller claimed – Ivy could have walked to one of those houses.

'Come,' said Marigold, taking Ivy's arm as the piskey

men led the way up the slope. 'We mustn't keep the others waiting.'

The old Engine House stood at the top of the ridge, its broken chimney jutting into the sky. Even after a century of neglect its walls held strong, but their tops ended in nothing but air; the roof had crumbled away long ago. Two of its windows still gaped like empty sockets, but the others were long smothered in a mass of the same plant that had given Ivy her name. From a distance the ruined mine building looked desolate, even haunted.

But that was an illusion, meant to keep intruders away. In reality the place was anything but neglected, for the piskeys of the Delve had been using it as their feasting and dancing ground for decades. They'd piled rocks and soil beneath the lone doorway to make it easy for their people to climb in and out, and smoothed out the precipitous drop in the floor. Now the Engine House was filled with light and festivity, as the piskeys of the Delve bustled about setting up chairs and laying the tables. On the far side of the dancing green her father Flint was tuning his fiddle, while Mica and the other piskey-boys played a game of chase-the-spriggan around the pile of wood that would soon become their wakefire.

'I'm going to talk to Nettle,' said Marigold, drawing her shawl closer around her shoulders. 'Jenny's over there; why don't you go and see her?'

'I will in a minute,' said Ivy, surprised. Lately Marigold

had been staying close to Ivy whenever there was a crowd, in case she felt sick or needed anything. But perhaps her mother had finally understood what Ivy had been telling her for months – that she could manage perfectly well on her own, and there was no need to fuss over her.

She watched her mother make her way to the bench along the far wall where most of the older piskeys were sitting, chatting comfortably to one another. What would Marigold want with Nettle? The old woman had attended the previous Joan and managed to outlive her, and since then she'd been serving Betony as well. But other than that, Ivy knew little about her.

'Boo!' yelled a voice, and Ivy let out a shriek as Keeve leaped in front of her. 'Got you!' he said, grinning.

Disgusted, Ivy pushed him away and headed towards Jenny. But Keeve affected a wounded expression and fell into step beside her.

'I just wanted you to notice me, that's all,' he said. 'Pretty Ivy, won't you dance with me tonight?'

Ivy faltered. The wicked glint in Keeve's eye had vanished, and his expression was earnest as she'd ever seen it. 'Do you…you don't really mean that, do you?' she asked.

Keeve chortled. 'Got you again!' he said, and scampered off.

Ivy ground her teeth. Most piskeys loved pranking, especially the younger ones – and especially on nights like this, when the one who played the most successful pranks would win a prize. But she'd never liked being tricked, or trying to trick others either, and she wished her fellow piskeys would leave her out of it.

'There you are,' said Mica, jogging up to her. He was growing broad and strong like their father, his black hair thick over his forehead and his eyes dark as cassiterite. 'Did you see the giant?' He pulled Ivy over to the doorway and pointed into the distance, where a pair of baleful lights swept the landscape. 'See his eyes glowing? He's looking for piskeys to eat…'

This time, Ivy was prepared. 'Oh, no!' she exclaimed. 'And let me guess – those flashing lights I just saw overhead? They must be wicked faeries spying on us!'

Mica scowled. 'Jenny told you.'

'Well,' said Ivy, 'it's not my fault you play the same trick every year.'

Her older brother sighed. 'Fair enough. You know what those lights are, then?'

'Human things,' she replied. Not that she'd ever seen a *car* or an *aeroplane*, or had any clear idea how they worked. But everyone knew that there was nothing to fear from the Big People; most of them didn't even believe in piskeys any more.

'Keeve and I have a bet on,' said Mica. 'He says as soon as he becomes a hunter, he's going to disguise himself as a human and get a ride in one of those cars. I told him they'll never stop for him, but he thinks all he has to do is—'

'All gather for the Lighting!' bellowed a voice, and the rest of the conversation was forgotten as Ivy and Mica hurried to find a seat. Mica wriggled his way in between Keeve and Mattock, while Jenny patted the bench beside her and leaned closer as Ivy sat down.

'Wait until you see this,' she whispered, nodding at the far side of the circle where the Joan stood with her consort by her side. 'I can't believe she's your *aunt*.'

Betony was a strongly built woman with hair as black as Ivy's, though longer and not so curly, and their kinship was evident in the angles of her cheekbones, her pointed chin. With grave dignity she extended her arms over the woodpile…

And flames exploded from her hands.

Ivy jerked back, nearly upsetting the bench in her shock. She'd known that the Joan would light the wakefire, but she'd never expected her to do it like this. Jenny patted her shoulder, reassuring, while Betony lowered her blazing palms to touch the kindling. The twigs glowed bright as molten copper, and soon the whole heap of wood was alight.

'All hail!' shouted the piskeys together. 'Hail Joan the Wad!'

Wad was the old Cornish word for *torch*, and until now Ivy had thought it just a ceremonial title. But no, her aunt could literally conjure fire from the air. How had Betony learned to wield such amazing power? 'You never told me,' she said, turning reproachful eyes to Jenny.

'Of course not,' replied the older girl, smiling. 'Surely you didn't want me to ruin *all* the surprises for you?'

Around them, the other piskeys were getting up and moving closer to the fire – not for warmth, but for light. This was their opportunity to replenish the natural luminescence of their bodies, which would serve them better than any lamp in the dark tunnels underground. As Ivy stood to join them a tingle ran over her skin, and her lips curved in a proud smile. Now she too would glow when she returned to the Delve, and she could go anywhere she wanted.

Where was her mother? She should be here, sharing this special moment. On the other side of the wakefire, her father Flint nodded and returned Ivy's smile – but Marigold was nowhere to be seen. Was she still talking to Nettle? No, Nettle was with the Joan, pouring piskey-wine into a bowl for the next part of the ceremony.

Probably Ivy's mother had just forgotten something underground, and gone to fetch it. Or maybe she just wanted to make sure Cicely was safely asleep. After all, she'd seen the Lighting many times before, and the fire would burn all night. Telling herself it was childish to feel hurt about it, Ivy returned to her seat.

The rest of the evening passed in a blur, one magical moment dissolving into another. Ivy ate and drank and laughed with Jenny and the others, watched the dancers whirl and leap to the music of her father's fiddle, and basked in the light of the wakefire until her skin could hold no more. Finally, tired and happy, she tumbled down by the old droll-teller's feet with the other children, and lay half-drowsing while he told stories.

As usual, all the tales revolved around a single theme: how clever piskeys of the past had outwitted their enemies. The first story was about a foolish human miner who tried to trick the knockers out of their treasure and ended up with nothing but a sore knee – all the children laughed at that. Then came the tale of a faery who met a wandering piskey-lad and tried to allure him into marrying her, a dark and sinister tale that made Ivy hold her breath. But fortunately, the boy saw past the faery's pretty face to her cold heart and escaped.

'Yet wickedest and most deadly of all,' said the droll-teller, bending close to his audience as though telling them a secret, 'are the spriggans.'

The younger children squirmed and cast uneasy glances at the doorway as the droll-teller went on, 'Like us, spriggans can change their size at will, and they love to play magical tricks. But they're the ugliest, skinniest, most maggoty-pale creatures you can imagine, and all their pranks are cruel.'

It wasn't the first time Ivy had heard about spriggans, but still the description made her shudder. She could picture them lurking in the darkness all around the Engine House, rag-wrapped monsters with glittering eyes and long bony fingers, waiting for the first careless piskey to pass by. And not only to frighten them, either. Her father had told her that spriggans were hungry all the time and would eat anything – or any*one* – they could catch.

'Spriggans love treasure,' the droll-teller continued, 'but they're too lazy to dig for it. So in the old days when we piskeys lived in villages on the surface, the spriggans would wait until the knockers went off to work in the mine – and then they'd attack.' His voice dropped to a dramatic whisper. 'They'd kill the guards and the old uncles and even the youngest boy-children, and cast a spell over all the women that would make them think the spriggans were their own menfolk. Then they'd settle in to feast and gloat over their treasure.'

Ivy's nose wrinkled in revulsion. It was horrible to think of being caught and eaten, but to be tricked into living with a spriggan as your husband was even worse. She was wondering how such a dreadful tale could end happily when Mattock spoke up from the back of the crowd:

'But then the knockers would come home and find the spriggans there. Wouldn't they?'

'They would, indeed,' said the droll-teller. 'Tired as they were, they'd pick up their hammers and their thunder-axes and fight. Sometimes they lost the battle, though more often they won, because a good knocker is braver and stronger than three spriggans put together. But even once all the spriggans had been killed, their evil spells were so strong that the knockers' wives and daughters didn't recognise their own menfolk any more. Instead they'd weep and wail over the ugly spriggans – and they'd accuse the knockers of being spriggans instead!'

The girl beside Ivy whimpered and buried her face in her hands. Ivy didn't feel like crying, but she did feel a little queasy. She was glad when Mattock raised his voice again: 'But the spell would wear off in a few days, isn't that right?'

By then the droll-teller seemed to realise he'd gone too far. He patted the weeping child and said, 'Yes, surely it would. No magic lasts forever, after all. But it wasn't long before some of the piskeys decided they'd had enough, and that it was time to make a new home for themselves deep in the rock and earth, where their enemies were too cowardly to follow. And that's how the Delve came to be.'

He smiled and sat back, as though this was the happy ending. But Ivy wasn't satisfied yet. 'What about the other piskeys?' she asked. 'The ones who didn't go to the Delve?'

'The spriggans went on attacking them,' said the droll-teller, 'just as before. But now those other piskeys only won the battle sometimes, and before long they hardly won at all. They were too proud to ask the folk in the Delve for help, you see. So they fought alone, and most of them died. But once our people heard of a piskey village coming to grief, we sent our bravest fighters to rescue the women and children and offer them a safe home with us. So the Delve grew and the other clans of piskeys became smaller, until we were the only piskeys left.'

On the far side of the circle Mica sat up eagerly, as though he could hardly wait to become a hunter and fight spriggans. Mattock looked solemn and a little troubled. Keeve, meanwhile, appeared to have fallen asleep – but that was no great surprise, since the droll-teller was his grandfather and he must have heard all these tales a hundred times.

The droll-teller launched into another tale, but by now Ivy was too tired to enjoy it. She searched the crowd for her mother, but there was no sign of her. And now her father had gone missing as well, for his chair was empty and his fiddle propped idle against the wall.

'Mica,' she whispered, leaning across to her brother. 'I'm going back to the cavern.'

'What for? It's not nearly daybreak yet.'

'I want to make sure Cicely's all right.' And their mother too, though Ivy didn't say it. Surely something unusual must have happened, to keep Marigold away from the Lighting so long.

'Well, you can't go now,' said Mica. 'Not by yourself. You'll just have to wait for the rest of us.'

Much as it galled Ivy, he was right. The closest entrance to the Earthenbore was well down the slope, too far for any woman or child to go alone. And it was no use asking Mica or Mattock to go with her; they hadn't even got their hunter's knives yet, let alone learned to use them. Sighing, Ivy leaned her elbow on a jutting stone and dropped her head against it. She was slipping into a doze when a cry from the other side of the Engine House shocked her awake. Was that her *father* shouting?

Mica was on his feet and running, pushing through the crowd. The music had stopped and all the dancers stood frozen, staring at the doorway. There stood Flint, his hair dishevelled and his face a mask of anguish, cradling a bundle of fabric against his chest. He stumbled forward and dropped to his knees.

Ivy scrambled over the green and flung herself down beside him. 'Dad, what is it? What's wrong?' Then she saw the cloth that her father was holding. It was, unmistakably, her mother's shawl – but now the pink roses were splotched with ugly gouts of red, and one corner was in tatters.

'Stand back,' commanded Betony, and the crowd parted to let the Joan through. She swept Ivy and Mica aside and stooped over her brother. Then she straightened, her expression grim.

'The Lighting is over,' she said. 'Everyone into the Delve. Now.'

At once the piskeys scattered, abandoning half-finished plates and cups of wine, gaming boards, musical instruments, and even shoes and jackets in their haste. Shouts of 'Hurry!' and 'Watch out!' rang through the night, as the knockers snatched up their thunder-axes and the hunters drew their knives. Mica grabbed Ivy's arm and hauled her towards the doorway, but she struggled against his hold, crying, 'Dad!'

'Don't be stupid,' snapped Mica, giving her a shove. 'The Joan will look after him. Move!'

Ivy stumbled out onto the hillside, tears burning her eyes. 'Mum,' she sobbed, but there was no answer – and though her gorge rose at the thought, she knew why.

Her mother had been taken by the spriggans.

one

Five years later

Ivy stood poised on her toes like a dancer, but there was no merriment in her face as she pulled the iron poker from its slot by the hearth and raised it high. A few paces away, a black adder twice her length squirmed across the cavern floor, blood oozing from the gash on the back of its head that should have killed it – but unfortunately, hadn't.

Why hadn't Mica cut the snake's head off before he brought it down from the surface? He'd been hunting for four years now; he should have known better than to *assume* the adder was dead. But he'd been in such a hurry to get to tonight's Lighting, he'd merely stuffed his catch into a bag, tossed it through the cavern door and left. And worse, he hadn't even tied the sack properly, so now Ivy had to finish off the snake herself.

There was no use shouting for help. Not that her

neighbours wouldn't be willing – they'd always been glad to lend a hand whenever Ivy could swallow her pride long enough to ask for it. But by now even the last stragglers had left their caverns and were hurrying towards the surface. In fact, if this wretched snake hadn't poked its head out as Ivy was getting dressed, she and Cicely would be running right along with them.

'Oh, Ivy, hurry!' Her little sister crouched at the edge of her bed-alcove, only her head poking between the curtains. 'We're already late!'

'Stay where you are, Cicely,' warned Ivy, edging closer to the snake. 'I'll be done in a minute.'

Mind calm and hands steady, that was the way. She mustn't think about what would happen if the snake bit her; she just had to strike as quickly as she could. The wedge-shaped head turned towards her, tongue flickering out to taste the air—

And with one savage two-handed blow, Ivy smashed the poker down.

The adder's body whipped into a frenzy, tail lashing around so fast it nearly knocked Ivy off her feet. She leaped backwards, holding the poker ready for another strike. But gradually its convulsions subsided, and Ivy let out her breath. The snake was dead.

'You can come out now,' she said to Cicely, dropping the poker with a clang onto the polished granite. The floor was a mess and the adder meat would spoil if she left it sitting, but there was no time to fret about that now. 'Let me finish getting dressed, and we'll go.'

'It's no use,' moaned Cicely, knuckling her eyes. 'We'll never get through all those tunnels in time.'

'We're not going through the tunnels,' Ivy said, pulling up her breeches. The dress she'd been working on for months still lay across the foot of her bed, but she could hardly climb in that. 'I know a faster way. Come on.'

'*Please* hurry!' Cicely hovered next to Ivy, her dappled wings fluttering with agitation. 'They'll be lighting the wakefire any minute, and Jenny says it's the best part!'

Ivy dug her fingers into the next handhold, hauling herself up the side of the Great Shaft with stubborn will. She didn't pause to explain that she was already climbing as fast as she could; excuses were for the lazy, or so Aunt Betony always said.

Though if it hadn't been for Mica's carelessness, she'd have got Cicely to her first Lighting in plenty of time and found her a good seat into the bargain... But if dwelling on what *should* have happened made any difference, Ivy would have sprouted wings long ago. She set her jaw and kept climbing.

'Oh, it's not fair,' wailed Cicely, as sounds of music and laughter drifted down from above. 'Ivy, let me go ahead, I don't need a light, there's plenty of room—'

'You can't fly the Shaft blind,' said Ivy firmly. True, compared to the piskeys' own neat tunnels the Great Shaft was enormous. But there was a cap of concrete and metal over the top, and if Cicely didn't see it coming she'd knock herself senseless. 'When you've got your own glow, you can go ahead if you want. But right now, you stay with me.'

Cicely whimpered, but made no further protest. Ivy reached for a grip and pulled herself up again, her muscles trembling with the effort. By rights she shouldn't be climbing the Great Shaft at all, and if anyone found out she'd be in serious trouble. It would have been safer to go through the tunnels – but that would have taken twice as long, even if she and Cicely were running. And besides, it gave Ivy a private thrill to know that she alone, of all the piskeys in the Delve, *could* climb like this.

At last her groping fingers brushed wood, slimy and rough with age. She had reached the old ladder. Ivy hooked one arm over the bottom rung and gazed up at the half-rotted wood and rusted metal before her, chewing her lip in consideration. Once this ladder had carried human miners down the shaft to their day's work. Then the tin mine had closed, and its shafts were caged off to keep careless humans from falling in. Now and then some idle passer-by shoved a stick or a stone between the bars and let it drop, but apart from that no one had touched this ladder in well over a century. She'd have to make herself human size to climb it, but would it hold her weight?

Well, she'd soon find out. Ivy took a deep breath and willed herself to grow.

It would have been easier if she'd practised first. The shift in size threw her off balance, and she grabbed the next rung just in time. But she had no time to waste on panic. The moment her body stopped tingling she was on the move, scrambling for the top of the shaft. 'We're nearly there,' she gasped to Cicely. 'It's not too—'

'All hail Joan the Wad!' came a muffled shout from above them, and the top of the shaft flared with golden light. Cicely's face crumpled. 'We missed it.'

Guilt and frustration tumbled like rocks in Ivy's stomach. She'd done her best, but it hadn't been good enough. There'd be another Lighting at midwinter, but what consolation was that to Cicely now? And as usual Mica was to blame but he'd never admit it, and Cicely would never dream of reproaching him. Not the older brother who brought her berries and bits of honeycomb, and gave her piskey-back rides around the cavern. In Cicely's eyes, Mica could do no wrong.

'Well,' said Ivy, and then she couldn't think of anything else to say. She reached for the next rung, and continued climbing towards the surface.

'People of the Delve, be welcome,' Betony declared, with a disapproving glance at Ivy and Cicely as they crept to a seat at the back of the crowd. She took the copper bowl from Nettle's hands and raised it high, so that everyone around the wakefire could see it.

'This is the draught of harmony,' she declared. 'Let us drink and be one in heart, proud of our heritage and true to our ancient ways, so that enemies can never divide us. A blessing on the Delve, and a curse on faeries and spriggans!'

'A curse on the spriggans!' the others chorused – and Ivy loudest of all. The very mention of those filthy creatures made her burn inside, an old ember of rage and bitterness that would never go out. First they had taken her mother from her, and if that weren't bad enough, they had stolen her father as well.

Or at least they might as well have. After Marigold disappeared Flint had spent days blindly wandering about the countryside, until the Joan took away his hunting privileges and confined him to the Delve for his own safety. Since then he had done little but work in the mine, hammering away night and day with his thunder-axe. He seldom spoke, and never laughed; he ate the food Ivy cooked for him without seeming to taste it, and slept poorly when he slept at all. He still came to every Lighting, but only long enough to replenish his glow. And he never played his fiddle any more.

'Curse them,' Ivy whispered, but Cicely remained silent, her eyes on her lap. Guilt pricked Ivy again, and she gave her sister an apologetic squeeze before reaching for the copper bowl now making its way around the circle. The draught inside was clear as spring water, sparkling lights dancing across its surface; Ivy tipped the bowl and drank a mouthful before helping Cicely to do the same.

'Oh, it's *wonderful*,' breathed her little sister, surfacing with flushed cheeks and wide brown eyes. 'I had no idea piskey-wine was so nice. Can I—'

'Not until you're older,' said Ivy, and handed the bowl on. Cicely's lower lip jutted, but she seemed a little less gloomy as the drink passed from one piskey to another and finally made its way back to Betony, who poured the dregs hissing into the fire.

'And now,' the Joan proclaimed, 'let us eat!'

At once Ivy and Cicely jumped up, following the other piskeys towards the long tables. All Ivy's favourite dishes were here tonight – from pasties stuffed with rabbit and chopped roots, to roasted woodlice with wild garlic, right down to the thick slabs of saffron cake waiting on a platter at the far end. And to drink there was spring water and chilled mint tea, as well as several bottles of the sparkling piskey-wine – though it would be another year before Ivy was old enough to drink more than a small cup of it, and Cicely was too young to have any more at all. But that scarcely mattered with so many other good things to enjoy.

As they ate, Ivy glanced at Cicely and was relieved to see her sister's mood improving with every bite. Soon she was chattering to Jenny and giggling at the faces Keeve made at her across the table, and Ivy's own spirits began to rise as she realised she hadn't entirely spoiled her sister's first Lighting after all.

But then she glimpsed Mica strolling by with plate in hand, and her smile faded. There he was, relaxed and dressed in his Lighting best – and here Ivy sat with her breeches and her bare grimy feet. The old aunties gave her pitying looks over their shoulders, and she could practically hear what they were thinking: *What a shame young Ivy can't take proper care of herself, especially when her brother and sister look so fine. But she's always been sickly, and with no mother...*

'What's the matter?' asked Cicely around a mouthful of saffron cake. 'You look like you've eaten gravel.'

'Never mind,' said Ivy. 'It's nothing you need to worry about.'

'One-two-three-four!' called the crowder, and the musicians struck up a lively tune that twanged Ivy's muscles and tugged at her bones. As a child, she'd been too shy and short of breath to dance in public. Even when all the other children were skipping about, she'd hung back and pretended she didn't care. But Marigold had seen through her diffidence, and as soon as they got home she'd held Ivy's hands and skipped around the cavern with her until the two of them collapsed in a giggling heap on the floor.

Marigold hadn't worried so much about Ivy's health in those days; she'd told Ivy that her lungs were just a little slower to grow than the rest of her, and they'd soon come right. And she'd promised Ivy that one day she'd be able to dance just as well as any piskey in the Delve, if not better.

Well, now Ivy could. But not to this tune. This was a flying dance, where the males tossed the females high in the air and stepped to one side as their partners fluttered down, and Ivy could not have taken part even if someone had asked her. She walked over to Cicely, who was watching the dancers with the same wistful longing, and sat down by her side.

'What is it?' she asked. 'Don't you want to dance?'

'I don't have a partner,' said Cicely glumly. 'And it's already started.'

Ivy jumped up and thrust out both her hands. 'Then dance with me,' she said.

'Me and you? But you're—'

'Stronger than I look,' said Ivy, grabbing her little sister under both arms and heaving her into the air. Cicely let out a giggle, her moth-wings fluttering as she drifted back to earth – only to have Ivy whirl her around and toss her up again. Lifting her sister wasn't nearly as easy as she pretended; Cicely was on the sturdy side, and Ivy's muscles already ached from climbing up the shaft. But it was worth the effort to see those brown eyes sparkle, and hear Cicely's squeals of delight.

No sooner had the Flying Dance ended than another merry reel took its place, and Ivy and Cicely kept dancing. The two of them whirled arm in arm beside the bonfire, Cicely stumbling over her own feet with laughter, until Ivy was winded and panting.

'I'm done,' she gasped, waving a hand. 'I've got to sit down.'

'Me too,' said Cicely, collapsing beside Ivy with a happy sigh. Then she sat up again and said, 'Is that the moon? I thought it was supposed to be round.'

Well, at least she wasn't terrified. Ivy had seen more than a few piskey-girls shriek and hide their faces at their first glimpse of the night sky. 'It is, sometimes,' said Ivy.

'It's beautiful anyway,' Cicely said. She ran a hand over the moss-covered stones. 'Everything out here's soft, and smells so good. I wish…'

'What?' asked Ivy, with a distracted glance over her shoulder. The place where her wings should have been had just tingled, as though someone were watching her. But the only thing behind her was the fire, and the benches on the other side were empty.

'I wish we could do this all the time.'

Ivy gave a short laugh. 'Do you have any idea how much work goes into a Lighting? Collecting enough wood to burn all night, and setting up the tables, and—'

'I don't mean that.' Cicely tugged a loose thread on her skirt. 'I mean…being here. Up above. The boys get to do it when they're old enough, so why can't we?' But before Ivy could answer she made a face and said, 'I know. Because of the *spriggans*.'

Gooseflesh rippled over Ivy's skin. Had someone pranked her little sister into thinking spriggans weren't real? Who would do such a terrible thing? 'Cicely,' she said, fighting to stay calm, 'you know what happened to our mother.'

'I know she disappeared,' said Cicely. 'And all they ever found was her shawl. But have you ever *seen* a spriggan? Has anybody? How do we know they took her, and not… something else?'

'Like what? Giants?' Ivy frowned. 'Those are just stories, Cicely.'

'No, not that. I mean that maybe…' Her eyes slid to the doorway, and the darkness beyond. 'Maybe she didn't want to be with us any more.'

Ivy choked. '*No*,' she said fiercely, when she could speak again. 'There is *no way* she would ever have left us like that. And spriggans are real, whether anyone's seen one lately or not. Who put these ridiculous ideas into your head?'

'He didn't mean to,' said Cicely, shrinking back. 'I overheard him and Mattock talking, when they thought I was asleep—'

Mica again. Fury scorched through Ivy, and she leaped to her feet. Where was he? Her eyes raked the crowd until she spotted him by the far wall, one arm braced not-quite-casually against the stone as he coaxed one of the older girls to dance.

'Stay here,' she told her sister flatly, and stalked to confront him.

*

35

'I need to talk to you right now,' Ivy said as she stepped between Mica and his would-be partner, who gave a nervous titter. 'Shall we go somewhere private, or do you want me to shout at you in front of everyone?'

For an instant Mica looked startled. Then his expression hardened. 'If that's what you want,' he said, and with that he seized Ivy's arm and pulled her out the door.

'Are you mad?' exclaimed Ivy, twisting back towards the light. 'We're not supposed to leave the Engine House!'

'You're safe enough with me,' said Mica. He marched her down the path nearly to the bottom of the slope, then let her go. 'All right, we're private. What is it now?'

'You!' Ivy shoved him as hard as she could, too angry to care that he barely moved. 'How *dare* you tell Cicely that our mother left us on purpose? How could you be so stupid?'

'I didn't tell her that!'

'Maybe not, but you said it where she could hear you. Or are you going to deny that as well?'

Mica folded his arms and looked away.

'You disgust me,' said Ivy. 'You never think about other people at all, do you? You get some slurry-brained idea in your head and you have to blather it to Mattock, no matter who else might be listening. And if spilling dross about our mother wasn't bad enough—'

'I wasn't spilling—'

'Now Cicely thinks there's no reason to stay in the Delve, because spriggans don't even exist!'

That struck a vein, if nothing else did. Mica paled, and now he looked worried – even frightened. 'All right,' he said. 'I'll talk to Cicely and set her straight. First thing tomorrow.'

'Good,' said Ivy grimly.

'But I'm not going to lie to her, either.'

'Nobody asked you to lie!' Which was a good thing, because most piskeys could only tell a direct untruth if they were joking, and this was no laughing matter. 'I'm asking you to stop being so careless, and take some responsibility for a change!'

'Responsibility?' Mica snorted, colour flooding back into his face. 'That's a fine speech from someone who showed up late, dressed in dirt and patches—'

'I wouldn't have been late if you hadn't chucked a live adder through the door! What was I supposed to do, walk off and leave it there?'

'Adder?' Mica's shock was convincing, as was the look of dawning fury that followed it.

But Ivy wasn't about to be distracted. 'And I wasn't the only one who ended up late. Cicely missed the start of the wakefire, because of you. So don't—' She broke off, startled, as her brother shoved past her. 'Where are you going? Mica!'

But her brother was already sprinting up the path, bellowing, 'Keeve, you little spriggan! I'll wring your neck!' And before Ivy could call out again, he vanished inside the Engine House.

Ivy stared after him, appalled. He'd left her alone at the foot of the slope, well outside the circle of the Joan's protective spells. How could even Mica be so reckless?

Still, the night seemed peaceful enough. Surely there was no need to call for help – that would only give her fellow piskeys more excuse to pity her. All she had to do was walk up the slope. It wasn't that far.

Yet she'd only taken a step when her spine prickled with the same uncomfortable feeling she'd had in the Engine House, the sense of being watched by someone just out of sight. Her stomach knotted as she remembered how her mother had disappeared, so swiftly and silently that no one even noticed she was gone until it was too late...

Ivy blew out an exasperated breath. This was ridiculous. She wasn't weak or helpless; she'd faced down an adder and won. There probably weren't any spriggans lurking on the hillside, but even if there were a thousand, she wouldn't give them the satisfaction of seeing her panic. She squared her shoulders and started up the path again.

'*Ivy*,' said a voice behind her.

She stiffened, then relaxed. So Mica hadn't left her alone after all. There was another piskey out here, probably one of the wood-gatherers or water-carriers for the Lighting, and they could walk back to the Engine House together. She turned, ready to greet him and explain – but the words died on her lips.

It was too big to be a piskey and too small to be human, a

spidery figure wrapped in dark clothing. It wore a hood, no doubt ashamed of its hideous features, but no shadow could hide the sickly pallor of its skin, or the hunger in those glittering eyes.

Spriggan.

two

If Ivy had wings, she might have been tempted to risk everything on a dash for the Engine House. But though she was quick on her feet, she wasn't sure she could outrun a spriggan. Especially since he'd crept up behind her so stealthily that she'd never even heard him coming – if he could do that, there was no telling what else he could do.

She took a step backward, feeling the dirt crumble beneath her bare feet. All at once she was acutely aware of the hairs standing up on her forearms and the nape of her neck, the *boom-boom-boom* of her heartbeat, the stench of her own cold sweat. 'How—' Her voice wavered. 'How do you know my name?'

The spriggan moved closer, teeth gleaming in the shadows of his hood. 'That's good,' he said. 'I didn't even have to tell you not to scream. I think we're going to get along very well.'

The amusement in his tone made Ivy feel sick. She could

smell him now, a sharp dry scent like fir needles, and all her instincts screamed at her to turn invisible. But what good would that do? He'd still be able to hear her, and probably smell her as well. She retreated another step, groping with her toes for a loose stone, a clod of earth, a bit of gravel. Anything she could kick that might hurt him, distract him, buy her a few precious seconds to escape—

'Ivy!' came a shout from up the slope, and the spriggan hissed a curse and darted away. Sagging with relief, Ivy turned to face Mattock as he sprinted down to her, his hair shining copper in the light of their shared glow.

'Are you all right?' he exclaimed. 'When Mica came back without you, I knew something was wrong. But I didn't expect to find you all the way down here!' He seized her by the shoulders and gave her a shake. 'What were you thinking?'

She'd nearly been captured by a spriggan, and he was giving *her* a lecture? Indignant, Ivy cuffed him across the head. Then she jabbed a finger emphatically in the direction the spriggan had gone.

But the slope was empty, its clumps of heather and bracken undisturbed. The only sign of life was a single tiny bird, fluttering towards the horizon.

'I know what I saw,' Ivy insisted as she and Mattock walked back to the Engine House. 'It was a spriggan, I'm sure of it.'

'Well,' said Mattock, rubbing his ear where she'd clipped

him, 'if you're that convinced, I suppose you'd better tell the Joan. But I wouldn't mention it to anyone else.'

'But if there's one spriggan out there, there could be more,' she said. 'We have to warn the others—'

'They're safe enough inside the Engine House,' said Mattock. 'I'll keep watch if it makes you feel better, but no spriggan's going to take on a hundred piskeys at once.' He quickened his stride as they reached the doorway, where Mica was leaning with a sour expression on his face. 'Did you find Keeve?'

'No,' said Mica. 'But when I do, I'm going to give him the thrashing of his life.' His gaze shifted to Ivy. 'What are *you* doing here?'

'You left her down in the valley,' said Mattock before Ivy could answer. 'You're lucky I was the one who found her, or you'd be explaining yourself to the Joan right now.'

'*Left* her?' Mica said. 'She's got legs, hasn't she? If she didn't have enough wits to follow me up the hill, that's not my fault.' He straightened up, gave Ivy a contemptuous glance, and strode inside.

'I hate him,' said Ivy flatly.

Mattock put a hand on her shoulder. 'He's half-drunk, and angry at Keeve for pranking him. In a few hours he'll think better of it.'

'And I'll still hate him then.' She shook him off. 'I'm going to find Cicely.'

*

Ivy found her little sister sitting by the droll-teller's feet with the other children, listening raptly as he spun a tale about a tribe of piskeys who could magically leap from one place to another at will. Ivy had heard the story before and dismissed it as wishful thinking, like the legends that claimed her piskey ancestors had power to heal every kind of injury and disease, or that they could transform their bodies into any shape they wished. Surely, if her people had been able to do such wonderful things in the past, they'd still be able to do them now.

But the spriggan had come out of nowhere, and Ivy was beginning to wonder if there might be some truth to the old legends after all. Maybe piskeys couldn't transport themselves from place to place with a thought, but what if spriggans could? It would explain how Marigold had vanished so quickly, and why they'd never found any trace of her but her shawl...

Suppressing a shudder at how close she'd come to sharing her mother's fate, Ivy sat down next to Cicely. She couldn't tell her sister what had happened, not yet: Cicely was in no danger at the moment, and it would be cruel to steal away her joy in her first Lighting. But if Mica didn't talk to Cicely soon, or if he couldn't convince her to take the threat of spriggans seriously, then Ivy would have no choice but to tell her. A few nightmares were a small price to pay for Cicely's safety.

She glanced across the Engine House to where the Joan

sat with her consort, Gossan – the Jack O'Lantern by title, though unlike his wife he wasn't the sort to stand on ceremony. By rights Ivy ought to tell her story to him as well, for he was the leader of the hunters, and it would be his duty to direct the search if they decided to track the spriggan down. But right now he was engrossed in conversation with Keeve's father Hew, while Betony was hearing a dispute between two of the women who'd done the cooking, and it would be difficult to talk to either of them without being overheard.

Maybe Mattock was right. Maybe Ivy should hold her peace until tomorrow, when she could talk to the Joan in private. After all, the spriggan was gone, and what were the chances of anyone finding him now?

'Now then,' said the droll-teller, sitting back with his bony hands on his knees. 'What would you like to hear about next?'

'Giants!' piped up one eager listener, and 'Gnomes!' shouted another. Ivy, who was interested in neither, was about to get up and leave when Cicely called out, 'Faeries!'

'Ah, I can't refuse a pretty lass,' the droll-teller said. 'Faeries it is.' Some of the boys groaned, and he gave a chuckle. 'No worry, lads, there's something for you in this story as well. Let me tell you of the last great battle between the piskeys and the faery folk, many years ago…'

He went on to tell a story that even Ivy hadn't heard

before, about a time when the piskey clans of Cornwall – or Kernow, in the old speech – had banded together to defend their territory against an invading army of faeries. The fight had been long and bitter, with terrible magics wielded on both sides, but in the end the piskeys had won and the faeries had retreated to their own lands.

'And after that day,' he finished, 'they never dared march upon our borders again. Once or twice a troop of them came sneaking across the Tamar, claiming some patch of woodland as their *wyld* and pretending they'd always lived there. But they soon thought better of it once a few of our boys paid them a visit, and now there's hardly a faery to be found from Launceston to Land's End.'

Which was probably for the best, Ivy thought. Faeries might not be as vicious as spriggans, but they were far too cunning and ruthless to be trusted. Still, she couldn't blame Cicely for being curious about them, because they were said to be eternally young and beautiful, with graceful bodies and wings clear as crystal, and as a child Ivy had often longed to see a faery herself.

'Where's Mica?' asked Cicely, as the droll-teller wandered off in search of a drink. 'He said he'd play jump-stones with me – oh, there he is.' She moved to get up, but Ivy caught her arm.

'He's in a foul mood right now,' she said. 'I'd leave him alone, if I were you. Why don't we play a game instead?'

*

As usual, the Lighting ended with the first rosy glimmer of dawn. The last of the piskey-wine was poured out on the ashes of the wakefire, and the tables and benches whisked into storage. The Joan pronounced her blessing on the company, and with that all the revellers – yawning musicians and sore-footed dancers, pranksters and victims, knockers and hunters, aunties and maidens – headed back into the Delve for some well-earned sleep.

'I'm telling you, it was a spriggan,' Ivy said, as Mica laid the slumbering Cicely in her alcove. 'If Matt hadn't shown up when he did…'

'And I'm telling you it was Keeve, hiding in the gorse-bushes with a tablecloth over his head,' said Mica. He sat down on the edge of his bed and started pulling off his boots. 'He did the same thing last year, remember? Jumped up behind the droll-teller and made everyone scream.' He flopped onto the mattress. 'I should have throttled him then.'

'It wasn't Keeve,' said Ivy. Keeve's eyes were black and bright with boyish mischief, nothing like the slate-grey stare that had so chilled her. 'And I know what a tablecloth looks like. Why can't you believe—'

But Mica's eyes were closed, and a snore was bubbling up between his lips. He wasn't pretending, either. Mica could drop off into a deep slumber in an instant, and Ivy, who often struggled to sleep, found it one of the most infuriating things about him.

Meanwhile, the adder's body still lay in the middle of the cavern, its blood pooling on the granite. And though Ivy realised now that Mica wasn't to blame, she resented him for not even offering to clean up the mess.

Flint wouldn't be any help either, even if she'd had the courage to ask him. He'd left the Lighting early and his thunder-axe was gone from its place by the door, which meant he'd already slept as much as he needed to before heading off to the diggings again.

Resigned, Ivy crouched by the snake's limp body, pulled the sack over its mangled head and started shoving the rest of it back in. She'd stick it in the cold-hole for now, and give it to Keeve once they all woke up – along with a good piece of her mind. Maybe then he'd think better of switching sacks on his fellow hunters, especially without making sure the snake was properly dead first.

The cavern was still quiet when Ivy woke several hours later, the only light her own glow reflected in its copper-tiled walls. It had taken her father years to refine all that metal and hammer it into shape, but he'd worked every spare moment until it was done. He'd also polished the floor to bring out every fleck and ripple in the granite, and as if that weren't enough, he'd begun inlaying the stone with silver all around the edges.

He'd only finished half the cavern when Marigold disappeared. A few chiselled swirls continued where the silver left off, but they'd never been filled, and in the end Ivy had dragged an old trunk over those forlorn two paces of stone so she wouldn't have to look at them.

She padded to the water-channel and washed her face and hands, then opened the clothespress she shared with Cicely and took out a sleeveless blouse and skirt. Closer to the surface the Delve could be cool, but not here, and where Ivy was going it would be warmer still. Once dressed, she studied herself critically in the mirror. Should she leave her shoulder-length curls down, as she usually did? Or would she look older and more serious with her hair up?

'You look nice,' said Cicely sleepily from her alcove. 'Where are you going?'

Ivy put the mirror aside. 'To talk to the Joan,' she said.

'What about?'

She didn't like to frighten Cicely, especially since Mica hadn't even had a chance to talk to her yet. But she couldn't lie to her, either. 'I saw a spriggan last night, outside the Engine House,' she said in an offhand tone, hoping Cicely would assume she'd only glimpsed it from a distance. 'It ran away before I could point it out to anyone, and Mica thinks it was only Keeve playing a prank. But I thought the Joan and Jack ought to know.'

'Oh,' Cicely said in a small voice, and Ivy could tell the news had troubled her. Well, maybe that was for the best – it would make it all the easier for Mica to talk to her when the time came. Ivy slid a copper arm-ring up above each

48

elbow and pinched it tight, then stooped to kiss her sister's forehead.

'I'll be back soon,' she said. 'Wish me luck.'

'You'll need that and a hammer to get Aunt Betony to listen to you,' said Mica from his alcove. He swept the curtains aside and clambered out of bed, scratching his bare chest. 'What's for dinner?'

'There's plenty of adder in the cold-hole,' said Ivy sweetly, and walked out.

As Ivy headed down the stairs to the next level, she was struck by how quiet the Delve was. Usually at this time of day there'd be children chasing each other through the corridors, matrons carrying baskets of laundry up from the wash-cistern, knockers returning from the diggings with their thunder-axes over their shoulders. But right now most of her fellow piskeys were still sleeping, and Ivy walked the passages alone.

Soon another set of stairs took her down to Silverlode Passage, where threads of the precious metal still shone bright against the granite. The tunnel was wider here, as it was one of the main thoroughfares of the Delve, and the most direct route to the cavern where the piskeys held their market. Yet even this passage was empty, which made Ivy feel lonely and strangely liberated at the same time. She appreciated the close-knit community of the Delve, where everyone looked out not only for their own interests but also for everyone else's. But there were times when her fellow piskeys' company became stifling, and it was a relief to be by herself for a while.

The Joan's stateroom was at the far end of the Silverlode, the entrance marked by lit torches on either side – a sign that Betony was inside and ready to hear her people's petitions. But the door was closed, and Ivy had to knock three times before anyone answered.

'All right, all right,' said Nettle's gravelly tones from within, 'I'm a-coming.' The door opened with a creak, and her thin, wizened face appeared. 'Right then, what's your business?'

'I need to talk to the Joan. I think...' No, she didn't just think. She'd looked into those cold eyes, and she *knew*. Ivy stood a little taller and said, 'I saw a spriggan last night.'

For an instant Nettle seemed taken aback, but then her expression softened. She leaned closer and murmured, 'Ah, Ivy-lass, your mother was a good woman, and what happened to her was a terrible shame. But you can't go about—'

'Let her in, Nettle.' Betony's voice carried across the cavern. 'I'll deal with this.'

Nettle shut her mouth so hard her teeth clicked, and opened the door at once. Ivy walked through into a broad, firelit chamber, its daunting size made cosy by copper panels, a patterned rug, and draperies in rich, earthy hues. The far end of the room was dominated by a table of carved granite, and Ivy's aunt was seated in the chair behind it.

'So you think you saw a spriggan,' said the Joan. 'Where?'

There was something about Betony that always made Ivy feel small. Her aunt's strong bones and striking features, the smooth waves of hair falling over her shoulders, made Ivy keenly aware of her own unruly curls and slight, unpiskeylike figure. And then there were those creamy wings with their shimmering patterns of bronze, so much like Cicely's that Ivy could never look at them without being reminded of what her own wings might have – *should* have – been.

'In the valley below the Engine House,' she said, subdued.

'And what were you doing there?'

This was the awkward part. Exasperating as Mica could be at times, he was still Ivy's brother, and she didn't want to make trouble for him. But she wasn't about to take the blame for his carelessness, either. 'Mica and I needed to talk in private,' she said at last. 'He said I'd be safe as long as he was with me.'

'So he was with you when you saw the spriggan?'

Ivy winced. 'No.'

'I see,' said the Joan. 'Go on.'

'He didn't mean to leave me,' Ivy said. 'He thought I was right behind him when he ran up the hill. But the spriggan arrived before I could catch up, and then…'

'Arrived how? From which direction?'

All these pointed questions were making Ivy feel defensive. 'I don't know. He turned up behind me, all of a sudden. It was like he was just...there.'

'And yet he didn't touch you, or put a spell on you, or harm you in any way?'

'No,' Ivy said, 'but I'm sure he would have if Mattock hadn't come looking for me.'

'So Mattock saw the spriggan, then?'

'No. It ran off before he arrived. I tried to point it out to him, but—' She spread her hands, feeling more foolish than ever. 'It was already gone.'

The Joan leaned back in her chair, fingers tapping the edge of the table. 'And when you told Mattock and your brother about this spriggan, what did they say?'

'They said it was Keeve playing a prank. Only I know it wasn't, because—'

She was about to say *he talked to me*, but Betony cut her off. 'Clearly you feel that wasn't the case. But for a spriggan to appear the moment you happened to be alone, frighten you without doing you any harm, and vanish before anyone else could see him... It does seem unlikely, don't you think?'

'But I felt him watching me, when I was sitting by the wakefire,' Ivy said in desperation. 'He could have singled me out then, and waited until I was alone to—'

'But how could he know that you would go outside the Engine House, much less that your brother would leave you alone? And when he had his opportunity, why didn't he take it?' She paused, then went on in a gentler tone, 'No one could blame you for hating the spriggans, or wanting to see your mother avenged. But you were not yourself last night, and the mind can play tricks sometimes.'

What was *that* supposed to mean? Just because she'd showed up late to the Lighting with old clothes and dirt on her face, the Joan thought she was losing her wits? Ivy gripped her arm-rings, calling on their cold strength. 'I didn't imagine it! Why doesn't anyone believe me?'

But her aunt only looked at her, a faint pity in her gaze. And all at once Ivy remembered Cicely's words: *Have you ever seen a spriggan? Has anybody?*

She drew in her breath. 'You don't believe in spriggans.' And neither did Mica or Mattock, judging by their reactions. How could she have been so naïve?

'You mistake me, Ivy. I would never deny that spriggans exist.'

'Oh, really?' Ivy was angry enough for sarcasm, though she knew she might regret it. 'When was the last time anyone saw one?'

'Must be thirty years ago,' came the rasping answer, and Ivy started; she'd forgotten Nettle was there. 'A thin, miserable bit of a thing it was too, all by its lonesome. But it fought like a demon till young Hew smashed its head in, or so he and the other lads said.'

Thirty years… Could it be true? She'd spent her whole life terrified of spriggans, and all the while they'd been practically extinct?

'Then why are we still hiding underground?' Ivy asked, rounding on her aunt. 'If I only imagined what I saw, and my mother wasn't taken by the spriggans after all—'

'There are more dangers in the world than spriggans,' said Betony, with a hard look at Nettle. 'And good reason for our people to stay underground, even now. As for your mother... I would let that be, Ivy, if I were you.'

'You think she left us,' Ivy said, struggling to breathe. 'Don't you. You think my mother went away on *purpose*.'

'I don't know what became of Marigold when she left the Engine House that night,' the Joan replied, unruffled. 'She may indeed have been caught by the spriggans, for all I know.' She rose and walked around the table. 'But you will not bring her back by making yourself miserable – as I have told your father many times.' She put her fingers under Ivy's chin and tipped her face up. 'You have been working too hard. It would do you good to get more rest. Let Mica and Cicely look after you for a change.'

I'm not sick, Ivy wanted to protest, but she'd heard the warning in her aunt's tone: the discussion was over. And Nettle was holding the door open, in case she hadn't taken the hint. Hiding her resentment, Ivy bowed her head. 'Yes, my Joan.'

*

It wasn't self-doubt that made Ivy pause halfway through her journey home and choose a different route. It was sheer stubbornness, and as she turned west into Tinners' Row where Keeve and his family lived, Ivy clenched her fists in anticipation. She'd get to the bottom of this, never mind what Betony said; she'd *prove* she hadn't been pranked, or imagining an enemy that wasn't there.

'Keeve!' she shouted at his door, her knocks loud as a thunder-axe in the narrow tunnel. 'Wake up! I need to talk to you!'

'He's not here,' came the muffled reply.

Ivy was surprised. Last night Keeve had danced harder and drunk more piskey-wine than anyone else she knew; it didn't seem possible that he'd recovered so quickly. 'Where is he, then?'

The door creaked open and Keeve's mother, Teasel, looked out, her face pinched with anxiety. 'He didn't come back last night. Hew's gone looking for him.'

That was even more odd. Keeve had good reason to fear Mica's wrath after that prank with the adder, but he liked a comfortable bed as much as anyone. 'I'm sorry to trouble you, then,' Ivy said. 'But when Keeve gets back, would you let me know? I've got something of his I need to return, and—'

Teasel didn't wait for her to finish. She gave a tight-lipped nod, and shut the door.

*

'He's still not back,' said Mica several hours later, as he returned to the cavern. 'And they didn't want the adder.'

By then it was night-time, and Ivy was brushing out Cicely's hair before they went to bed. Not that any of them would be likely to sleep well, knowing Keeve was still missing.

'So Hew couldn't find him?' Ivy asked as she gave Cicely's hair a final stroke and started to braid it again. 'Are they going to send out a search party?'

'Two of them,' Mica said shortly, heaving the adder back into the cold-hole. 'Gem and Feldspar are leading the first, and Matt and I'll be on the second. But I doubt it'll be worth the trouble. He's probably just gone off to town for a pint.'

'You mean with the humans?' asked Cicely, twisting around so eagerly that Ivy lost hold of her braid. 'Do you really think so?'

'It wouldn't be the first time,' Mica said. But Ivy could see the crease between his brows, and knew that he was more worried than he let on. And rightly so – Keeve might be reckless at times, but he'd never stayed away from the Delve this long before.

'They've checked the milking barn, I suppose?' Ivy asked. The piskeys kept no cattle, but one of the nearby human farmers did, and Keeve was an expert at coaxing the cows to give up a few extra pints for the piskeys. 'The cows are bound to miss him, if nobody else does.'

She'd tried to make light of the situation for Cicely's sake, but her little sister wasn't fooled. 'Do you think the spriggan took him?' she asked in a small voice.

Mica's eyes flicked to Ivy's and then away. 'What would a spriggan want with Keeve?' he said. 'He wasn't carrying any treasure, and he's far too tough to be good eating. Now off to bed with you, skillywidden.' He tweaked Cicely's nose and went out.

That was all the reassurance Cicely needed, and she went to sleep without so much as a whimper. Even Ivy managed to argue herself into a few hours' rest, telling herself there'd surely be good news in the morning.

But the search parties found no sign of Keeve, and by the time another day had passed, even Mica stopped acting casual. The atmosphere in the Delve grew tense and the piskeys spoke in whispers, as though at a funeral. Gifts began to pile up in front of Hew and Teasel's cavern.

And before long, Ivy's story about the spriggan wasn't a story any more. Mattock came to the door and apologised, his square face sober beneath his mop of rusty hair. Betony called Ivy back to the Joan's chambers and questioned her again, this time without condescension. Cicely woke sobbing that a spriggan had come to get her, and when she found Mica pulling on his boots for the evening hunt, she clung to him and begged him not to go.

'Don't be such a pebble-head,' he said in a gruff tone, prising her off. 'I'll be safe enough with Mattock at my back, and we can always jump down a hole at the first sign of trouble. Or run like rabbits, if it comes to that.'

It was the right thing to say to Cicely, who managed a wavering smile. But Ivy wasn't so reassured. Mica might be lazy and given to boasting, but he was no coward; what he could do if a spriggan came after him and what he *would* do were two different matters. 'Be careful,' she said, as Mica headed for the door.

Two days ago, her brother would have rolled his eyes and told her not to be such an old auntie. Now he gave a sober nod, and left without another word.

'Ivy! Wake up!'

What time was it? It surely couldn't be morning. Ivy raised her head blearily from the pillow to find Mica stooping over her. 'Ugh,' she said, 'you stink. What have you been doing?'

'Guess,' said Mica, wiping sweat off his brow and baring his teeth in a grin.

Ivy sat up, abruptly wide awake. 'You found him?' Alive, it would seem, or Mica wouldn't look so pleased with himself. 'Is he all right? Can he talk?'

Mica gave her an odd look. 'After Mattock and I jumped on him and beat him senseless, I should say not. Why, did you want to question him? I'd leave that to the Joan, if I were you.'

'*Beat* him—' For a moment Ivy was too shocked to speak.

Then her sleep-addled brain caught up with her, and she understood. 'You don't mean Keeve.'

Mica gave a snort. 'I wish,' he said. 'No, we didn't find him, or at least not yet. We caught the spriggan.'

three

'Won't speak a word, I'm told. Just sits there with his ugly mouth shut, and stares.' Keeve's mother tugged a fresh coil of roving onto her shoulder, her drop spindle whirling as she spun the soft mass into yarn. Only someone who knew her well would have noticed the tremor in her hands.

'Maybe he doesn't know how to speak,' piped up one of the younger girls from her seat on the rug. Teasel's cavern was as cosy and well-furnished as any in the Delve, but not even she had enough chairs for twenty. 'Has anyone ever *heard* a spriggan talk?'

I have, thought Ivy. But the memory of that soft, insinuating voice made her feel slimy all over, and it wasn't as though he'd said anything useful. Teasel needed answers, not mockery.

'Tch! You'd get more sense out of an animal,' said another woman. 'It's useless, if you ask me – meaning no offence to you, Teasel,' she added as Keeve's mother bristled. 'Of course we all want to see your lad safe home again. Only that I can't see how that nasty creature down below is going to help us find him.'

'Well,' said Teasel, pinching the yarn tight between finger and thumb, 'if the creature won't give me back my son, then at least we can make him pay for it. That's what I say, and Hew's of the same mind. My man killed a spriggan all by himself once, you know. Stove its head in with his thunder-axe, and kicked its carcass into the sea.'

The other women exclaimed and sat up, eager for details, but Cicely edged closer to Ivy. 'I don't like it when people talk about killing,' she whispered.

'It's a spriggan,' Ivy replied, not looking up from the wool she was carding. 'And if he won't tell what he did with Keeve, then he deserves it.'

Yet later that evening, after she'd tucked Cicely into bed, Ivy found herself wondering *why* the spriggan wasn't talking. Perhaps he was afraid of being executed for his crimes, but he must realise that he was never going to get out of the Delve anyway...

Make him pay for it, murmured Teasel in her memory, and then with grim relish, *My man killed a spriggan all by himself once.*

But that had been thirty years ago, according to Nettle. If the spriggans had managed to elude the hunters of the Delve for so long, how had her brother and Mattock caught this one so easily? Especially if he'd killed Keeve and eaten him right down to the bones, as no one was saying but everybody feared. Surely after committing such a horrible murder, he'd want to put as much distance between himself and the Delve as he could?

'How am I supposed to know what goes on in a spriggan's head?' asked Mica irritably, when Ivy asked him. By that time Cicely was sound asleep, so they could talk freely. 'Ask the Joan, if she can get him talking before he starves to death.' He poured himself a tankard of small beer and sat down at the table. 'Anyway, why should you care? I thought you'd be happy to see him caught. Revenge for our mother, and all that.'

'And *all that*?' Ivy repeated in disbelief. 'You caught a spriggan with your own hands! How can you talk as though—' She dropped onto the bench across from Mica. 'You can't still think our mother left us on purpose.'

'Why not?' he snapped, then flinched as Cicely mumbled and turned over. 'All I'm saying,' he went on more quietly, 'is that nobody knows what happened that night. And I don't see how you can keep on about spriggans, when you of all people should know—' He broke off and pushed back from the table, his lip curling. 'Oh, what's the point? You never listen to me anyway.'

'I'm listening now,' said Ivy, making an effort at patience. Maybe Mica had forgotten the tenderness in Marigold's face as she kissed her children good night, or her radiant smile as she danced to the music of Flint's fiddle. Maybe he truly thought there was some reason their mother would have wanted to leave. 'Go on. What is it I'm supposed to know?'

'About the fight, of course.'

'What fight?'

'Between Dad and Mum, the night before she disappeared.' He glanced at the archway to their father's bedchamber – the only separate room in the cavern. 'They were in there with the door closed, so there's no telling how it started. But once they got going you could hear nearly every word. Don't you remember?'

Her parents, fighting? It seemed impossible – Flint had always doted on Marigold, and neither of them were the quarrelling sort. Ivy was tempted to suggest it had just been a nightmare, but the look on Mica's face forestalled her. She shook her head. 'You're going to have to remind me. What were they fighting about?'

'She said she was leaving, and she wanted to take you and Cicely with her.' His voice wavered on the last phrase, and he made a face at his tankard. 'Dad was furious. He said he couldn't stop her throwing away her life, but she wasn't taking his children anywhere. Then she started to cry and I couldn't make out what she was saying any more, and he didn't say anything at all. And when she came out of the chamber she was still crying, but quietly, like she didn't want any of us to know. So I pretended I was asleep.'

Ivy's stomach felt heavy, as though she had swallowed a stone. 'I don't remember any of that,' she said.

'Well, you should. Because you sat up and asked her what was the matter. And then she climbed into your alcove and shut the curtains, and the two of you were whispering in there for ages.' He ran a finger around the rim of his cup. 'So you knew she was going away, like I did. You just couldn't bear to face the truth, so you...' He shrugged. 'I don't know, blocked it out somehow. Made yourself believe it was the spriggans who took her instead.'

'I didn't *make myself* do anything!' Ivy knotted her fists in her lap, so furious she felt sick. 'What makes you think your memory is any better than mine? Maybe it was you who couldn't bear to think that our mother was taken by the spriggans, so you invented this story and talked yourself into believing it! You think she bled all over her shawl on purpose, then left it on a gorse-bush for Dad to find so she could...do what? Go dancing with the faeries?'

Mica hunched his shoulders. 'I don't know why she wanted to leave,' he said. 'And I don't know what happened to her either. Maybe the spriggans did get her in the end. But I'm not going to waste my life brooding over someone who—'

'Don't you dare,' warned Ivy. 'If you want to tell yourself that Mum was selfish and uncaring and that we're well rid of her, then I can't stop you. But I remember what she was really like, and I will never believe that. *Never.*'

'It doesn't matter,' Mica muttered into his beer. 'Either

way she's gone, and she isn't coming back. Believe whatever makes you happy.'

And all at once Ivy thought she understood. 'Is that why you never said anything to me about it?' she said more softly. 'Because you thought I was happier not knowing?'

'No,' said Mica. 'I never said anything because I knew you'd be like this.' He drained his tankard, shoved it towards her, and marched off to bed.

Ivy sat unmoving, staring into the foamy dregs. She felt numb and a little dizzy, as though she'd cut herself by accident and was just beginning to feel it. Could she really have forgotten something so enormous, so shattering? Even if she had, shouldn't she be able to remember it now?

Yet when she forced her mind back to that evening five years ago, she found only a blank fuzzy space – nothing to confirm or deny anything Mica had said. Could she really have been so weak, so desperate, as to erase her own memories? She'd never heard of anyone doing such a thing, but maybe...

No. She wasn't going to blame herself, or her mother, until she could be certain that Mica's story was true. Which meant she'd have to wait until her father came home, and ask him.

Or better yet, she could go find him herself, and settle the question at once. After all, what was the worst Flint could do to her? Even a blow or a curse would be better than the silence she lived with every day.

Ivy pushed back her chair. 'I'm going for a walk,' she said. 'Don't wait up for me.'

By the time Ivy left the cavern, it was so late that most piskeys were in bed, and the others were on their way there. But Flint had given up regular hours a long time ago, so there was no telling where he might be.

Most likely he was working in the depths of the mine, but by now he'd tunnelled so far that Ivy hardly knew where to begin looking for him – a problem that became clear the instant she climbed down the ladder to the diggings. If the other knockers had been working, she could have asked one of them to point her in the right direction. But without being familiar with the labyrinth of tunnels that the piskey miners used, she could wander half the night before she heard the telltale crack and rumble of her father's thunder-axe.

She called his name as loudly as she dared, but there was no answer. If her father had been any less capable, Ivy might have been worried about him. But Flint was a true knocker, able to sense every strength and weakness of the surrounding granite, and he never caused a rockfall unless he meant to. He was safe enough, and he'd come home when he was ready. But who knew how much longer that would be?

Frustrated, Ivy climbed up the ladder and shut the trap-door behind her. What was she going to do now?

It was no use going home to bed in this state: she'd be tossing and turning for hours.

At last she decided to take a walk around the Delve. Perhaps she'd bump into her father, or at least hear him working, along the way – and even if she didn't, at least it should make her tired enough to steal a few minutes' rest before he came in.

Over the next hour Ivy made two long winding circuits of the tunnels, climbing every ramp and staircase she found. But by the time she'd finished she felt no closer to sleep than before.

There was only one place she could think of that she hadn't visited already. Ivy walked the length of the adjoining tunnel and braced her hands on the iron railing at the edge of the Great Shaft, gazing up at the faint glimmer of moonlight high above. Should she climb to the top? The effort would certainly tire her out, but—

'*Bind up my wounds,*' rasped a voice from the darkness.

Ivy jumped back, clapping both hands over her mouth to stifle a cry. 'Who's there?' she tried to ask, but her lips could barely form the words. The sound hadn't come from the tunnel behind her – it was floating up from the depths of the shaft, from the old human workings where no piskey had reason to be.

'*Soft! I did but dream. O coward conscience, how dost thou afflict me!*'

Nobody in the Delve talked like that. Not even the oldest

piskeys used such formal language, and the droll-teller himself had never spoken with such tortured passion. Ivy clutched the railing and leaned out over it, dreading what she might see. She'd never believed in ghosts, but...

'The lights burn blue. It is now dead midnight. Cold fearful drops stand on my trembling flesh...' Then the speaker faltered and began to moan, 'Light! *Light!'* with increasing desperation, like a feverish child begging for water. It was the most pitiful thing Ivy had ever heard.

Might it be a human, who had wandered in through one of the old adits and got lost in the depths of the mine? Ivy would have been relieved to think so, for in that case it would be easy to play will-o'-the-wisp and lead him up to the surface again. But in her heart she knew better. The words might be strange and garbled, but the voice was all too familiar.

It was the spriggan.

She'd never suspected that his cell was so close to the Great Shaft. All she'd heard was that he was being held somewhere far away from the piskeys' living quarters, and that only the Joan and Jack were allowed to see him. But she'd also been told that the spriggan wasn't talking...and he was definitely talking now.

'What do I fear? Myself? There's none else by: Richard loves Richard; that is, I am I...'

He'd calmed down now, at least enough to stop wailing for light and start talking to himself again. Richard? Was that his name? It sounded weirdly human. Ivy hadn't thought of spriggans as having names before; to her they were all just spriggans, as snakes were snakes.

But if he had a name, then he had a personality. If he could talk about feeling pain and guilt and fear, there was a chance that he might be willing to talk about other things, as well. Like what he'd done with Keeve...

Or what had happened to Ivy's mother.

Did Ivy dare? Could she climb down into the dark recesses of the shaft, find the tunnel where the spriggan was being held prisoner, and walk right up to his door? If she offered him a glimpse of the light he craved, would he tell her what she wanted so badly to know?

Mind, if anyone found out she had gone near the spriggan, Ivy would be in big trouble. But he could hardly hurt her while locked up in his cell. And if she didn't take her chance with him now, she might spend the rest of her life wondering what would have happened if she had...

'*I am I*,' the spriggan repeated, then muttered, 'Whatever that means.' And with that he let out a laugh – but it dissolved into coughing, and ended in a breath like a sob.

Ivy inhaled slowly, summoning strength and courage. Then she swung her leg over the railing, and lowered herself into the darkness.

She had never climbed this part of the Great Shaft before,

much less backwards. Every new foothold had to be carefully tested, lest it crumble away and send her plummeting into the fathomless sump below. After several minutes of spidering her way down the rock, Ivy's curls were plastered to her forehead with sweat. Yet she thought of her mother, and kept on.

She swung her left leg sideways, toes groping for another ledge. But her foot dangled into empty air, and no matter how far she stretched she could find no place to stand. Had she reached the lower tunnel already? Digging her fingers into the rock, Ivy eased herself downwards, then arched her back, swung her hips, and let go.

The adjoining tunnel was deeper than she'd anticipated, and for a heart-stopping instant Ivy feared she'd made her last mistake. But then her bare feet smacked stone, and she landed with only a slight stagger. Sighing relief, Ivy straightened up –

And found herself face to face with the spriggan.

At first she was too stunned to speak. Not only because she'd never expected his cell to open straight onto the Great Shaft, but because he was so utterly different from the monster she'd imagined. Pale as a dead thing, yes, and woefully thin – he could never have passed for a piskey. Nor was he pleasant to look at, not with one eye swollen half-shut and a split lip distorting his mouth into a sneer. But apart from that there was nothing gruesome about him, and he was *young*. Older than Ivy to be sure, more a man than a boy – but he couldn't be more than a couple of years older than Mica.

Yet he was still a spriggan, and that made him dangerous. Even crouched against the wall with one arm cradled to his chest, he had a menacing air about him, a lithe tension that could explode at any moment into violence. Ivy dimmed her glow and backed towards the shaft, though she knew it was too late: he'd heard her land, seen her skin shining in the darkness, and at any moment...

'*Is there a murderer here?*' he whispered, pushing himself to his feet. He lurched forward – but then came a rattling noise, and he jerked to a halt mid-step.

So that was why the Joan hadn't been worried about him escaping, even with an open shaft mere paces away. While he was still unconscious, Mica and Mattock had clapped an iron manacle around his ankle and chained him to the floor. He couldn't go more than a stride in any direction, so Ivy was well out of reach – and if she remembered the legends right, the iron would keep him from using magic, too. Only those with knocker blood could endure the touch of iron.

'You tell me,' she said, bolder now. She could see him well enough with her night vision, but to him she'd be nothing more than a ghostly shape – a tantalising hint of the light he yearned for. 'Are you a murderer?'

The spriggan let out a shuddering breath. His head drooped, and he muttered, '*No. Yes. I am: Then fly...*'

If only she could. 'I'm not here to play riddle-games,' said

Ivy. Had he lost his wits? 'Did you or did you not kill Keeve?'

A long pause, while the spriggan watched her sidelong out of one grey eye. '*I am a villain*,' he said at last, then added quickly as Ivy tensed: '*Yet I lie. I am not.*'

'Stop talking nonsense and tell me the truth, then!'

The spriggan leaned against the wall, his distorted mouth closing tight. He did not reply.

Had she been too harsh with him? Would he refuse to say any more? Ivy took a step forward – though not too close, since she had no desire to feel those fingers around her neck. Then she said gently, 'You want light, don't you?'

His breath caught, just the briefest hitch, but it was as good as an answer. 'I'll give it to you,' Ivy said, 'if you answer some questions for me.'

She waited, but the spriggan didn't respond. Did he not believe her? Or was he too slurry-brained to understand?

Ivy increased her glow a little, hoping to tempt him. 'See?' she said. 'I'll give you more, if you'll tell me what you did with Keeve. And even more than that, if you can tell me what happened to my mother. She was beautiful, with light brown hair, and her wings…'

What had Marigold's wings been like? She couldn't remember. Ivy cleared her throat and went on, 'Anyway, she disappeared five years ago. Did you spriggans take her? Is she still alive?'

The prisoner raised his head to hers, lips parting as

though to speak. But then his chin dropped and he looked away.

Ivy threw up her hands. 'This is useless.' The stench that hung around him was making her queasy, and she was tired of looking at those hollow cheeks and sunken eyes. The spriggan was either delirious or mad or both, and she wished that she had never come. 'I give up. You can stay here and rot for all I care.' Defiantly flaring brighter so he'd never forget what he'd missed, she turned and strode away.

'*Ivy.*'

Startled, she looked back to find the spriggan stretching out his one good hand. 'Don't go,' he said, and now his voice sounded ordinary, the formal cadences lost. 'I didn't know... I couldn't be sure it was you, until now.'

Was he trying to make her pity him? If so, it wasn't going to work. And she wasn't going to ask again how he knew her name, either – he'd probably just overheard it, back at the Lighting. Ivy tapped her foot. 'Well?'

'I didn't kill Keeve.' He rubbed his temple, as though concentrating were an effort. 'I don't know where he is.'

'But you were there, the night he disappeared,' Ivy said. 'Who else could have taken him?'

'I have no idea. But it wasn't me.'

'Why didn't you say that to the Joan, then?' Ivy asked. 'Did you think she wouldn't believe you?'

'I had to give her some reason to keep me alive,' he said. 'Until I could talk to you.'

'Me?' Ivy was startled. 'Why?'

The spriggan straightened, brushing the sweat-darkened hair from his brow. 'Because,' he said, 'your mother sent me to find you. She's alive, and safe. And if you let me go…I'll take you to her.'

four

Ivy stood still, wide green eyes fixed on the spriggan. For a moment there was no sound except the slow drip of water down the Great Shaft and the creature's laboured breathing. Then she said in a strangled voice, 'You're lying.' She didn't even know if spriggans could lie, but what other explanation could there be?

'I'm not lying.'

'Yes, you are.' She spoke quickly, almost gabbling in her panic. She had to stop this before it got out of hand – before she was tempted to believe him. 'You heard me say I was looking for my mother, and now you're using that to try and trick me—'

'Her name is Marigold.'

His quiet certainty shook her, but Ivy wasn't about to give in. There were any number of ways he could have learned her mother's name – including under torture. 'Why would she send *you* to me?' she demanded. 'If my mother was alive, if she wanted to see me so badly, she'd come and see me herself.'

'I didn't ask about her motives. Marigold asked me to deliver a message to you, and I agreed because I owed her a debt, nothing more. If you want an explanation, you'll have to ask for one when you see her.' His look turned sly. 'Unless you don't *want* to see her.'

Ivy barely resisted the urge to hit him. 'Of course I do,' she snapped. 'Or would, if I believed a single word of what you've told me. Where did you see my mother, then – in the bottom of your stewpot?'

'Actually, it was in Truro.' He paused and added with a hint of condescension, 'That's a human city and not a recipe, in case you were wondering. I don't eat piskeys, even irritating ones.'

'That's ridiculous,' Ivy said, folding her arms so he wouldn't see her hands shake. 'My mother would never live with humans, not when she could be here with us. And even if she couldn't come back to the Delve for some reason, she'd never make a bargain with a – a filthy, lying *spriggan.*'

She expected an angry retort, but the prisoner only pinched the bridge of his nose, as though she had given him a headache. Then he said with infinite weariness, 'I don't even know what a spriggan is.'

Ivy's legs wobbled. 'What? But then…what are you?'

'A faery. What else?'

What else, indeed. Between the dirt and blood that smeared his body, the ragged clothes and unkempt hair, she would never have taken him for one of the so-called Fair Folk. Yet now that he mentioned it, he did look more like a faery than he ever had a spriggan…

'Oh,' she said faintly.

'Marigold warned me to be careful about showing myself to anyone. She said your people had been living underground for a long time, and that they didn't take kindly to strangers. But even so—' He touched his injured arm and grimaced. 'I wasn't expecting quite this level of hostility.'

He sounded reasonable now, even sane. But Ivy wasn't ready to let her guard down yet. 'Is it broken?' she asked.

'Out of joint.' He moved his hand, revealing the ugly swelling around the elbow. 'Your brother seemed to think he could make me talk by trying to rip my arm off, but I can't say it inspired me to much more than yelling.'

Ivy almost asked how he'd known Mica was her brother, but then she remembered: he'd seen the two of them arguing outside the Engine House. 'So why didn't you tell him you knew my mother?' she asked.

'Because I was too busy yelling, perhaps?' He spoke mildly, but the words were tinged with sarcasm. 'Not to mention fighting for my life.'

Even Ivy's distrust couldn't keep her from feeling a twinge of sympathy. Faeries might be deceitful and self-centred as the legends claimed, but the stranger was clearly in pain. Maybe that was why he'd been raving earlier.

'Mica…doesn't always think before he acts,' she said, resisting a traitorous impulse to add, *I'm sorry.*

'I got that impression, yes,' said the faery dryly. 'I don't suppose you have some kind of magical healing elixir that would put my arm right?'

'Not really,' said Ivy. Yarrow's herbs might ease the pain and bring down the swelling, but they wouldn't solve the underlying problem. 'And even if I did, don't you think the Joan would notice that someone had healed you?'

'I doubt it, unless she can see through rock.' He jerked his head at the ceiling-high wall of rubble behind him. 'She hasn't bothered to look at me once since I woke up in here. And it seems she's not planning to give me any food or water either, unless I start talking.'

Ivy was silent, troubled by the revelation. Did Betony really mean to starve the spriggan – or faery – until he confessed to killing Keeve? But what if he hadn't?

'I don't know what you've heard about faeries,' said the prisoner, 'but if there's one thing my people honour, it's a bargain. Help me now, and I'll do you a favour in return.'

'Like you did for my mother?' Ivy asked, moving a little closer. After all, he could hardly overpower her with only one working hand. 'What exactly did you promise her, anyway?'

'To tell you that she was alive, and wanted to see you,' he said. 'And if you were willing, to bring you back to Truro with me.'

Ivy had no idea how far away the city of Truro was. But she'd never heard Mica or any of the other hunters mention it, so it must be out of their usual range – at least a day's journey on foot, if not more. How could she possibly travel so far from the Delve without anyone noticing that she was gone?

And yet, if her mother was truly alive…how could she *not* go?

She was still wrestling with the question when she noticed the stranger extending his injured arm towards her, wincing all the while. 'What are you doing?' she asked.

'I told you. Help me, and I'll help you. Just do as I say.' He hesitated, then added with obvious reluctance, 'Please.'

Ivy sighed. 'What do you want me to do?'

'Take my hand, and slide your other hand under my elbow.'

Suppressing her distaste, Ivy reached out and took his limp, white fingers in her own. She had half-expected to find his skin cold and slimy, as a spriggan's ought to be – but his hand was warm, even feverish, in her grip. Gingerly she slipped her other hand beneath his swollen joint, feeling the dislocation. 'What now?' she asked.

'Hold my elbow steady,' said the prisoner between his teeth, 'and pull my wrist towards you. Not too fast, but –

79

aaaaah!' There was a sickening pop beneath Ivy's palm and he staggered against her, gasping. But when he lifted his head again, the relief on his face was close to ecstasy.

'You have my *profound* gratitude,' he breathed, flexing his arm. 'So does this mean we have a bargain?'

Ivy's thoughts and feelings were in a tangle, and she had no idea how to reply. Had she really just helped one of her people's oldest enemies? What would happen to her, if anyone found out? She sat down heavily on an outcropping. When she'd left the cavern looking for answers about her mother, she'd never imagined it would turn out like this. 'I don't know,' she said. 'I don't know what to do.'

'Yes, you do.' He dragged his chain across the floor and crouched beside her. 'It's perfectly simple. You get me out of here, and I take you to Marigold.'

He made it sound so easy. 'But how would we get there? And when would we leave?'

'As soon as you like, or near enough. As for how...' He tapped a finger against his teeth. 'It would be easiest to travel by magic, but you've never been to Truro before, so that won't work. And you haven't got wings, so...' He shrugged. 'I'll just have to carry you on my back.'

'*Carry* me?' asked Ivy, in baffled outrage. 'I can walk perfectly well, in case you hadn't noticed! What kind of—'

'Of course you can walk. But you can't fly, which is more to the point.'

'And you expect me to believe that you can?' Faery or not,

he had no more wings than she did. Was the stranger mad after all, or did he really think she was that stupid? Disgusted, Ivy pushed herself to her feet. 'I've had enough of this. I'm going to bed.'

'Wait.' His voice sharpened. 'You can't leave me here.'

'I don't see why not,' Ivy said. 'You've had your fun, and got your arm fixed into the bargain. What else do you need me for? Wait a few days, and you should be thin enough to slip out of that manacle and *fly* out of here.' She made a cynical flapping motion and turned away.

'You really don't know what I'm talking about.' He sounded incredulous. 'I knew piskeys were different, but I had no idea... Ivy, listen to me!'

Annoyed as she was, his desperation brought her up short. She stopped, waiting.

'I know I don't have wings any more than you do,' he said. 'Not in this form. But I can change shape – all male faeries can. And if I turn myself into a bird, and you make yourself small enough, I can fly you to Truro and back again before anyone knows you're gone.'

'That's ridic—' Ivy started, but the word dissolved on her tongue as she remembered the little bird she'd seen flying away, right after the spriggan had disappeared. Was it possible? Could that have been him?

She wanted to believe. Not only that magic could turn a wingless faery into a bird, but that everything else the stranger had told her was true as well. That Marigold was alive and longing to see her, and that one short flight over the countryside would bring them together again.

And that was exactly why Ivy couldn't listen to the spriggan any longer. Because if she did, she might end up making the worst mistake of her life.

'I have to go,' she blurted, and fled.

'I shall despair. There is no creature loves me; And if I die, no soul shall pity me...'

Wearily Ivy raised her head from the pillow, the stranger's parting words still echoing in her mind. She'd had to listen to him all the way up the shaft last night, gabbling about villainy and murder and vengeance, and guilt had stabbed her as she realised he was already tumbling back into madness. Even without the agony of a dislocated elbow, being locked up in the pitch dark with an iron band around his ankle must be unbearable for a creature used to fresh air and sunlight, and if that weren't cruel enough, he was dying of hunger and thirst as well...

Ivy kicked back the bedcovers and pulled open the curtains of her alcove, grimacing at the dirty smears her fingers left behind. She'd been so tired when she got back to the cavern, she'd fallen into bed without washing or changing her clothes. Had Mica and Cicely noticed? What would she tell them, if they asked where she had been?

She hopped down onto the rug and glanced in both directions. All the beds were empty, and the door to their father's bedchamber stood open; bowls and spoons littered the table, and Cicely had forgotten to put the cream back in the cold-hole. It was mid-morning, and they'd all left hours ago – what must they have thought when they woke up and found Ivy still asleep?

She heated water for a bath and scrubbed herself clean, then tidied up the dining table and made the bed Mica had left in disarray. It irked her that he never did it himself, but if she didn't look after it Cicely would, so there was no point leaving it. After that she'd sweep the floor and make some bread, and finish curing the skin from Keeve's adder, and then…

Ivy collapsed into a chair, fingers worrying at her black curls. It was no use trying to distract herself, or pretend that her conversation with the spriggan hadn't happened. What if Marigold really had sent him? Could Ivy let him starve and miss what might well be her only chance to find her mother, simply because she was afraid of being taken in?

Yet she had to find a way to protect herself, before she agreed to anything. Faeries might consider a bargain sacred, but if the old stories were true, they also had a knack for finding loopholes in nearly any bargain they made. And the last thing Ivy wanted was to risk her life for this stranger, only to end up betrayed…

'You're up,' said Cicely, peering in the doorway. 'I thought you were ill. I was going to ask Yarrow to come and look at you.'

Ivy forced a smile. 'I'm well enough. I just got to bed later than I should have.' She climbed to her feet. 'Why don't we make some bread?'

'Did you talk to him?' asked Mica that night at supper, taking the last roll from the basket.

Ivy choked. 'What – who?'

'Dad. It was him you were looking for, wasn't it?' He gave her a pointed look. 'To ask him about...you know.'

She hid her face in her cup and took a long drink, only partly relieved. Why was Mica always oblivious to her feelings except when she *didn't* want him to notice? 'Oh. No, I didn't. I couldn't find him, so I went for a walk instead.'

'What are you talking about?' asked Cicely.

But Mica didn't answer, and the silence thickened until Ivy said, 'Just something that Mica remembered and I didn't. I thought he was mistaken, so I was going to ask Dad. But then I realised maybe he was right after all.'

'Took you long enough,' muttered Mica, but she could see that he was both surprised and pleased. It must have been frustrating for him these past five years, hearing Ivy claim that their mother had been taken by the spriggans when he was certain that deep down she knew better. Not that it excused his attitude towards her – he still deserved a good smack around the head for that, and Ivy wished she were tall enough to give it to him. But it explained a lot about the way he'd been behaving.

'It's about Mum, isn't it?' Cicely turned accusing eyes to Ivy. 'You always get that look on your face when you're thinking about her. What did he say? Was it the same as—'

'Leave it,' Mica cut in. 'Ivy's tired of talking about it and so am I. It's not going to change anything.' He stabbed another slice of rabbit and began cutting it up. 'Matt and I are going into Redruth tomorrow. Is there anything you want?'

Ivy poked at her meal, torn between gratitude and guilt. Every now and then, along with the small animals they hunted, the fish they caught and the wild greens, mushrooms and berries they foraged, the hunters of the Delve took human-shape and journeyed to the nearby towns for more exotic fare: glittering white sugar and flour ground fine as dust, currants and saffron and citrus peel, slabs of chocolate or sweet marzipan. It was always a pleasant surprise when Mica remembered to ask Ivy what she needed, but if he knew where she'd been last night, he wouldn't be offering to do her any favours.

'I'm running out of cinnamon,' she said at last. 'And I wouldn't mind a couple of oranges.' Cicely loved oranges, so perhaps that would be enough to keep her from brooding over Mica's reprimand – though judging by the mulish look on her face, it was already too late.

'I told Yarrow I'd help her grind herbs tonight,' Cicely said, pushing her plate away. 'I should go.'

'All right,' said Ivy. She waited until her sister had left, then turned to Mica. 'Have you heard anything more about the spriggan? Has he talked to the Joan yet?'

Mica shook his head in disgust. 'I told Gossan they should hang him up by his ankles over a smelting-pot and see what he has to say then, but he said *we piskeys ought to be better than that*, whatever that's supposed to mean. They're going to leave him alone for a couple of days before they question him again.'

'And if he still won't talk?'

He shrugged. 'Gossan said they'd mine that vein when they came to it.' Though the contempt in his tone said how little he approved of the Jack's forbearance. 'But whether he tells us what he did with Keeve or not, there's no way that spriggan's going to see daylight again. If the Joan doesn't make sure of that...' His hand dropped to the hilt of his hunter's knife. 'Then I will.'

It was raining that night as Ivy descended the Great Shaft, slow droplets falling between the bars and pattering into the stagnant water below. But she'd brought a rope this time, fastening one end tight at the foot of the iron railing and the other around her waist, so even if she slipped she wouldn't fall far.

She'd expected to hear the spriggan talking, as he had the night before. But the shaft was silent, and as she lowered herself into his cell the only sounds were the rasp of hemp on stone and the scuffing of her own bare feet. 'It's me,' she whispered, brightening her glow so he could see her. 'Are you awake?'

The prisoner sat against the wall, hands dangling between his knees. He looked like a corpse at first, eyes glazed and features slack, but as Ivy approached he stirred and gave a feeble smile. *'But soft!'* he murmured. *'What light through yonder window breaks?'*

'What are you talking about?' asked Ivy, sharp with the effort of hiding her relief. 'There aren't any windows here.'

'It's a line from a play by Shakespeare,' he replied. He must have seen Ivy's blank expression, because he went on patiently, 'Shakespeare was a human writer who lived a few centuries ago. Plays are stories made up of speeches and acted out in front of an audience. You understand the concept of theatre?'

'You mean a droll-show,' said Ivy. 'Like at midwinter, when the children dress up and pretend to be warriors, or… monsters.' She had almost said *spriggans*.

The prisoner's nostrils flared. 'I suppose. In a crude fashion.'

Time to change the subject, before he made her feel any more ignorant. 'I've been thinking about what you said to me. And…I'm ready to make a bargain.'

At once his expression changed. 'Go on.'

'I'll take the iron off your ankle and help you get out of

here, so you can take me to my mother. But I won't ride on your back.'

She spoke the words firmly, determined not to betray even a hint of weakness. After all, even if he could transform himself into a bird, there was no guarantee that he wouldn't fly off without her – or worse, take her somewhere she didn't want to go.

'Ivy,' said the stranger in exasperation, 'you can't expect me to *walk* you there. Even at human size—'

'No.' Her heart was fluttering, but she kept her voice calm. 'Teach me to change shape, like you do. I won't go anywhere with you, until I can fly.'

He stared at her. 'You? But you're a piskey. A *female* piskey, at that. And you think I can teach you to become a bird?'

'Why not? You learned to do it.'

'Piskey magic and faery magic aren't the same,' he said with forced patience. 'There are all kinds of things my people can do that yours can't. And even among faeries, changing shape isn't something females do.'

'How do you know that? Just because you've never seen one do it? I wouldn't bother turning myself into a bird either, if I had wings of my own. But I don't, so I have to try.' She folded her arms. 'And if you ever want to get out of here, you're going to have to try too.'

He made a faint, disbelieving sound. 'You drive a hard bargain, lady.'

'Harder where there's none,' she said.

'Even if you're right, it's not going to be easy. Before you can take the shape of a bird or animal, you have to know every part of it. You have to be completely familiar with the way it looks and moves, and know its habits as well as you know your own.' He spread his lean hands, inviting her to look around. 'Do you see any birds in here?'

Ivy hesitated. She'd thought changing shape would only be a matter of technique – that all he had to do was explain the steps to her and she'd be able to try it right away. But if she had to actually *look* at a bird, in order to become one...

'You'll have to go up to the surface,' the stranger went on, 'in the middle of the day, and spend a few hours following birds around before you find the one that calls to you, the one you *need* to become. And that's only the first step.' He shifted his weight, wincing as the iron band tugged at his ankle. 'Are you ready to do that?'

To go above in broad daylight, under the merciless eye of a sun she'd never seen before? To defy the rules and traditions she'd been raised with, risk the Joan's wrath and her fellow piskeys' disapproval, and make herself a hypocrite for telling Cicely that it was dangerous to go above? To take the chance that Keeve's murderer was still out there, waiting for another careless piskey to cross his path?

Any one of those ideas was terrifying, let alone all of them together. And yet to trust herself completely to a stranger, to climb onto his back and let him take her wherever he pleased, was even more unthinkable. Either way she'd be taking an enormous risk – but better to choose her own path than to have someone else choose it for her.

And besides, if she *could* do this, she wouldn't only have a chance of finding her mother, she'd have wings as well...

'Yes,' said Ivy, lifting her chin. 'Whatever it takes, I'm ready.'

five

The good thing about sneaking out through the Earthenbore was that it gave Ivy plenty of places to hide. Smaller tunnels branched off in every direction, so she could always duck into a side corridor if she heard someone coming.

The unfortunate thing was that Ivy couldn't be sure she wouldn't get caught anyway. Turning invisible would keep her from being seen, but it couldn't mask her scent, or prevent her bumping into someone by accident. And since she couldn't see unless she glowed at least a little, it would be pointless turning invisible unless she wanted to grope her way through the tunnels with no light at all.

But right now it was early afternoon, the time when the older knockers taught the younger men to refine and work metal, and piskey-wives did their washing and sewing while their daughters looked after the Delve's small menagerie of livestock, and all the youngest children were at lessons. As long as Ivy didn't stay away from home too long, there was no reason anyone should notice her missing.

She followed the passage to its final branch, as far from the Delve as she could go while still remaining underground, and began climbing the slope to the surface. Soon the scent of sun-baked earth wafted towards her, and the blackness around her began to lighten. Ivy crept forwards until the ceiling became so low she had to stoop, and then go on hands and knees. At last the tunnel ended in a latticework of brilliant green foliage, with a sliver of sky above it so blue it hurt to look at. She winced and turned her face away.

All her instincts told her to go back, that she wasn't prepared for this. To leave the earth's cool embrace and step out into that blazing emptiness, unarmed and unaccompanied, was more than any piskey she knew had ever done. Even Mica had been guided by two seasoned hunters on his first daylight trip, and he'd come back with a headache so fierce he'd spent the rest of the day in bed.

But if Ivy didn't go out there, she'd never learn to fly.

Keeping her head low to avoid the prickly overhang, Ivy crawled out of the tunnel. Only when the underbrush stopped rustling and she felt the sun's heat on her black curls did she sit up and slowly crack her eyelids open.

She'd only seen this landscape before at night, when its colours were soft and soothing. Now it shone with a hectic, fevered intensity that made her exhausted just looking at it.

How would she ever spot a single bird at this rate, let alone get close enough to study it? She could barely see. If an enemy crept up on her, she wouldn't know until it was far too late.

Yet Ivy wasn't about to give up. Learning to climb hadn't been easy either, and she'd had to start small, scaling the walls of an abandoned stope. And even once that ceased to be a challenge, climbing the Great Shaft had been a terrifying prospect. But Ivy would never forget the thrill when she pulled herself up onto the concrete lip at the top, and leaned out through the bars to feel the rain falling on her upturned face. Fresh air had never tasted so sweet.

She was stronger than anyone knew. She could do this. Ivy squinted, shielded her eyes with one hand, and began edging down the hillside one step at a time.

Some time later Ivy sat cross-legged in the shade of a holly bush, gazing into the sky. Her head throbbed, and sweat trickled down her spine. But her eyes had adjusted to the sunlight now, so she no longer feared that anyone would sneak up on her unnoticed. And she'd already spotted several kinds of birds.

Some had been solitary, winging past with smooth, masterful strokes; others had arrived in clusters, dipping and soaring in patterns intricate as any six-hand reel. She'd seen birds as big as Mica and birds smaller than Flint's fiddle, birds with long beaks and stubby ones, birds pale as the spriggan's hair and others dark as her own. But though she'd listened intently to their chirps and cries, none had stirred any answering call in her heart.

Maybe she was just too distracted to concentrate. A few minutes ago a horse and rider had come plunging out of the wood – both of them tiny with distance, but still the sight sent a stab of envy into Ivy's heart. Even though she'd only seen them in pictures, the love of horses was in her piskey blood, and she longed to leap to her feet and run after it.

But a horse couldn't take her to Truro and back again before anyone knew she was missing – not like her own wings could. And that was why Ivy had to stay focused until she found the right bird, and learned how to take its shape. So that even if the spriggan turned out to be lying, at least she'd have gained *something* from meeting him.

Time passed, and more birds with it. But still none of them seemed right to Ivy. She told herself to stop being fussy and choose the next bird that came along, but the moment she saw it – a ragged black creature with a scrap of carrion in its beak – her soul rebelled. No matter how badly she wanted to see her mother, she couldn't shape a bird like that.

The shadows were growing longer now, the sun slipping towards the horizon. If Ivy didn't get home soon, Cicely would wonder where she'd gone. Disappointed, she got to her feet and began climbing back up the hill. But at least now she knew she could visit the upper world without getting caught by spriggans or blundering into some unforeseen disaster, so perhaps tomorrow…

Something dark flashed across her vision, and instinctively she whirled to follow it. A little bird with wings like a bent bow, body tampering smoothly to a two-pronged fork of a tail. It swooped over the valley, moving so fast that Ivy's eyes barely had time to focus before it was out of sight.

Swee-ree, swee-ree, swee-ree, came its song from the distance, a piercing call that plucked at Ivy's heart. 'Wait!' she cried. 'Come back!'

And to her amazement, it did. Rounding the treetops, it soared towards her and flew a circle above her head, bright eyes watching her all the while. She'd heard that piskeys had a special rapport with animals, but she'd thought that was something only hunters did. She'd never guessed that she could do it, too.

'What are you?' she asked, her voice soft with wonder. The bird didn't answer, of course, but it dipped a little lower. And then a second bird of the same kind came flashing across the hillside to join it, and the two of them chased each other in dizzying spirals across the sky.

It was like magic, and music, and dancing, all at once. And as Ivy's heart soared with them she knew, as surely as she knew her own name, that this was the bird she wanted to be.

'Are you sure?' asked the faery that night, tearing a piece off the loaf Ivy had brought him. 'Small, forked tail, dark all

95

over?' And it stayed aloft the whole time, without coming to land?'

Ivy nodded. She'd stayed as long as she dared studying the little birds, so late that she'd nearly bumped into Mica and Mattock coming back from their trip to Redruth. A quick invisibility spell had protected her, but she still felt sick every time she thought about how close she'd come to being caught. 'So what kind of bird is it?' she asked. 'Does it have a name?'

'It's a swift. They're not resident birds. They winter in Africa and stay here only four or five months of the year. You're *certain* that's the one?'

'Why do you keep asking me that?' asked Ivy. 'I thought you'd be pleased. If I fly then so do you, remember?'

'Believe me,' said the prisoner, 'I haven't forgotten for an instant.' He chewed another mouthful before going on, 'It's just a bit unusual. I've never met anyone who shaped a swift before. So are you ready for the next step?'

'Of course,' said Ivy.

'Then tell me. What do swifts eat?'

'I'm…not sure. Insects?'

'Well, you'd better find out, because you're going to be eating it yourself.' His gaze held hers, relentless. 'How does a swift drink? Where does it sleep? How long can it fly, how high, how far? What predators does it fear, and how does it avoid them? How does it behave around other swifts?'

She had no answers for any of those. 'Why does any of that matter?' she asked. 'All I want to do is fly.'

'Because,' he said, 'swifts are communal birds. If you don't behave like a proper swift the other swifts will sense it, and instead of welcoming you into their midst, they'll attack. Predators will notice too, and come after you because you're easy prey. At best you could be driven miles off course, or end up injured and never reach your destination. Do you want to take that chance?'

Ivy blew out a frustrated breath. 'But I don't know *how* to find out all of that,' she said. 'I can't spend all day chasing swifts around the countryside—'

'Then find out as much as you can. But there's no way you're going to be able to turn yourself into a swift until you know a lot more about them than you do right now.'

It wasn't what she'd wanted to hear. But he had no reason to lie about it, especially with his own freedom at stake. So she nodded, and held out her hand for the water bottle.

'You're going already?'

'Why not? What else do we have to talk about?'

His mouth flattened. 'What indeed.' He handed her the bottle and turned away.

'Richard...' began Ivy, then faltered as he shot her an incredulous look. 'You mean that isn't your name?'

The prisoner started to laugh, a dry and horrible laughter like bones clattering down a mineshaft. *'I am justly served with mine own treachery,'* he gasped.

Disturbed, Ivy started to back away, but he held up a hand. 'No, don't run. I'm not angry with you. *Richard...*' He rolled the two syllables around in his mouth. 'Why not? It's as good a name as any.'

But not his usual name, obviously. 'So what do the other faeries call you, then?'

'It doesn't matter. Richard will do.' He stretched his arms above his head and yawned. 'Now if you'll excuse me, I'm going to sleep.'

Ivy's gaze travelled across the back of the cavern, taking in the rough-hewn floor without so much as a heap of straw to soften it, the chain that restricted the prisoner's movements to no more than two small steps in any direction, the iron band clamped around his ankle. Not to mention the acrid stench from the corner — if it was unpleasant now, in another day or two it would be unbearable.

Yet she didn't dare do anything more to help him, not yet. Bringing him food and water was risky enough.

'Good night, Richard,' Ivy said quietly, and left.

'You're awfully brown,' said Cicely in a tone that was half puzzlement, half admiration. 'Have you been rubbing something into your skin?'

Ivy looked up from the water-channel, the wash-cloth still in her hand. 'I...no, I haven't,' she said, too flustered to think of a better answer. She'd returned from her second trip to the surface in plenty of time, and taken care to brush off her clothes and comb her wind-blown curls. But she'd never realised what all that sunlight had done to her complexion. 'Why would I want to do that?'

Cicely blushed. 'I…I thought you might be trying to make yourself look pretty. Not that you aren't – I mean, I know you don't usually fuss about that sort of thing, but you've been away from the cavern a lot these last few days and Jenny said – I mean, I was wondering—'

'Jenny said what, exactly?' Ivy dropped the cloth and put her hands on her hips. 'And when did the two of you start talking about me behind my back?'

'It wasn't like that!' said Cicely, indignant now. 'I was feeding the chickens when Jenny came to get some eggs, and she asked me where you were and I said you were at home, and she said you weren't because she'd knocked and got no answer, and then she said she hadn't seen Mattock either and maybe…'

So Jenny thought she and Mattock were sweethearts, sneaking away together. Well, Ivy couldn't blame her for that, even though the idea was laughable – not only because Matt was Mica's best friend and Mica would probably thump him for even considering it, but what piskey-boy would want a mate with no wings?

'I'm not prettying myself up for Matt, if that's what you're asking,' Ivy said. 'I've been…working on something.'

99

Cicely's face lit with excitement. 'Is it a surprise? Will I get to see it when it's done?'

For one wild moment Ivy was tempted to tell her the truth. Keeping secrets was a lonely business, and Marigold was Cicely's mother too. But then she'd have to explain about her night-time visits to Richard, and that was too much dangerous knowledge for any ten-year-old to carry.

No, it was too soon. Better to leave it until she'd learned to fly, until she'd found Marigold. There would be plenty of time to share the good news with Cicely and Mica then.

'Maybe,' she said, smiling at her sister. 'Wait and see.'

'I'm ready,' Ivy told Richard as she dropped to the floor of his cell. 'And I've brought your supper.'

Richard's lips moved, but only a croak came out. He had to take a long draught from Ivy's water bottle before he could speak. 'Lovely,' he rasped, wiping his mouth on the back of his hand. 'I trust you've been enjoying plenty of sunshine on my behalf.'

Ivy took a loaf from her pack and set it down beside him, along with a hunk of cheese she'd saved from her own supper. 'Ask me what I know about swifts,' she said. 'Anything you like.'

'I'll take your word for it,' said Richard. 'Why don't you ask me some of the things you *don't* know?'

That was better than Ivy had expected. In truth she knew the answers to fewer than half of the questions he'd originally asked her, but she couldn't think how to learn more on short notice. 'Do they ever land?' she asked. She'd watched a swift skimming over a river to scoop up water with its beak, and seen another snatching insects from the air in mid-flight. But though there were plenty of trees and shrubs nearby, they hadn't stopped to perch on any of them.

'Only to nest,' he said. 'They eat, drink, mate and even sleep in flight. Have you seen their legs?'

'They're short.'

'Yes. Far too short to allow them to land safely on the ground, or even in a tree. They only perch on vertical surfaces – rock faces and such. And they build their nests under the eaves of barns and houses – the higher, the better.' He broke off a piece of cheese, popped it into his mouth and said around it, 'Anything else you want to know?'

'I'm not sure about predators,' Ivy admitted. 'I saw a few bigger birds that looked dangerous, but they didn't seem fast enough.'

'Most of them aren't. But watch out for the hobby – it's a kind of small falcon that can dive very quickly. That's about the only thing that can catch a swift.'

Ivy waited for more, but he only tore off another chunk of bread and kept eating. 'So,' she said, 'what now?'

Richard swallowed with an effort. 'Picture,' he said, 'a swift in your mind. Every detail, from beak to tail-feathers. Don't let any other thoughts come in.'

The moment he said that, it was impossible *not* to be distracted. All Ivy could think about was Cicely's quizzical expression as she said, *You're awfully brown…*

'You've lost it already, haven't you?'

'Don't talk to me,' she said irritably.

'You're going to have to do this with every kind of noise and distraction around. You might as well start learning now.'

Ivy scowled, trying to marshal her scattered thoughts. Meanwhile Richard, blast him, started *whistling* – no, not so much whistling as trilling, a persistent chirrup-noise she'd never heard before. What bird sang like that?

And now the swift-image was gone again. She groaned, and screwed her eyes shut for another attempt. Mentally she traced and retraced every line of the swift's small body, right down to the tiny patch of white feathers beneath its chin – until Richard exclaimed aloud and Ivy opened her eyes to find a perfect illusion of a swift flashing around the cavern.

She threw up her hands, and the glamour vanished. 'That's not what I meant to do!'

'No,' said Richard, 'but it's not a bad start.' He ran a finger thoughtfully across his split lip. 'Maybe if you create the illusion first, and focus on that…'

'And then what?'

'Then you will yourself into its form.'

That didn't sound so hard. Ivy brushed a curl back from

her forehead, conjured the swift-image again, and silently commanded her body to take its shape. Harder and harder she concentrated, until her skin began to tingle. It was working! She could feel her muscles shifting, her bones beginning to shrink...

But when she opened her eyes, she was still in piskey-form. She'd made herself as small as a swift, but she hadn't taken its shape. 'Ugh!' said Ivy, changing back to her usual size. 'Why isn't it working?'

'I was afraid of this,' said Richard. 'Without being able to show you how I take bird-shape, it's impossible to teach you how to do it. Did your mother ever have to explain to you the steps that go into creating a glamour? Of course not. You watched her a few times, and you *knew*.'

It was true. Magic was a matter of instinct rather than learning, for piskeys and all magical folk. But Ivy could see where this was leading, and she didn't like it. 'So you're saying that unless I take the iron off your ankle and let you go, I'll never be able to fly.'

Richard opened his mouth, made a face and closed it again. Finally he said, 'There are a couple of things you can try first. You might find it easier to change shape outside, where there are no walls or ceilings to hold you back. That alone might work – but if it doesn't, then try it again by moonlight.'

'Moonlight? What difference will that make?'

'It'll make your magic stronger,' he said. 'A full moon on

a clear night would be best, but even a little moonlight's better than none.'

Ivy glanced back at the darkened shaft. She wasn't sure she had the energy to climb all the way to the top right now – not after so many long nights and daytime trips to the surface. And Mica had come back to the cavern even later than usual tonight, so there wasn't much time left in any case.

'All right,' she said. 'I'll try it.'

'Then I wish you good luck,' said Richard. 'But if you could speed up your experiments a little, I'd appreciate it. One meal a day isn't much to go on, and I'm not sure how much longer your Joan is planning to keep me alive.'

He spoke lightly, but there was a wildness about his eyes that reminded Ivy of how he had looked when she'd first seen him, clutching his injured arm and babbling Shakespeare. Battered, starving, and desperate for light, he might not keep his sanity much longer – and then what would Ivy do?

'I can't promise anything,' she said as she reached for her rope. 'I have to be careful, or my family will get suspicious. But I'll do the best I can.'

When Ivy returned home the first sound that greeted her was Mica's rattling snore, and for once she was grateful for it. Keeping her glow as dim as she could, she tiptoed across to her bed-alcove, pulled off her shirt and grabbed her discarded nightgown from beneath the pillow. If she could stop fretting about swifts and Richard and her mother for a few minutes, maybe she'd be able to—

'Ivy?'

It was only a sleepy mumble, but Ivy's heart dropped into her stomach. It took her several seconds to collect her wits and whisper, 'It's all right, Cicely. I'm here.'

She waited, but there was no answer, and finally Ivy relaxed and lay down. Most likely Cicely was just talking in her sleep again, and would remember nothing of the conversation in the morning.

'Sleep well, little sister,' she murmured, and closed her eyes.

SIX

Tired though she was, Ivy managed to wake up at her normal time the next day – early enough to rouse Mica for his morning run, though he looked even more sour than usual about it.

'You were up late last night,' she said, as she packed up a cold pasty and a bottle of small beer for Flint's lunch. His thunder-axe was still propped outside the bedroom door, so maybe she'd be able to get some breakfast into him before he vanished again. 'What happened?'

Mica poured himself a mug of hot chicory and gulped about half of it, making a face as he set it down. 'I brought coffee back from Redruth,' he said. 'Why are you still making this muck?'

'If you don't like it, make the coffee yourself,' said Ivy. 'Why are you changing the subject?'

Mica shot her a baleful glare. Then, with a glance at Cicely's curtained alcove, he leaned closer and muttered,

'Gem and Feldspar spotted someone – or some*thing* – sneaking about the Engine House last night.'

Ivy's lips formed a silent *oh*.

'But it disappeared before they could get a proper look at it. So Gossan sent a few of us out to see if we could track it down, but...' He shrugged, and took another swig of chicory. 'No luck. Whatever it was, it came and went like the wind.'

'You think it's another spriggan?' asked Ivy. She'd been so caught up in watching the swifts, she'd forgotten that Keeve's murderer could still be out there.

'Maybe.' Mica dropped the empty mug onto the worktop and picked up his hunter's knife. 'But we're not supposed to say anything about it yet, so keep that to yourself.'

'Ready, Mica?' The question came so quietly through the crack in the door that only piskey ears could have heard it. It always amazed Ivy that a boy as big and broad-shouldered as Mattock should be so soft-spoken.

'I'm coming.' Mica swung his pack over his shoulder, gave Ivy a last warning glance and disappeared.

Ivy returned to the hearth and stirred the porridge, her brows creased in a frown. Who was the shadowy figure that Gem and Feldspar had seen creeping about the hillside? Could Richard have had a companion, who was now looking for him? It seemed unlikely that two strangers would turn up around the same time, if they weren't somehow connected...

'Is there any porridge left?' asked Cicely, climbing out of her alcove. But her gaze was downcast, and she spoke without her usual spirit. Had she overheard Mica talking? Or had she merely sensed Ivy's troubled mood?

'Yes, of course,' Ivy said, doing her best to sound cheerful. 'With berries and cream too, if you like.'

The two of them were sitting down to eat when Flint emerged from his bedchamber, dressed in the same dusty clothes he'd worn the day before. Once he had been handsome, and so like Betony that the two of them might have been twins. But now his features sagged as though his skin were too big for him, and his eyes were dull as pebbles.

'Come and have some porridge, Dad,' Ivy said, offering him her bowl. But he shook his head, and reached for his thunder-axe.

Ivy wanted to grab her father and shake him, but she knew it would do no good. She heard him coughing in the night sometimes, but he'd never let her give him any of Yarrow's herbal remedies to make it better. His hands shook whenever he gripped anything lighter than a pick or shovel, and his teeth had turned yellow with neglect – yet he didn't seem to care about those things, either. So why should he bother eating a proper breakfast?

'Take this, then,' she said, pushing the packed lunch against his chest. He curled his arm around it, swung the magical pickaxe onto his shoulder and walked out without another glance.

Oh, Mother, Ivy thought, leaning wearily on the edge of the table. *Even if you stopped loving him, surely you never wanted him to end up like this?*

Going up to the surface today could be the biggest risk Ivy had taken yet, especially with the hunters already on the alert. But she couldn't let that stop her, especially now. Because if Marigold was alive, she needed to know how much her family missed her, and how desperately they needed her to come back.

Ivy waited until Cicely went off for her lessons, then crept out of the Delve with all her usual caution. All seemed well at first, though as she turned into the Earthenbore she had an uncomfortable suspicion that she was being watched. But no one stepped out to challenge her, so after a brief hesitation she ignored the feeling and kept on.

Once outside she found a good spot on the hillside from which to launch herself, and went through the steps Richard had taught her. *Picture the swift. Focus on the swift. Become the swift.* Yet after several minutes of jaw-clenching effort, Ivy knew it was no use. No matter how hard she concentrated or how much magic she put into the effort, she was still the same wingless piskey-girl as before.

Ivy hugged her knees to her chest, doubt snaking into her mind. When she'd seen her first swift and felt that powerful sense of connection, she'd felt certain that she was meant to fly. But what if Richard had been right all along, and she *couldn't* change shape? What if her piskey blood, or some quirk of her female nature, made it impossible?

Well, she'd know tonight, one way or the other. Maybe Richard was right, and moonlight was the key. But after so many failed attempts, it was hard to believe that such a small thing would make any difference.

Ivy was back in the cavern, making a fish pie for supper, when Cicely came in. 'Did you have a good lesson?' she asked, but Cicely didn't reply. She kicked off her shoes and climbed into her bed-alcove, pulling the curtain shut.

That wasn't like Cicely at all. Ivy wiped her hands on her apron and followed. 'What's the matter? Are you all right?' She opened the curtain and found her little sister lying on her side, her eyes squeezed shut. Her cheeks were flushed, her forehead warm to the touch.

No wonder she'd been so quiet earlier. 'Does your stomach hurt?' Ivy asked. 'Or is it your chest? Shall I get Yarrow to make you a potion?'

'No,' mumbled Cicely. 'I just want to rest. Please go away.'

With some reluctance Ivy stepped back and let the curtain drop. Perhaps her sister had become overheated running around with the other children, and would be better in an hour or two.

'I'll get you some water,' she said. 'Drink as much as you can. If you're not well by suppertime, I'll call for Yarrow.'

To Ivy's relief, Cicely seemed to have recovered by the time supper was on the table. She still wasn't her usual talkative self, but she ate a generous helping of fish pie, and helped Ivy clean up afterwards. She spent the rest of the evening working on the jumper she was knitting for Mica, then climbed into her bed-alcove without complaint.

By the time Mica returned, Ivy had snuffed out the day-lamps and was pretending to be asleep. She waited until his breathing deepened into the usual full-throated rumble, then dropped lightly to the rug and tiptoed out.

All seemed quiet as she made her way through the tunnels, but halfway up the Hunter's Stair she froze, her skin prickling. Had that been a footstep? She turned, ready to confront her pursuer and brazen it out. But she saw nothing in the darkness behind her, not even the tiniest flicker.

Ivy set her jaw and climbed faster, silently rebuking herself for letting her nerves get the better of her. Yes, it would be disastrous if she were caught sneaking out of the Delve, but she'd already taken that risk three times by daylight and survived.

When she emerged onto the hillside, she had to turn nearly a full circle before she spotted the moon. Only half-full, and dimmed a little by the ragged clouds, but it would have to do. Now, where to begin? She couldn't return to the launching place she'd used earlier, with its too-gentle slope that reeked of fear and failure. If this were her last chance to change shape, she had to be bolder than that. Ivy set off at an angle across the hill, crunching through the heather and bracken.

After a few breathless minutes she reached a spot where the rocks broke through the soil and the ground dropped steeply away. It would have been a long jump to the bottom even for a human, and at piskey size it was high enough to make her nervous. But it was the perfect place to launch herself from, if she became a swift.

Ivy tilted her head back, closing her eyes as the moonlight tingled on her skin. Summoning the familiar image in her mind, she spread her arms wide, stepped forward...

And a scream rang out from behind her.

Startled, Ivy twisted around – and her foot slipped. Arms flailing, legs tangled together, she let out a cry of her own as she toppled over the edge. But the shout became a shriek, keening high in her ears, and her skin changed into feathers even as she fell. She skimmed a hand's span over the rocks and zoomed upward, into the open sky.

She was flying! Joy filled Ivy from her crown to her forked tail-feathers. Even though she'd never flown before, she felt no fear or awkwardness; her new body was the perfect shape to bend the air currents to her bidding, and she could change speed or direction with the merest flick of a feather. How could she ever have thought of wind as an insubstantial thing? The updraught beneath her wings felt as solid as the earth itself.

Daring, she rose higher, the landscape dropping away beneath her. Her swift's eyes were as sharp as her piskey ones had ever been, and she could pick out every feature of the countryside below – hills and valleys, cottages and barns, and here and there the silhouettes of old whim-engine and pumping-engine houses, remnants of the hundreds of mines that now lay abandoned and overgrown. Lights dotted the ground and sprinkled the horizon like bits of shattered crystal – not merely the small clusters of human dwellings she'd grown accustomed to seeing from the hillside, but entire towns and cities glittering in the dark. And in the distance lay more cottages, more towns, more stretches of open country both wild and tame...and beyond them, the grey rolling line of the ocean.

Excitement surged in Ivy's breast. She could go anywhere she wanted now. In fact, if she'd known where Truro was, she could have flown to her mother this very minute...

Then she remembered the cry that had startled her off the ledge, and the warmth inside her turned chill. It might have been an animal or the shriek of a passing bird, but what if it wasn't? Ivy doubled back towards the familiar hillside, searching for signs of life. But she saw no frenzied movements or splashes of unexpected colour; all that met her gaze were the dull hues of wild greens and shrubberies, earth and clay and stone. And though she listened closely with her bird-keen ears, the only sound was the wind whispering through the leaves.

Perhaps Ivy had only imagined the scream – it would be a relief to think so. She'd hardly begun to stretch her wings, and there was still a glorious infinity of open sky to explore. But the night wouldn't last forever, and now that Richard had proved himself a man of his word, Ivy owed it to him to set him free. Maybe, if she moved quickly enough, there'd still be time for him to take her to her mother.

Ivy hurried towards her home cavern, still giddy with the thrill of flight. Before heading underground she'd transformed into a swift and back again several times over, until she could leap into flight as easily as blinking and land with barely a stumble. Changing shape was so easy now, she felt certain that even without moonlight she'd be able to do it again.

I can fly! Ivy's heart sang out. She wanted to burst into the cavern and shout her triumph, wake up Mica and Cicely so they could see the miracle. But she couldn't do that yet – it was too risky. She had to at least free Richard first. Dimming her glow to the barest hint of luminescence, she eased the door open and tiptoed in.

Flint's thunder-axe was propped against the wall in its usual place, with his well-worn boots beside it. Ivy glanced at the bed-alcoves, reassuring herself that all the curtains were drawn. Then with painstaking care she lifted the magical pickaxe, and carried it out the door.

*

Lowering herself and the thunder-axe down the Great Shaft at the same time was an agonising business. Every time the pick's weight shifted Ivy held her breath, fearing the precious tool would slip free of her makeshift harness and drop into the flooded depths below. But at last she made it safely to Richard's cell.

'I did it,' she panted as she loosened the ropes around her chest and lifted the thunder-axe free. 'Now let's get that iron off your ankle.'

Richard looked blank, and Ivy wondered if he'd understood. 'I said,' she began more loudly, but he cut her off.

'I heard you,' he replied. 'I'm just a bit unused to *pleasant* surprises, that's all. Are you really planning to strike off my manacle with that thing? From the way you're staggering about, it seems more likely that you're going to smash my foot to bits with it.'

'I'll try not to,' said Ivy tartly. She crouched beside him, examining the iron band. 'How did they put this on you?'

'I don't know. I was unconscious when—' But then Ivy slipped her fingers between the manacle and his skin, and his words ended in a gasp.

'Did I hurt you?' Ivy pulled her hand away. 'I didn't mean to.'

'No, not that.' Richard sounded shaken. 'It's – you. You touched iron on *purpose*.'

Oh, of course. She'd forgotten what a shock that would

be to him. 'My people have been working with rock and metal for centuries,' Ivy said, feeling her way around the band. 'If we lost our magic every time we touched iron, how would we get anything done?' She sat back. 'I can't find a hinge or a keyhole anywhere. They must have spelled it right onto your ankle.'

He stared at her. 'You mean piskeys can use magic on iron, too?'

'Some of us can. Unfortunately for you, I'm not one of them. That's why I borrowed this.' She nodded at the thunder-axe. 'But we'll need to put some padding around your ankle first.'

Without hesitation Richard pulled off what was left of his shirt and handed it to her. His skin was sickly-pale beneath the bruises, his collarbones jutting and his ribs clearly visible. 'Try not to swoon,' he said dryly.

'I've never swooned in my life,' said Ivy. She tore the shirt into strips, and pushed as much of the worn fabric as she could between the manacle and the faery's ankle. 'Ready?' she asked.

Richard looked apprehensive, but he nodded.

'Just one thing,' Ivy said as she hefted the pickaxe. 'And I want you to tell me the truth. When you came here looking for me, on Lighting night – did you bring someone else with you? Or did you tell anyone where you'd gone?'

She watched his face, searching for even the tiniest hint of

116

guilt or fear. But he only looked puzzled. 'Your Joan asked me the same thing, this morning,' he said. 'But no, I came alone. And the only one who knew I was coming here was Marigold.'

If he was a liar, he was a very good one. 'All right,' said Ivy, and swung the thunder-axe down.

The blade struck with a ringing *clank* and a spark of brilliant blue light. Richard made a strangled noise, and she knew the blow had hurt him – but when Ivy's dazzled vision cleared, the band was still intact.

Obviously she hadn't figured out how to use the magical pickaxe quite right. Maybe if she pushed a bit of her own magic into it first... With barely a pause, Ivy raised the thunder-axe and brought it down again.

This time the spark was so bright, Ivy stumbled and nearly dropped the pick. The iron manacle cracked in two, and clattered onto the stone at Richard's feet.

'Finally,' the faery breathed. He slid away from her and rubbed his ankle, which was cruelly blistered where the iron had pressed against it. She waited for him to do something magical – heal himself perhaps, or spell himself clean, or mend his tattered clothes. But all he did was sit there.

'Well?' she asked. 'Are we going to fly? There might still be time, if we hurry.'

Richard raised his eyebrows. 'After wearing iron for over a week? It'll be hours – maybe even days – before I can do magic again. I'm not flying anywhere tonight.'

Ivy recoiled as though he had slapped her. 'You...you can't be serious. You said—'

'I said I'd take you to your mother if you let me go. I never said I could do it right away.' But there was no triumph in his tone, only resignation. 'I'm not going to try and escape, if that's why you're still gripping that pickaxe. I can't even get out of this tunnel, unless you lead me out yourself.'

Ivy's hands tightened on the thunder-axe. 'I can't do that,' she said. She'd been prepared for everything from passionate gratitude to cold-blooded betrayal, but she'd never anticipated this. 'If we were caught...'

'Then go, and leave me here.' He spoke wearily, as though he'd expected nothing better. 'Maybe your Joan will think I freed myself, when she comes to execute me tomorrow.'

Alarm stabbed into Ivy. 'Execute you? She told you that?'

'Oh yes. Quite matter-of-factly. I'm to be hanged in the Market Cavern, with someone called Hew knotting the rope, and my body left in the Engine House as a warning to my accomplice. Whoever that is.'

Ivy wished she could believe he was lying, but his story was far too likely. Keeve's family were still crying out for vengeance, and if Richard's body was left on the surface to deter whatever creature had been skulking about the Engine House, it would satisfy the hunters as well.

'But you never know,' Richard went on. 'Maybe before

then I'll be strong enough to fly out of here – though that's going to be a bit difficult, with no light to see by.' His mouth twisted ruefully. 'Pity I never learned to take bat-shape.'

He was right about that too, unfortunately. If she'd been worried about Cicely flying up the Great Shaft without a glow to light her way, how could she expect Richard to do any better? The only way to be sure of getting him safely to the surface was to take him out of the Delve herself.

Yet to free a prisoner that the Joan had condemned to death, and lead him to the surface through tunnels that no one but a piskey had ever been allowed to see – it was unthinkable, unforgivable. If Ivy were caught, it would not only bring disgrace on her entire family, but she'd probably be executed as well.

I can't, her mind cried out, *I can't do this, there has to be another way*. But it was too late for that. First she'd healed Richard, then she'd fed him, and now she'd freed him from his chains. And she'd promised to help him get out of the Delve.

Ivy drew a deep breath, willing herself strong. Then she hefted Flint's thunder-axe up onto her shoulder and said, 'All right. Come with me.'

seven

If carrying the thunder-axe down the shaft had been hard for Ivy, getting it back up was even more of a challenge. Growing a couple of hand-spans taller made the pick a lighter burden, but it also made her heavier – not to mention putting more strain on the rope. She'd only climbed a little way before she had to shrink to her customary size, and by the time she reached the iron railing she was wheezing.

'I'm up,' she panted to Richard as she clambered over, making her glow as bright as she dared so that he'd have enough light for his own climb. 'Tie the rope around your waist, and I'll—'

But Richard was already pulling himself up the shaft towards her, feet braced wide on the rock. His strength surprised Ivy – if he could manage such a climb even in his weakened state, how strong had he been before? But when he reached the railing he stopped, leaning back on the rope.

'That's iron,' he said flatly. 'I can't touch it.'

'You have to,' she whispered, but he shook his head.

'Touching iron's like an electric shock to a faery – it doesn't just take away our magic, it *hurts*. It can even knock us unconscious. If I grab it, I may not be able to hang on.' He shifted his footing on the rock and reached a hand up towards her. 'I'll have to jump as high as I can, and let you pull me over.'

This was ridiculous, thought Ivy. They'd never get out of the Delve at this rate. Still, there was nothing else but to try it, so she leaned as far over the railing as she could and gripped his hand in her own.

'One,' mouthed Richard, crouching against the rock. 'Two. *Three*—'

He sprang upward, while Ivy braced her feet against the railing and hauled with all her might. The iron groaned as Richard's weight landed on it, then blazed white as it touched skin. He gasped and convulsed – but in the same moment Ivy dragged him over, and the two of them landed in a heap on the floor of the adjoining tunnel.

'*Ow*,' Richard breathed, rolling away from her and pressing one hand to his stomach. Dizzy with relief, Ivy sat up and crawled over to the railing to untie her rope. She coiled it up, slung it across her body and reached for the thunder-axe again.

'Come on,' she told him. 'We've got a long way to go.'

*

'This is incredible,' murmured Richard. 'Is that *silver*?'

She'd told him to stay close and put his hand on her shoulder, so she could keep her glow dim. Not only because she feared they'd be seen if she shone more brightly, but because no outsider should ever see the treasures of the Delve. Unfortunately, the faery's night-vision was a lot better than she'd thought. 'Stop it,' she hissed, quickening her pace. 'Keep your eyes down.'

He obeyed, or at least kept silent, until they turned the next corner. But then he made a disbelieving noise, and Ivy knew what he'd just seen – the thousands of tiny gemstones embedded into the tunnel walls. Only total darkness could have hidden them, and she didn't dare extinguish her light or they'd never get anywhere at all. But hearing Richard's intake of breath and slow, wondering exhale made Ivy feel even more like a traitor than before.

She hugged the thunder-axe closer, arm muscles burning with the strain of carrying the heavy pick so long. She didn't dare try shifting it to a more comfortable position – if she dropped it, the crash would be loud enough to wake the whole Delve. Richard might be willing to take it from her, but she hated to appear weak, and she didn't trust him enough yet to hand him something he could use as a weapon. Besides, she was almost home now, so she'd be able to put it down soon enough...

She'd only taken a few more steps when a loose stone spiked into her heel, throwing her off-balance. With a gasp

Ivy staggered sideways, bumping into the tunnel wall. The thunder-axe's head tipped away from her, and she felt the haft twist out of her grip –

Richard leaped forward, his hands locking over hers and catching the pickaxe a mere hand-span from the floor. For a few uneven heartbeats the two of them stared into each other's eyes, breathing hard. Then Ivy drew herself upright, gave him a shaky nod, and hefted the pick again.

By the time they reached her family's cavern, all Ivy's nerves were jangling. Little shivers ran over her skin as she crept inside to put the rope away and prop the thunder-axe in place, and she felt horribly sure that at any moment Mica or Cicely would fling open their curtains and confront her. When her brother stirred and mumbled just as she was lowering the pick to the floor, she had to clamp her teeth shut on a scream. But then the familiar snore started up again, and she managed to quell her panic and carry on.

'Done it,' she whispered to Richard as she slipped out, easing the door closed behind her. Then she grabbed his arm and hurried up the corridor. She couldn't bear to creep and skulk any more; it was too unnerving. Better to make a bold rush for the exit than waste any more time on secrecy.

They'd just passed the Narrows and were starting up the Hunter's Stair when Richard seized her wrist and jerked her to a stop. Shocked by his rudeness, Ivy was just about to order him to let go when she heard it. Voices.

There was no time to discuss a plan. Leaping down the

stair, Ivy pulled Richard into the only hiding place she could find – a shallow curve of the tunnel, barely wide enough for the two of them. Flattening him against the wall with one outstretched arm, she pressed herself next to him, extinguished her glow, and fervently willed them both invisible.

'…doesn't mean he won't be back again,' said Feldspar's voice from above. 'Next time he'll bring others with him, and we'll have a battle on our hands.'

'You think so?' That was Gem, boots clomping as he headed down the steps. 'I can't see it. We've always kept our heads down when their kind were about, and we haven't lost a hunter in years. Excepting young Keeve, of course. But he always was a wild one, and I wouldn't be surprised—' He stopped. 'What?'

'Hush a minute.' Feldspar sounded tense. 'Did you hear something?'

Ivy's heart was pounding so hard, she felt sure it would smash right out of her chest. She closed her eyes, pushing all her concentration into holding the invisibility glamour steady. Any second now the two hunters would pass by, their combined glows banishing every shadow, and if she let the illusion falter even for a moment…

'What's to hear?' asked Gem with a snort. 'You think a spriggan could follow us right into the Delve? If he's that crafty and we're that blind, we may as well surrender and hand over our treasure right now.'

Richard's chest rose sharply against Ivy's arm, and she could practically read his thoughts: *Treasure?* Her lips flattened. If he turned out to be a spriggan after all, she'd never forgive herself.

Above them, Feldspar chuckled. 'All right, I'll quit trying to prank you. But I'm not joking about there being more of those creatures. Two sightings in a week – that can't be a coincidence. And who's to say that killing one won't just make the rest of them angry?'

'Ah, you're a twitch-nosed rabbit. We're safe enough in the Delve, so let 'em come, is what I say...'

Still lost in friendly argument, the two hunters continued down the steps into the Narrows, passing so close to Ivy that she could feel their glows warming her skin. But they never broke stride, or looked around. And soon the sound of their footsteps faded away.

Ivy relaxed, but her mind was still racing. So Gem and Feldspar had been out all night looking for spriggans. How close had she come to meeting them when she'd gone out earlier? Had they heard the scream that had startled her into flight?

Richard gave a little cough, and she realised she was still pinning him against the wall. Embarrassed, she dropped her arm and let him go.

'We'd better hurry,' she whispered as she stepped out into the corridor, rekindling her light. 'It should be safe now, but there isn't much time.'

*

When Ivy and Richard climbed out onto the surface the moon had vanished, and a light rain was falling. Ivy rubbed her bare arms, but Richard flung his wide as though to embrace the sky.

'Finally,' he exulted. 'I thought I'd never breathe fresh air again.'

This was the moment Ivy had dreaded. He was stronger and faster than she was, even in his weakened state; if he chose to betray her now, she'd be unable to stop him.

'You taught me to fly,' she said. 'Now I've set you free, as we agreed. But there's one more thing. Swear to me that you'll tell no one what you saw in the Delve tonight. *No one*.'

'A good mouth-filling oath?' Richard turned, his smile fading to seriousness as his pewter-grey gaze met hers. 'I swear it,' he said. 'By my blood and by my name. My *true* name.'

Ivy's apprehension eased a little. Maybe she could count on him after all. 'But you still have to take me to my mother,' she said. 'I'll come as soon as I get the chance, but—'

'You're not coming now?'

'I can't.' It hurt to admit how badly she'd miscalculated, but she couldn't deny it now. 'If I don't get home soon, my family will wake up and find me missing. And when they realise you're gone as well…'

'They'll think we've eloped?' said Richard with a quirk

of the eyebrows, but when Ivy glared at him he relented. 'My apologies. They'll think I've taken you hostage, of course.'

Ivy nodded. 'That's why I have to go now. But...' She drew in her breath. 'I risked my life for you tonight, and I hope you won't make me regret it. Promise that when I call for you, tomorrow night or the next, you'll be here.'

A muscle jumped in Richard's cheek. He wrapped his arms around himself, as though he'd only just remembered he was only half-dressed. 'Tomorrow *or* the next, you say. And if you haven't come by then?'

'Then you're free to go.' She couldn't expect him to wait forever, after all. 'But if you leave a note telling me where my mother is, I'll be able to look for her on my own. And then you'll have kept your word to both of us.'

Richard gave her a narrow look. 'Not to the letter, which is how we faeries make our bargains. But perhaps Marigold will see it differently. As you wish.' Without another word, he turned and walked away.

'That's gratitude,' called Ivy after him, but the faery didn't look back. Telling herself it was foolish to feel hurt – what more could she expect from someone who wasn't even a piskey? – Ivy swept the bracken aside and ducked into the Delve.

Ivy dreamed that she was flying, and at first she didn't want to wake – until she remembered that she *could* fly, and broke into an involuntary smile. But her bones ached, and her eyelids felt so heavy she could barely force them open. Surely it couldn't be morning yet?

But there was no doubting her sense of time; it was as unfailing as her sense of direction. And if she didn't get up and wake the others, they'd know something was wrong. Repressing a sigh, Ivy struggled out of bed and lit the day-lamps. She prodded Mica with the broom handle until he swore and slapped it away, then crossed to Cicely's alcove, opened the curtains...

And found the bed empty.

'Cicely?' Ivy turned, searching the cavern for her sister's glow. She passed a hand over the pillow, then the bedclothes, but felt not a trace of warmth. 'Mica, did you hear Cicely get up a while ago?'

Mica poked his head out between the curtains, his black hair tousled from sleep. 'What? No.'

A fearful suspicion stirred in Ivy's mind. She went to the door and opened it, looking both ways down the passage. 'Cicely! Are you there?'

'Don't be ridiculous,' said Mica, muffled by the shirt he was pulling over his head. 'Where would she go at this hour?'

He had a point, but Ivy wasn't about to acknowledge it. She grabbed her wrap off its hook and flung it around her. 'I'm going to look for her,' she said, and dashed out.

An hour later she had visited all of Cicely's favourite

places, knocked several sleepy families awake, and walked a circuit of the neighbouring tunnels, calling all the while. Jenny joined her, as did Mica and Mattock, and between them they searched the Delve from Market Cavern to Earthenbore.

But there was no sign of Ivy's little sister anywhere. Cicely, like Keeve before her, had vanished.

eight

Ivy sat shivering by the hearth in the Joan's stateroom, one of Cicely's hair ribbons crumpled in her hand. She barely noticed Betony pacing the rug as she questioned Mica about when he'd last seen Cicely, or Gossan's frown as he listened, or Flint standing in the doorway with a face as stony as his name. All Ivy knew was that her little sister was gone, and that it was her fault.

After the first shock of Cicely's disappearance, it hadn't taken Ivy long to realise what must have happened. The uneasy feeling she'd had yesterday, both times she went to the surface...she ought to have trusted her instincts. Because, of course, it had been Cicely following her all along.

Perhaps it had been Ivy's sun-browned skin that roused Cicely's suspicions, or perhaps it was hearing her slip back into the cavern in the middle of the night. Perhaps she'd simply been eager to find out what surprise Ivy was preparing. But for whatever reason, Cicely had made herself invisible and followed Ivy all the way to the surface, only to discover that her older sister had been sneaking out of the Delve without her.

Cicely probably hadn't gone outside the first time – the afternoon light would have blinded her. Instead she'd retreated to her bed, to brood over what she'd seen. But when she heard Ivy getting up later that night, it was the perfect chance to follow her a second time, and find out what she was up to.

It sickened Ivy to think that she'd led her little sister into danger. But more dreadful still was knowing that the scream she'd heard on the hillside – that thin, wailing cry that had startled her into flight – must have come from Cicely. If she'd gone to investigate straight away, she might have been in time to save her. But Ivy had been caught up in the joy of her new swift-form, and by the time she turned back her sister had already vanished...

'WHAT?' exploded Mica, and Ivy nearly dropped Cicely's ribbon in the fire. 'That's impossible! I chained that spriggan up myself – there's no way he could have escaped!'

'And yet he did,' said Betony crisply. 'Perhaps the iron was not as pure as you believed, or perhaps he found some way to weaken it. But the prisoner has gone, and taken Cicely with him.'

No, thought Ivy in dismay. *He couldn't have, he was with me.* But how could she tell them that?

131

'I'll kill him,' Mica's voice was savage, his big hands clenched so tight they shook. 'I'll track him all the way across Kernow if I have to, but I swear I won't rest until I break his skinny neck.'

'There's a search party heading to the surface,' said Gossan, 'and our most seasoned hunters and trackers are among them. They will do everything in their power to find Cicely.'

'No doubt,' Mica said flatly, 'but they can only search for a few hours before they have to come back again. And that's not good enough.' He dropped to one knee. 'Jack O'Lantern, Joan the Wad,' he said formally to Gossan and Betony in turn, 'I ask permission to track the spriggan myself, and stay out as long as it takes to find him and get my sister back.'

'Alone?' asked Betony. 'Leaving Ivy with no one to provide for her?'

She didn't even glance at Flint; they all knew that Ivy's father was of no fit mind to look after anyone. He was safe enough working in the mine, but send him to the surface and he might well drown himself in a bog, or walk off a cliff into the sea.

'Mattock would take care of Ivy, if I asked him,' said Mica quickly. 'Or Jenny's clan could take her in, until I get back.'

And there it was again. Just because Ivy was wingless, because she was small and skinny, they were talking about her as though she were an invalid. Never mind that she'd been managing a household for five years and doing the bulk of the chores as well – that didn't count as real work, apparently.

Betony and Gossan shared a look. Then the Joan said, 'Cicely must be found, yes, and her kidnapper punished as he deserves. But this is not a matter for any piskey to undertake alone.'

'Then I'll put together my own search party,' pleaded Mica. 'I'll take Mattock with me, and Gem and Feldspar too if you want. But you have to let me go!'

'*Have* to?' Betony said coldly. 'The Jack and I will do what is best for the Delve, Mica. Not only for you, but for *all* our people.' She walked behind her desk and sat down, wings folded primly behind her. 'I will consider your request, and inform you when we reach a decision. Until then, you may leave.'

Mica's expression turned mutinous. He sprang to his feet and stalked out.

'That one will make trouble,' warned Nettle, as she poured the tea and handed a cup to Gossan. 'He's moody, like his mother. And if he's not kept busy…'

'He will be,' said the Joan, and now she sounded weary. Then she turned to Ivy and said, 'Did you bring something of Cicely's with you?'

Silently Ivy got up and handed her the hair ribbon. Betony smoothed it out upon her palm, then laid her other

133

hand over it and closed her eyes. She must be casting a spell to try and find Cicely, Ivy realised, and held her breath. Of course the Joan would have tried the same thing when Keeve went missing, but perhaps this time...

'Nothing,' said Betony. 'I fear she is already beyond the range of my spells.' She laid the ribbon down. 'Tell me, Ivy. You said you and Mica had both warned Cicely against going to the surface. Do you have any idea what drew her there, or what made her disobey?'

'I—' Ivy's throat was so tight she could hardly speak. 'I don't—'

'My love.' Gossan leaned close to his wife's ear. 'She has already lost her mother, and now her sister as well. Give her time to grieve.'

Gratitude rushed into Ivy, followed by a hot wave of shame. She didn't deserve the Jack's compassion, not after the things she'd done. But if she confessed, they'd lock *her* up in the dungeon. And then she'd never get the chance to go outside and search for Cicely as only a swift could do.

'Very well,' said Betony, waving a hand at Ivy. 'You may leave.'

As Ivy walked to the door, Nettle followed her. 'I know how it feels, to lose a sister,' she said in a cracked whisper. 'It's a hard, hard thing. I'll never see my poor Gillyflower again, but I hope you find your Cicely.' She gave her a last, sad smile, and closed the door.

Ivy was left alone with Flint, who stood like a statue with his thunder-axe over his shoulder. 'She's gone, Dad,' Ivy said, clutching at his free hand. 'Cicely's gone. What are we going to do?'

She searched his face for a change in expression, but Flint didn't even blink. He pulled out of her grip, hefted his pickaxe, and walked away.

'What is wrong with you?' Ivy's voice rose high, breaking on the final word. 'Don't you care about Cicely, or anything? Is this all you can do – bury yourself in the ground and hammer away until you drop dead, and we're left with no parents at all?'

Flint's head drooped a little, but he didn't answer. He kept walking past the stairs and the entrance to the Market Cavern, heading for the trapdoor that would take him down into the diggings.

Ivy stared after him until he was nothing but a blur in the distance. Then she wiped her eyes angrily on the back of her hand, and ran to catch up with Mica.

'I can't believe Aunt Betony just dismissed me like that.' Mica paced around the cavern, kicking at the rug. 'Cicely's my sister; I should be the one to look for her. And I was the one who caught the spriggan in the first place. But from the way *she* was acting, you'd think it was my fault he'd escaped!'

Ivy sank into a chair, arms wrapped around her chest to

hold the hurt inside. 'I know,' she said unevenly. 'It's not fair. You're not to blame.'

'I can't understand how he got out of there,' muttered Mica. 'The iron was pure – I made sure of that. He couldn't have got past that pile of rocks in the tunnel, and he couldn't climb the shaft either, not without a rope...'

Apprehension stirred in Ivy. If she let him go on like this, it wouldn't be long before he came to the obvious conclusion – that someone had deliberately helped the prisoner escape. 'What are you going to do?' she asked, to change the subject. 'If Betony won't let you go...'

'She will. She's *got* to.' Mica flung himself onto the sofa across from her, fists clenched on his knees. 'I know the surface as well as any hunter in the Delve. I'm not afraid of spriggans. And I won't give up until I find Cicely, however long it takes. Who else can say that?'

I can, Ivy thought, but she didn't dare say it. Not until she knew she could trust him. 'But if she decides not to listen? What will you do then?'

His face creased with anguish. 'What do you want me to say? That I'd disobey the Joan and Jack, break every rule in the Delve if I had to, just for a chance of finding Cicely again? You know I would. I know you would, too.'

Ivy's eyes prickled, and she looked down at her lap. So Mica did understand how she felt, after all. If she could only explain to him that she'd felt the same way about finding their mother...

'Then if someone told you that she was alive, and they knew where she was,' she said, 'then you'd do whatever it took to get to her? Even if – if everyone else said it was dangerous, and you shouldn't go?'

'Of course.' His voice sharpened. 'I'm not a coward. What are you getting at?'

She must be careful now, so very careful. If Mica guessed that Ivy had anything to do with Richard's escape, he'd turn against her in a heartbeat. 'I've heard stories,' she said. 'About our ancestors, and other magical folk. How some of them could change into the shapes of animals, or—'

His face twisted with revulsion. 'You want me to try and turn myself into an *animal*?'

Ivy hadn't even considered that possibility; she'd only meant to prepare him for the shock of seeing her change into swift-form. But perhaps it was a good thing he'd misunderstood. 'Is that so bad?' she asked.

'Of course it is!' He flung himself to his feet and began to pace again. 'If you'd ever *seen* a wild animal, let alone hunted one—'

'I don't understand.'

Mica made an exasperated noise and raked his fingers through his hair. 'Look, it's common sense. Piskeys have a special relationship with animals – you know that much?'

Ivy nodded.

'Well, when we become hunters, we swear to help any sick or injured creature we find, and never kill any animal

137

for sport. But they're still animals, and we still have to eat. If we started turning ourselves into them, how could we hunt them? That's why it's forbidden.'

'Who says so?' asked Ivy. 'I've never heard such a thing. And anyway, animals eat each other all the time. Maybe you wouldn't want to kill the exact kind of animal you become, but—'

Mica cut her off. 'It's not just a bad idea, it's against our nature. We piskeys are solid like the earth, not changeable like air or water. That's how we've survived all these centuries.'

That sounded like something Aunt Betony would say, though it made no sense to Ivy. If shape-changing was impossible for piskeys, then why bother forbidding them to do it? 'But the droll-teller said that our ancestors used to change shape sometimes,' she protested. 'And some faeries still—'

'Faeries!' Her brother's mouth worked as though he were about to spit. 'We don't go near their kind. Why should I want to do anything they do?'

'Because,' said Ivy, controlling her impatience with an effort, 'if you could turn yourself into a bird and fly over the countryside instead of having to search on foot, you might have a better chance of finding Cicely.'

Mica gave a harsh laugh. 'A bird! Do you have any idea—' Then he stopped and repeated softly, 'A *bird*,' as though it were a revelation.

Had he finally understood what Ivy was saying? It was on the tip of her tongue to tell him he was wrong about piskeys not being able to change – or even prove it, by transforming into a swift before his eyes. Maybe then he'd realise how foolish it was to cling to some old hunters' superstition, and let her help him look for Cicely.

'So that's how he did it,' Mica went on, gazing past Ivy as though entranced. 'I wouldn't have thought he could, but maybe…'

'Mica?' asked Ivy, wary now. 'What are you talking about?'

He focused on her, eyes alight with fervour. 'I know how the spriggan got out,' he said. 'And I know how to catch him, too.'

'What? How?'

'Never mind that. This is hunter business. I'm going to talk to Gossan.' He started towards the door, then paused and turned back. 'But if I were you, I'd forget all that dross about shape-changing. If the Joan knew you'd even suggested it…' He gave her a bleak smile. 'Trust me. You don't want to know what she'd do.'

When Mica had gone, Ivy slumped in her chair, feeling more drained than ever. For one brief shining moment she'd dared to believe that she might not be alone after all, that she and Mica could put aside their differences and work together. And that if she explained it carefully enough, he might even understand why she'd gone outside the Delve and learned to change shape – because she'd truly believed it was the only way to find their mother.

But she'd been wrong, more wrong than she'd ever imagined. Because shape-changing wasn't merely unusual, it was forbidden. And if Mica saw Ivy turn into a swift, he wouldn't just be surprised – he'd be horrified.

And now she'd put Richard in danger, too. She'd never meant Mica to guess that the so-called spriggan could become a bird, much less use that knowledge to trap him again. Now he'd come up with a plan – a plan that might even work – and she had no idea what it was or how to stop it. All she could do was tell Richard what had happened, and urge him to be on his guard.

But how could she, without giving herself away? The whole Delve was buzzing with the news of Cicely's disappearance, and there'd be searchers going in and out of the Earthenbore all day – not to mention plenty of friends and neighbours coming by to offer Ivy their sympathies. Getting up to the surface would be impossible until tonight at the earliest, and it wouldn't be easy even then.

A knock at the door startled Ivy from reverie. She got up and opened it, to find Mattock standing there with a basket of flat cakes in one hand and a bottle of cream in the other. 'My mum sent these for you,' he said.

'Did she make the hevva cakes or did you?' asked Ivy, and he blushed. A few years ago Mica had caught Mattock

140

helping his mother make saffron buns and had never let him forget it. 'It's kind of you,' she added, managing a smile. 'We'll have them for tea, if Mica's back by then.'

'He's not here?' asked Mattock. 'I'd have thought…well, with everything going on, I expected you'd be together.'

'Mica doesn't like brooding over bad things,' said Ivy. 'He'd rather be doing something about them. Right now, he thinks he's figured out a way to catch the spriggan and get Cicely back before—'

Her throat closed up, and she couldn't finish the sentence. She took the bottle and basket from Mattock's hands and turned away before her face betrayed her as well.

He followed her to the kitchen, his big frame looming over her as she set the gifts down. She could feel his warmth like a solid wall against her back as he said quietly, 'Ivy.'

'I'm not crying.' She ground the words between her teeth. 'Cicely is alive, and I'm going to find her, so there's nothing to cry about.'

'*You're* going to find her? How?'

Ivy wanted to beat her head against the table and curse her own stupidity, but she managed to force a laugh. 'I mean we are. All of us. Working together. Each in our own way.'

And now she was babbling. Why wouldn't Mattock leave her alone? Surely he could tell she didn't want anyone's company, didn't want to eat his stupid cakes or drink the cream that only Cicely had ever really liked, didn't want anything except to find her sister, only nobody would give her the chance—

Then Mattock put his hands on her shoulders, and Ivy's resistance crumbled. She turned around and buried her face against his chest. 'I can't believe she's gone,' she whispered. 'I should have known, Matt. I should have seen it coming.'

He didn't say anything, only held her tight. It felt amazingly good to lean against him, feeling his strength like armour all around her – the last person she remembered ever holding her like this was Flint, and that had been years ago.

But she couldn't cling to Mattock forever, and surely he wouldn't want her to. Ivy straightened up, brushing at her cheeks. 'I appreciate you coming by,' she said with all the dignity she could muster. 'Please tell your mum I'm grateful.'

Mattock nodded and bowed out of the cavern, closing the door behind him with such exaggerated care that Ivy had to smile. Simple, honest Mattock. Sometimes she wished he were her brother instead of Mica, but that wouldn't be fair to him.

And it wouldn't be fair to involve him in her plan to look for Cicely, either. She could only hope he wouldn't guess, after her foolish slip of the tongue, that she planned to do anything at all.

It was a grim and mostly silent meal that Ivy and Mica ate that night. Without Cicely's bright chatter the atmosphere in the cavern was oppressive, and even phrases like 'pass the butter' fell with the weight of an anvil. Ivy soon found herself wishing that Flint would come and join them, just so she'd have someone else *not* to talk to.

But she hadn't seen her father since the morning, and when she'd met Hew coming up grimy-faced and coughing from the diggings, he'd told Ivy that Flint meant to stay even later than usual to make up for the time he'd missed. As though losing Cicely had been merely another interruption to his work. As though it mattered whether he dug any more tin or copper out of that tunnel, or dug any more tunnels at all.

'He's a knocker, lass,' Hew had reminded her gently. 'He's only doing what he's made for. And maybe it's the best thing for him. Same as your brother, with the hunting. It's how we menfolk grieve.'

What about me? Ivy wanted to shout at him. *I can't sense ore or shape metal. I'm not allowed to hunt. All I want to do is help look for my sister, but that's forbidden. How am I supposed to grieve?*

But there was no answer to that, at least not that Hew could give her. So she'd held her tongue and nodded, and then she'd gone back to the cavern and made about a week's worth of meat pasties to keep in the cold-hole, since that at least was something she could do.

'What did Gossan have to say about your plan?' she asked Mica, when he'd finished his last bite and she could endure the silence no longer. 'Did the Joan agree to let you start looking for Cicely?'

'They said I could go out tonight,' replied Mica, wiping his mouth, 'if Mattock and Gem go with me. Only we have to stay together and be home by sunrise, so what's the use of that?' He threw the napkin down. 'We might as well not bother.'

'But you will,' said Ivy. She knew Mica too well to believe otherwise, no matter how much he complained. 'When do you leave?'

'In a couple of hours.' He walked towards his alcove. 'But Matt said he'd come by and wake me when it's time, so you needn't worry about it. I'm going to sleep.'

Ivy spent a few minutes putting what was left of the food away, then climbed into bed herself. She was drifting in and out of consciousness, too miserable to sleep but too tired to stay awake, when the door creaked and she heard Mattock tiptoe in. Mica groaned, there was a rustle, and a few minutes later the two of them went out.

Now was her chance. Ivy waited a little longer, to be sure Mica and Mattock were well on their way. Then hurriedly she dressed and slipped out into the passage, heading for the Great Shaft.

The sky above the Delve was clear, the moon a neat half-circle among the stars. To the west, a trio of dim lights bobbed along the ground – Mica, Mattock and Gem. Secure in the knowledge that they'd never recognise her in swift-form, Ivy glided over the ruins of the Engine House, then angled off towards the nearby wood.

It wasn't a large wood: only a scattering of trees and undergrowth, with a well-travelled footpath through the middle. Ivy flew from one end to the other looking for signs of life, then landed in piskey-shape on the far side. 'Richard?' she asked, quietly at first and then a little louder. But though she listened until she grew impatient, there was no reply.

'Richard!' She was shouting now, not caring if anyone heard her. Surely Mica and the others wouldn't recognise her voice at this distance. 'I'm here! Where are you?'

Still no one answered, and Ivy's restlessness grew. She couldn't hang about here all night – she had to find Cicely. But she'd wanted to warn Richard about Mica's plan. Why didn't he answer?

Surely it was too soon to give up yet. Ivy walked to the centre of the wood, cupped her hands around her mouth, and yelled 'Richard!' one more time. Then she sat down on a fallen branch and waited.

Minutes passed, each more slowly than the next. Something rustled in the leaves above her, and Ivy looked up in hope – but no, it was only a squirrel. A little while later a bird began to sing, but it was a liquid, melancholy tune, nothing like the trilling noises Richard had made back in the dungeon.

Ivy rubbed her palms on her thighs, fidgeting with anxiety. What if Richard had decided not to keep his promise after all? What if he'd decided it was too dangerous to stay, and flown off to some faraway place?

'Richard!' she called hoarsely. 'You'd better come soon! I'm not going to wait forever!'

But still there was nothing. Not a word, not a sign.

The faery was gone.

Ivy took a deep breath and let it go. Then she leaped to her feet, snatched up a stick and hurled it into the underbrush. 'Curse you!' she stormed. 'You liar, you oath-breaker, you – you demon blackguard wretch of a *spriggan*!'

There was a long silence, while the wind murmured through the treetops. Then a light, ironic voice said, 'I see my reputation is at stake.'

Ivy spun around. There on the path, as though he had been there all along, stood Richard – but not Richard as she had last seen him, covered in filth and bruises and dressed in rags. His hair hung straight and clean almost to his shoulders, and his jacket and slim trousers looked new. If not for the purple shadow around one eye and the scab on his upper lip, she would hardly have recognised him.

But before she could speak, he vanished. A tiny bird with a blue-black head, shadowy wings and white underbelly flitted past, landed on her other side, and turned into Richard again.

'I was a few hundred feet up when I heard you calling,'

he said. 'And I needed to make sure that you'd come alone.'

Blood rushed into Ivy's face. She'd been so busy worrying that she might not be able to trust him, it had never occurred to her that he could have similar doubts. 'You thought I'd betray you?'

'Not willingly, no. But if your Joan found out that you'd helped me, she might not have given you a choice.'

He had a point. Ivy's fury subsided, and she gave a reluctant nod.

'Ready to go?' Richard asked. 'It's a little late, but we should be able to get to Truro in time.'

'I can't.' Ivy passed a hand wearily over her curls. 'My little sister Cicely's gone missing.'

He frowned. 'You mean she just disappeared? Like that other one – Keeve?'

Ivy hoped not, since she suspected that Keeve was dead. But she couldn't deny the possibility. 'Yes. Do you have any idea where she might have gone?'

Richard looked sober. 'None at all.'

No easy answers, then. She'd hoped she wouldn't have to do this, but she could see no other way. 'Then I'll have to say goodbye,' Ivy said. 'I can't go to my mother now, not until I find Cicely. Besides, my brother's figured out that you can change shape, and he thinks he knows how to catch you. It's not safe for you to stay here.'

'What do you want me to do, then? Go back to your mother, and tell her you aren't coming?'

How could a simple little word be so hard to say? 'Yes. But,' she added quickly, 'don't leave it at that. Tell her everything that's happened since you and I met – especially the part about Cicely.' If Marigold knew that her youngest daughter was missing, maybe she'd come and help with the search. 'And tell her that if she has any more messages for me, she'll have to deliver them herself. You've done enough.'

The faery's brows lifted, and he gave her an appraising look. Then he bowed to her without a trace of irony, and vanished. He didn't even turn into a bird; he was simply *not there* any more. Ivy stared at the place where he'd been standing until her eyes began to burn, and she realised she'd forgotten to blink. Then she shook herself into swift-form, and flew away.

nine

Ivy searched for her sister all night, gliding low over the uneven ground. She glimpsed a badger digging in the underbrush, and fox cubs tussling at play; she passed a field where rabbits browsed in the grass, and watched an owl wing silently by. The twin lamps of a human vehicle wound through the landscape, turned into the drive of a little farmstead and winked out, while in the distance hundreds of similar lights marked the boundaries of some great city. Yet she found nothing to suggest that Cicely had passed this way.

She turned westward and winged along the coast, skimming over sweeping curves of sand and coves where foam-capped breakers smashed upon the rocks. The sea-cliffs were riddled with holes, many of them adits from abandoned mine workings that likely connected to the Delve at some point. But still she could find no trace of Cicely.

Absorbed in her search, she scarcely noticed the tiny thread of gold creeping along the horizon. Not until the sky lightened from black to deep blue and the air began to fill with squawking gulls did Ivy realise that it was dawn – and that she should have been home ages ago. Cursing herself for being so careless, she wheeled south-east and flashed towards the Delve. Mica would be returning any minute, and if she didn't make it back to the cavern before he did…

Then she caught sight of her brother standing at the top of the ridge, with Mattock and Gem at his side. From the way he was waving his arms he must be angry, or at least passionate about something, but that was of no matter. All Ivy cared about was getting down the Great Shaft straightaway

Only she couldn't, because more birds were zooming towards her from every direction, warbling and squawking in a cacophony of avian language. A pair of swifts darted around her, their black eyes staring cold and bright into her own – and then the whole flock dived beneath her, a whirlwind of beaks and claws and feathers, heading straight for the hillside where Mica and his companions stood.

Bewildered, Ivy hung back and watched as the mixed multitude of birds spiralled around the hunters, still uttering their wordless cries. What were they doing? Had Mica sent them to look for the spriggan? Were they reporting to him somehow? She was still puzzling over it when Mica waved his hand and the flock scattered, flapping off as abruptly as they had come.

Except for the swifts. They hovered before him, uttering staccato shrieks of alarm, while Mica stood still as though listening. Then he made a sharp gesture, and the swifts shot away like twin arrows – straight at Ivy.

For an instant her mind went blank with disbelief. Then she remembered what Richard had said: *Swifts are communal birds. If you don't behave like a proper swift the other ones will sense it, and instead of welcoming you, they'll attack…*

Panic erupted in Ivy's breast. She whirled and fled, wings flapping frantically as she shot towards the Engine House and the capped shaft behind it. But the other swifts were more experienced fliers, and they quickly cut off her descent. Forced into retreat, Ivy swerved towards the wood, with the other swifts in close pursuit.

'No!' she screamed, but it came out as a shriek – and then the swifts were on her, stabbing at her with their beaks and beating her with their wings. Buffeted by the storm of their rage, Ivy struggled vainly to fend them off. Control was impossible, and hopelessness filled her as she realised they were steering her back towards Mica and the other piskeys.

Tsier-sier, sang another bird as it passed above, mocking her with its freedom. Ivy cried out again as a swift's beak jabbed into her breast, piercing feathers and skin. She had to get away, or they would tear her to pieces. She folded her wings and spiralled earthwards – then snapped them wide and shot up the slope in a last, desperate run for the Engine House.

Mica gave a shout, and the whizzing sound of his sling rippled the air. Ivy sensed the stone hurtling towards her and rolled – a fraction of a second too late. Heat scored across her back, and the muscles of her shoulder separated in a blaze of dazzling pain. The ground spiralled up to meet her, and she knew it would only be seconds before she hit—

A freak wind blasted the hillside, thrashing the gorse-bushes and rippling the heather in its wake. Still flapping her one good wing, Ivy felt herself tossed upwards on the breeze. Pain blinded her, and she was still trying to regain control when a dark form loomed up before her and ruthless hands snatched her from the air.

Ivy gave a final cry of agony as her injured wing twisted. Then she willed herself into piskey-form, and let the darkness claim her.

She had thought fainting would be like sleep, a quiet place where she knew nothing and no one could touch her. But though darkness hazed her vision and she had a fuzzy sense of being disconnected from her body, she could still hear someone talking to her, though faint and far away.

'—don't know where to find us yet, but they'll be here any—'

A moment of merciful oblivion, then it returned, louder and closer.

'—hide you somewhere. But if they find us—'

The words rose and fell in gasps, as though the speaker were running. Strangely, Ivy felt as though she were rising and falling, too. But she had no idea where she was, or who was with her. A dull throbbing spread through her shoulder and radiated out from her chest, but she couldn't think what it meant.

'—stop it. Do you hear me? You have to—'

She must have blacked out again, because the next time she became aware the up-and-down sensation had stopped. An earthy smell rose around her, dampness seeping into her clothes. She was lying in bed and someone was covering her up, but why was it so wet, and what was wrong with—

Then the darkness shattered, and pain smashed into her like rocks falling. Ivy would have screamed, but a hand clamped over her mouth, muffling the cry. 'Stop glowing!' her rescuer snapped. '*Now!*'

Ivy was too dazed to protest. She willed herself not to glow, and tried to breathe through the pain instead. And now all was black again except for a few glints of grey light above her, and she was half-buried in dirt, her head resting on something hard and warm that smelled like fir needles...

Richard.

'...can't have gone far,' said a soft voice from above, and

153

for a moment Ivy felt sure she must be dreaming, because it sounded like Mattock. 'But how could he disappear like that?'

'Quiet,' came the reply, lower and harsher. 'Keep looking. He could be anywhere.'

Mica. Ivy caught her breath, but agony stabbed her chest and she let out a feeble moan. The foliage above them rustled, and Richard covered her mouth again, all his muscles tensed for flight.

Don't move, his body told her. *Don't make a sound.*

Ivy dug her fingers into Richard's arm and bit her lip to keep from screaming. How long had she lain in this dank hole? It felt like forever, and the fiery knots of pain in her chest and shoulder blotted out all other sensation. She would have surrendered to Mica and Mattock gladly, if only it would make the hurting stop…

'…Ivy, it's all right. They've gone.'

She should have been relieved, but now it hardly seemed to matter. Was it getting brighter? It could be the sun's rays angling into the cave, but daylight had never seemed so inviting. It bathed her wounds, taking away the pain and lifting her tenderly as her own mother's arms.

'Ivy?'

The light was all around her now. A blissful peace enfolded her, and she could feel the world slipping away…

'Oh no, you don't.' Richard's voice was harsh. 'Stay with me. Ivy!'

She sighed, melting limp against him. Then a hand smacked onto her injured shoulder, and Ivy's eyes flew open. The golden light vanished, and cold fire seared through her body. She would have screamed, but the pain was so intense it took her breath away.

'Live!' Richard shouted, as a second wave of power shocked through her. Ivy convulsed, bolted upright – and slapped him across the face.

For a moment Richard froze, his eyes wide and his neck still twisted with the force of her blow. Then he collapsed against the back of the muddy hollow and broke into rasping laughter. Only then did it dawn on Ivy that the pain in her shoulder had faded, and her chest no longer stabbed with every breath. She felt weak and a little dizzy, but...

'I'm alive,' she whispered.

Her skin was glowing again, and now she could see everything: the burrow lined with soil and dead leaves, the mushrooms crowded into one corner, the roots that kept the ceiling from falling in. Some abandoned fox's den or badger scrape in the depths of the thicket, so shallow that Richard had been forced to shrink himself and Ivy as small as he could just to fit.

And yet he'd done it. She'd told him to go, but he'd stayed, and when he saw her in trouble, he'd been ready. He'd flown to meet her, cast a spell to throw off her pursuers, transformed into faery-shape to catch her as she fell. And now he'd brought her back from the very gates of death, and what had she given him in return? A smack hard enough to rattle his teeth.

The worst of it was, Richard was still laughing. There was more than a hint of hysteria in it, and Ivy was beginning to think she might have to slap him again just to make him stop. 'What's so funny?' she asked.

He let out a last snort of hilarity, wiped his eyes with one filthy hand and sat up. 'It's just…there's this delicious irony to you hitting me, that's all. *The law hath not been dead, though it hath slept.*'

Which meant nothing to Ivy, but she didn't really care. 'You saved my life,' she said, and her hand went automatically to her shoulder. It was stiff and tender, but the bones and muscles felt whole and even the skin was unbroken. 'I don't know how to…' No, she wasn't about to *thank* him, that would put her eternally in his debt. But she owed him a great deal, and it would take her a long time to repay it. 'I don't know what to say.'

'Then don't say anything,' said Richard. 'You saved my life too, when you freed me from that dungeon. Now we're even.'

His gaze held hers until Ivy began to feel self-conscious. She brushed the soil from her legs and backed away. 'Well,' she said, 'we're certainly evenly dirty.'

Richard climbed to his feet, one hand braced on the low ceiling. 'We need to get out of here,' he said. 'I don't think your brother saw you change out of your swift-form. But if we stay here much longer he'll realise that you're missing, and I really don't want to be around when that happens. Especially not now that I've seen what he can do.'

The fevered energy that had filled Ivy since her healing drained away, leaving her shaken. 'Mica,' she whispered. 'I knew he had a plan to catch you, but I never guessed…' She looked up at him miserably. 'Richard, I can't go home.'

'Why not?'

'I've been gone too long. Even if Mica hasn't guessed yet that I was the swift he shot, it won't take him long to figure it out. I'll be punished for going above – locked up, or put under guard at the very least – and then I'll never get the chance—'

She broke off, pushing her fingertips against her eyes. The realisation of how badly she had miscalculated, what a disaster she had made for herself and everyone she loved, shook her to the core. 'I can't go back,' she said. 'Not until I find Cicely. And maybe not even then.'

Richard was quiet a moment, his face unreadable. At last he said, 'It's your choice. But if I were you, I'd talk to Marigold first. You'll have a better chance of finding your sister with her help than you would on your own.'

Ivy wanted to agree, but at the same time she felt selfish for even considering it. She wanted to see Marigold so badly, to know the comfort that only a mother could give – but surely she didn't deserve anything good after the way she'd failed Cicely? Especially now that she'd abandoned Mica and Flint as well?

And yet punishing herself wouldn't help Cicely either. 'I suppose you're right,' she said. 'But...' She moved her shoulder, wincing at the tug in her muscles. 'I'm not up to flying yet. I'm not even sure I could hang on, if I were on your back.' Especially since his bird-form was so tiny, she couldn't believe he'd made the offer in the first place.

'Well, we can't go any farther by magic. I could take you into the wood because I knew you'd been there already, but after that it was back to running.' Richard tapped his fingers along a root, frowning as he thought. 'What if we make ourselves human size, and you turn both of us invisible? If we've got to walk, we'll cover more ground that way.'

Ivy still felt wobbly after her near-death experience, and the thought of casting two spells at once made her head ache. But what choice did she have? They couldn't stay here – the hunters of the Delve would be after them at any moment.

'All right,' she said, willing herself to sound confident. 'Let's go.'

On the far side of the wood the ground dropped away, sloping down into a little valley where a stream gurgled among the rocks. Richard set the pace, and Ivy did her best to keep up with him. But though nervous energy sustained her for a while, it wasn't long before her strength began to falter. She'd been up most of the night, eaten nothing in hours, and her shoulder had begun aching again – first in occasional spasms, then with a steady throb that made her feel queasy.

'So,' said Richard as the path turned away from the riverbank and began to angle upward, 'now that I've finally convinced you I'm not one, what exactly *is* a spriggan? Some kind of hideous creature, obviously – and I'm trying not to take that personally – but how are they different from other magical folk?'

'I don't know that much about them,' Ivy said, focused on putting one foot in front of the other. Her chest was hurting as well now, and she found it hard to breathe. 'Only that they're thin and pale and ugly, and bring bad luck and bad weather wherever they go. They love only two things – food and treasure – and they steal piskey-women because they haven't any women of their own.'

'And they only live in Cornwall? Nowhere else?'

'I'm not sure,' she panted, wiping sweat from her brow. 'Why?'

'Because I've been to quite a few places, in my time,' Richard replied. 'I've travelled across England and Wales, and I even spent a few months in Scotland once. This isn't the first time I've been to Cornwall, either. But I've never seen a single one of these so-called spriggans – *look out!*'

Head down, eyes half-shut, Ivy didn't even see the rock rolling towards her until she tripped over it. She lurched sideways, too startled to even cry out – but when Richard caught her arm, Ivy let out a swift's shriek of agony. Hastily the faery switched his grip to her other side and helped her to safer ground.

'This shouldn't be happening,' he said, as Ivy sank down on an outcropping. He crouched in front of her, seizing her chin and lifting her head up. 'How long have you been in pain?'

She averted her eyes. 'A while. I thought I was just tired.'

'I put a lot of power into that healing.' His fingers traced the purpling bruise on her shoulder, and Ivy flinched. 'Why is it coming undone?'

'I don't know.' She tried to get up, but her knees buckled and she fell back again. 'But I can't walk any farther. Just…go. Leave me here.'

'I don't think so,' said Richard. He slid one arm beneath her legs, lifted her from the ground and set off up the hill, carrying Ivy as though she weighed nothing at all.

Ivy wanted to tell him to stop, so she could make herself small and save him the trouble. But her head was already pounding with the effort of keeping them both invisible, and the pain in her arm was growing worse every minute. All she could do was hide her face against Richard's neck, and try not to be sick down his collar.

Then she lost consciousness altogether, and dropped into a bottomless shaft of oblivion.

*

Ivy woke to a world of dusty golden light. Above her spread a ceiling braced by dark, square-cut beams, while around her rose walls of stone and mortar. A human building of some sort — a barn perhaps? But if so, how had Richard brought her in here? She'd always heard that faeries couldn't enter human dwellings without permission.

There was an itch between her shoulders, right where her wings ought to be. Ivy squirmed and reached behind her with one arm and then the other, trying to get at the irritation. She was on her third attempt before she realised she'd twisted her injured shoulder to its limits, and hadn't felt any pain at all. Wondering, she lowered her hand and touched the place below her collarbone where the swift's beak had pierced her. There was no tenderness there, either.

So Richard had healed her again while she lay unconscious, and this time he'd succeeded. But it must have taken all his strength, because now he lay sprawled on the floor beside her, so deep in slumber that he didn't even twitch when Ivy spoke his name.

Well, let him sleep; he'd earned it. Ivy rose, brushing dust from her breeches. The building was old but in good repair, a low rectangle with a broad corridor along one side and the rest divided by wood and metal partitions. An earthy, pungent smell mingled with the scent of dried grass — animals? Ivy stepped out of the doorway, avoiding a heap of suspicious-looking muck in the middle of the corridor, and went to investigate.

161

She expected she might find pigs or goats in the neighbouring pens, perhaps even a cow. But when she reached the last box a shaggy brown head lifted to greet her, ears pricked and nose quivering. Ivy held out her human-sized hand, delighted when the horse lipped her palm. 'Hello, you beauty,' she whispered to it, rubbing the smooth arch of its neck. 'What are you doing in here?'

The horse gave a soft whinny and stamped one foot – but gingerly. And when Ivy leaned over the door she saw the problem at once: its left foreleg had been injured, and it couldn't gallop until it was better. 'Oh, what a shame,' Ivy said, unlatching the door and slipping inside. Rubbing soothing circles over the horse's chest, she crouched to examine the bandaged limb.

Even through the wrappings it felt swollen and hot to the touch, and the horse shied away from her fingers, neighing protest. 'It's all right,' Ivy murmured. She blew softly into the horse's nostrils, soothing it, and smiled when it tucked its head down against her chest. 'I can't heal you, but when Richard wakes up, maybe—'

A creak resonated through the barn, and Ivy froze as the outer door swung wide. Another horse came prancing in, an elegant dapple-grey with a haughty air that reminded her of Betony. And beside it walked a girl a little younger than Ivy, with a braid of dark hair swinging down her back.

Hastily Ivy made herself invisible, but not quickly

enough. The girl's head turned, her pert features creasing in a frown. 'Hello? Is someone there?'

The brown horse chose that moment to sidle over and squeeze Ivy against the wall. An *oof* escaped her, and she shoved at its curving ribs, but it refused to budge. She flattened herself against the wood and tried to edge sideways, but something sharp sliced into her calf and she let out an involuntary yelp.

'Right, whoever you are,' said the girl sternly. 'Come out of there.' With a slap she sent the grey mare trotting into the neighbouring box, then strode towards them. 'Budge over, Dodger.' She shoved the brown horse and it danced sideways, leaving Ivy backed against the wall with blood spiralling down her leg.

'What are you doing here?' the girl demanded – but the moment her eyes met Ivy's, her expression changed. 'You're a faery! No, wait, that's not right.' She cocked her helmeted head to one side, looking puzzled and awed at once. 'What *are* you?'

Gooseflesh prickled over Ivy's skin. How could a human see through her invisibility glamour like that? She was still trying to think of something to say when a laconic voice spoke up:

'She's a piskey, of course. And she's with me.'

The girl whipped around, and Ivy took advantage of the distraction to make herself small and dart out into the corridor, taking refuge behind a nearby bucket. Once more,

Richard had put himself between her and danger. But how were they going to get out of this?

'Faery man?' breathed the girl, unlatching her helmet and putting it aside. 'Is it really you?'

Without hesitation Richard stepped out of hiding to meet her. His clothes were still rumpled and muddy and there were bits of grass in his air, but his eyes were wickedly bright.

'Hello, Molly Menadue,' he said. 'It's good to see you again.'

ten

The situation had changed so fast, so unexpectedly, that Ivy felt as though she were lost in some strange dream. This human girl had recognised Richard at a glance – even knew that he was a faery – and he didn't appear to mind it at all. He'd even greeted her by name, as though she were an old friend. But how could that be?

'You came back,' the girl said. 'I thought I'd never…it's been so long…' She flung her arms around Richard and hugged him exuberantly, then shoved him away and exclaimed, 'You just disappeared! Without even a note!'

'Something came up, and I had to go,' he said, but his eyes had darkened, and Ivy could tell he wasn't nearly as indifferent as he seemed. 'There was no time to explain.'

'You don't know what it was like, coming in here and finding you gone.' Molly sniffed. 'It was *horrible*.' She scrubbed at her eyes, then went on in a brisker tone, 'But enough of that. You're here now. So what brought you back? And what are you doing with…did you say she was a *piskey*?'

'Her name is Ivy, and we're travelling together,' said Richard. 'We got into a bit of trouble and needed somewhere to hide. This was the safest place I could think of.'

'Safe from what?'

Richard hesitated, and for a moment Ivy thought he was going to tell Molly their whole story. But all he said was, 'That's faery business – or rather, piskey business. But you needn't worry, you're in no danger.'

Molly put her fists on her hips. 'I don't care about that,' she said. 'I'm just dying to hear what you've been up to. It's been *ages*.'

'It has,' Richard agreed solemnly. 'How old are you now? Eighteen? Twenty-two?'

Molly broke into a reluctant smile. 'Thirteen, silly. It hasn't been *that* long.'

Ivy couldn't restrain her curiosity any longer. She stepped out into the corridor and grew to human size. 'How do you know Richard?' she asked the girl.

'Richard?' Molly frowned and glanced at the faery, who gave a tiny nod. 'Oh. Well…he's my faery godfather.'

Richard made a spluttering noise, and Ivy was torn between disbelief and a mad desire to laugh. She was still wrestling with the impulse when Molly grinned at her, and after that it was hopeless: she had to smile back.

'I was out riding Dodger last spring,' Molly went on,

gesturing to the brown horse, 'and I saw a…a bird, falling out of the sky like it was hurt. So I went to see if I could help, and when I got there, I found him – Richard – lying in the grass.'

She hadn't been about to say *bird*, Ivy could tell. She'd started to say something else, but changed her mind. Why?

'He tried to act like a human,' Molly went on, 'but I knew right away he was a faery, and I got so excited. I'd seen a couple of faeries before when I was at the shops in Truro, but they ignored me, and my mum got really angry at me for talking to strangers. But he didn't seem to mind talking, even though it was mostly nonsense, and he looked so thin and ill that I felt sorry for him. So I invited him home.'

'*Home* in this case being the barn,' said Richard. 'Since we both agreed that her mother wouldn't think much of the arrangement. And then she wrapped me up in blankets and fed me until I could hardly move, which probably saved my life.'

Molly blushed, but she looked pleased. Ivy turned to Richard and asked, 'Why were you so weak? What happened to you?'

'That's another story,' said Richard shortly. 'Let Molly tell hers.'

'He wouldn't tell me either,' Molly confided. 'I think he likes being mysterious. But anyway, he stayed for a few days and we got to be friends, and I told him my mum wants me to be a teacher like her, but what I really want is to be an actress. And he turned out to know loads about theatre, and I did a speech for him and he told me I was really good, and a week later I tried out for our school musical and I got the lead. So that's why I call him my faery godfather.'

'Did you!' said Richard, with a warmth in his tone Ivy had never heard before. 'Well done, Molly. What did your parents say to that?'

'I emailed the video to my dad, and he said I was brilliant. But my mum said I shouldn't let it go to my head.'

Richard's lip curled. 'Your mother suffers from a grievous lack of imagination. Never mind her, Molly. There'll be more lead roles in your future.'

Molly beamed at him. 'I've got to head in for supper,' she said. 'But I'll come back as soon as I can – and I'll bring you something to eat, too.' She looked from Richard to Ivy and back again. 'You're not going to run away again, are you? You'll stay the night at least?'

'We can't stay long,' said Richard, with unusual gentleness. 'But yes. For now, we'll stay.'

The sun was slipping below the horizon, its last beams slanting across the fields. In the neighbouring boxes the two horses snorted and stamped, while Ivy and Richard lay on a makeshift bed of old blankets and sacking, waiting for Molly to return.

Richard's eyes were half-closed, with blue shadows beneath them, and the bones of his face stood out sharply in the fading light. Ivy wanted to say something about the way he'd carried her over miles of countryside to this place, and then poured the last of his strength into healing her a second time – if she'd owed him her life before, she owed him twice over now. But Richard hadn't mentioned it, and Ivy had a feeling that he'd rather she didn't either.

'How far from the Delve are we?' she asked. 'Are we safe here?'

'Not too far, but far enough that your people aren't likely to find us,' said Richard. 'And besides, there's some charm about this place that makes it difficult for magical folk to see – I'd never have found it myself that first time, if Molly hadn't shown me the way. Some old protective spell set up by her grandmother, perhaps.'

'You mean,' said Ivy, propping herself on one elbow, 'you think her grandmother was a faery?'

'Or her great-grandmother, I suppose,' Richard replied, gazing thoughtfully into the rafters. 'It's impossible to say. But there's magic in Molly's blood somewhere, if she's been seeing faeries all her life. On her father's side, probably – it doesn't seem likely to be her mother's.'

'Where is her father, then?' asked Ivy. 'Doesn't he live here?'

'Sometimes,' Richard said. 'But his work takes him away for weeks at a time, so Molly doesn't see much of him. I've never seen him at all.' He sat up, brushing dirt from his dark jacket. 'I think I could heal that leg of yours now.'

'I'd rather you healed Dodger's,' said Ivy, getting up and leading the way. She opened the door to show Richard the horse's bandaged leg, but the faery shook his head.

'I don't have your people's way with animals,' said Richard. 'And my sorry experience with this one is that he'd as soon bite me as look at me. He can heal on his own, as far as I'm concerned.'

Ivy wanted to protest, but she owed Richard too much to demand anything. She was about to close the door when a new thought occurred to her. 'I cut my leg on something in here,' she said. 'Maybe that's what happened to Dodger, too.' She slipped inside the box, pushing away the horse's inquiring muzzle, and crouched to examine the partition. At first she saw nothing unusual, but when she allowed her skin to glow a little brighter she caught the glint of some dull metal object protruding from the wood. She closed her fingers around it and felt the faint tingle that told her what it was: iron.

'An old nail,' said Richard. 'Probably worked its way out over the years and no one noticed it. Tell Molly, when she comes back.'

'Tell me what?' asked Molly from the doorway, and Ivy pointed to the nail. The human girl gasped. 'Is that how Dodger cut himself? We thought he did it outside, but we could never find where. *Thank* you!'

Ivy went rigid with shock at the careless thanks. By the time she recovered, Molly had found a hammer and tugged the nail out. 'You hurt yourself on it too, didn't you?' she said to Ivy as she held it up – a crude-looking thing, rusty with age. 'That's how I could see you.'

'I…hadn't thought of that,' said Ivy. She'd been immune to iron when she lived in the Delve, but perhaps Richard's healing spells had changed her more than she'd realised. Could he have made her part faery by accident? Ivy wasn't sure she liked that idea at all.

Molly tossed the nail into the wastebin and plopped down on an overturned bucket, crossing her ankles. 'My mum's in the study working on some project or other, so we should be all right for a while.' She pulled out a cloth sack and began rummaging inside. 'I found a packet of fairings—'

'Fairings?' asked Richard.

'Ginger biscuits,' said Ivy, helping herself to one.

'And some sausages – sorry they're cold. Oh, and pears.' Molly made a face. 'It's not much of a meal, is it? Sorry.'

'Don't apologise,' said Ivy. 'It's kind of you to bring us anything at all.'

Molly looked at her curiously. 'You're nothing like I expected,' she said. 'I thought piskeys were little brown men, all full of wrinkles and mischief.'

'That's just local legend,' Richard interrupted before Ivy could speak. 'Piskey women don't get out much, but they do exist. And magical folk don't have wrinkles. Unless you know what to look for, you wouldn't be able to tell the difference between a piskey of twenty and one who's two hundred.'

'Two hundred!' exclaimed Ivy. 'That's ridiculous. The oldest piskey I know can't be more than a hundred and ten. And she certainly does have wrinkles; all the older folk do.'

Richard looked surprised. 'My mistake, then,' he said. 'Perhaps faeries and piskeys are more different than I'd thought.'

'Tell me about your people,' said Molly, turning eagerly to Ivy. 'I want to know more about them.'

Ivy hesitated. She hadn't meant to give away any secrets, and she had a feeling she'd already said more than she should. Not that it worried her where Richard was concerned; by now she felt almost sure she could trust him. But although she liked Molly, she didn't know the human girl well enough to feel comfortable talking about the Delve in her presence.

'Well,' she said slowly, trying to think of an answer that was honest but harmless, 'piskeys do enjoy a good prank, or at least the younger ones do. It's a sort of game with our people, to play tricks on each other without being tricked ourselves. And if we can all laugh about it together, that's the best of all.'

Yet even as she spoke, Ivy had to admit that there wasn't nearly as much laughter and fun in the Delve as there had been when she was a child. The older folk had a weary air about them, and some of the oldest – especially the older knockers – looked positively grim. Was it Betony's strict rule that had sobered them? Or was it something more?

'Go on,' said Molly. 'Where do you live? Richard told me once about some faeries who lived in a hollow oak tree. Is it something like that?'

'No,' said Ivy. 'But it's a safe place. A good place. And it's…beautiful.' And with that homesickness welled up in her, and she couldn't speak any more. She had spent a night and a day out of the Delve now. Would she ever see her home, or her people, again?

'I'm taking Ivy to visit a relative,' said Richard, filling in the silence. 'Someone she hasn't seen in a long time. Once that's done, I'll be on my way.'

'Where?' asked Molly.

Richard shrugged. 'I couldn't tell you,' he said. 'I prefer to keep my options open.' But a shadow crossed his face as he spoke, and for the first time it dawned on Ivy that he might not be a wanderer by choice — that he might not have anywhere to go.

'I didn't mean where are *you* going,' said Molly reproachfully. 'I know not to meddle in your business by now. I meant Ivy. Where are you taking her?'

'Truro,' said Richard. 'There's a dance and theatre school in the city where her relative's been staying.'

Ivy sat up with a start, the blood draining from her face. That was where her mother had been all these years? Surely he must be pranking her. She opened her mouth, but Molly spoke first:

'Dance and *theatre*? Really? Can I come with you?' She

must have noticed Richard's dubious look, for she went on quickly, 'Mum lets me go to Truro on the bus sometimes, as long as I take my mobile and promise to call her when I'm coming home. And she likes it better when I'm out of the house anyway. She won't say no if I tell her I'm going with friends. *Please*.'

Richard glanced at Ivy, but she was too choked with hurt and anger to reply. So her mother had abandoned her family to go dancing after all – not with the faeries, but with the humans. No wonder Richard had kept this from her.

But why was he telling her now? Did he think it was safe to reveal Marigold's secret because Ivy had already committed herself, because she needed her mother's help too badly to walk away? He was right about that, but she hated the thought that he'd manipulated her so easily – and that she'd been fool enough to let him.

'You never told me what she was doing,' she accused, when she could speak. 'Did she ask you not to? Or was it your idea to keep me in the dark?'

Richard's jaw tightened, and she could see she'd offended him. But he said only, 'I don't think this is the time to discuss it.' Turning to Molly, he continued, 'I know we're in your debt. But I don't think it's a good idea. As you can see, Ivy's a little sensitive at the moment.'

'Oh, and now it's *my* fault?' exclaimed Ivy. How dare he make her seem ungrateful for Molly's kindness?

'I apologise,' she said hastily to Molly, who had turned pale and then very red. 'If there's anything else we can do to repay you, I'd be glad to know of it. It's only—'

'Don't bother,' Molly said, her eyes on Richard. 'I won't interfere in your faery – or piskey – business. But if you had any idea what mum's been like...' A spasm of anger distorted her face. 'Never mind. I suppose that's all just *human business* to you.' She leaped up from the bucket and ran out.

'Wait—' Ivy called, but Molly had already slammed the door behind her.

'Don't worry,' said Richard. 'She'll be all right by tomorrow. And so will you, once you've had a proper night's sleep.'

Ivy bristled. 'What's that supposed to mean?'

'I told you your mother was at a dance school,' he said. 'If I thought that was some kind of dark secret, I wouldn't have said it. I've never lied to you yet, Ivy. Not that I expect you to be impressed by that, but you should be, because I'm one of the few faeries who can.' He pushed himself upright and went to the window. 'Marigold will explain everything when you see her – tomorrow. Tonight, you need to rest.'

'I'm not tired.' Ivy spoke crisply, to deny the embarrassment crawling inside her. Perhaps she had leaped to the wrong conclusion, and perhaps she was being unfair – but she hated being so vulnerable, so easily caught off guard. 'Why can't we go to Truro right now?'

'Because you're not ready to fly again, even if you think you are.' His hands tightened on the windowsill. 'Do you have any idea how damaged your body must have been, to need two complete healings in a day?'

The reminder of how much she owed him shamed her, but she was determined not to let it hold her back. 'All right, then we'll fly slowly. But I'm not staying here.'

He gave an exasperated growl and pushed himself around to face her. 'Why are you always so stubborn? What are you trying to prove?'

'Cicely needs me!' she shouted at him. 'She's out there somewhere, and she's scared and she's hurting, and nobody's going to find her if I—'

Richard cut her off with a gesture – literally so, because though Ivy's mouth kept moving no sound came out. 'Quiet down,' he said. 'Or Molly's mother will hear us.' He held her gaze until she gave a sullen nod, then gestured again to remove the spell and went on, 'I know you want to find your sister. But you're not going to help her by killing yourself.'

So not only did he see her as sickly and fragile, he thought her too witless even to realise how weak she was. No wonder he'd taken such pains to protect her. 'I'm not stupid,' she retorted, barely controlling her fury. 'I know what I'm capable of.'

'If that were true,' Richard said, 'we wouldn't be here right now. It took a lot of power to heal you, and I'm not going to let all that effort go to waste. So stop behaving like a petulant child, and lie down.'

Ivy's fists clenched. 'And if I don't?'

'Then I'll knock you out myself.'

He would, too. She could see it in his face. 'Fine,' Ivy said bitterly. 'I'll do as you say. For now.'

'Good,' said Richard, and turned away.

'Where are you going?'

'Out,' he replied shortly. 'Don't wait up for me.' Then he was gone, and in his place was a little black-and-white bird. It flashed around Ivy, lighted on the windowsill to fix her with one coldly glittering eye, then flew away.

With her mind still raging at Richard, her clothing stiff with mud and nothing but a thin layer of horsey-smelling blankets beneath her, Ivy didn't expect to sleep well that night. But once she'd made herself small and dragged a piece of sacking over herself for protection, she dropped into a deep slumber almost at once.

Still, it seemed only a short time before the door to the barn creaked, and Ivy's eyes opened to the first pale light of morning. The horses stamped and neighed, and Ivy got up quickly, thinking it must be Molly coming in. But then among the earthy smells of grass and manure she caught a thread of an unfamiliar scent. Surely Molly had never smelled like that, all drenched in musk and strange spices? Ivy crept to the corner and peered around it, keeping small so as not to attract notice.

A woman stood before the second box, fitting a bridle over the grey mare's head. She wore trousers and a fitted jacket, and her auburn hair curved smoothly against the nape of her neck. Her skin was pale as cream, far lighter than Molly's. Still, she had the same upturned nose and determined chin, and there could be no doubt she was the human girl's mother.

The mare snorted and shied as her mistress led her out into the corridor, but the woman kept a firm hand on the bridle until the horse settled again. She lifted the saddle onto her back and cinched the strap tight, then led the mare into the yard. Keeping to the shadows, Ivy crept to the door and watched as Molly's mother swung herself up into the saddle and cantered off.

To ride like that must be glorious, thought Ivy with a tinge of envy. She retreated to the far end of the barn and sat down again, pulling her knees up and wrapping her arms around them. There was no sign of Richard yet, but surely he'd return soon.

'Hello?' came Molly's voice from the other end of the barn, and Ivy jumped to her feet. The sun had fully risen now, slipping its golden fingers between the shutters, and the place was growing stuffy with its warmth.

'I'm here,' Ivy said, her mouth watering at the rich, buttery scent rising from the paper sack Molly carried. Even after finishing off most of last night's provisions she felt as hungry as she'd ever been in her life, and when the human girl offered her the bag she took it eagerly.

Molly glanced about the barn and frowned. 'Where's, er, Richard?'

'I don't know,' Ivy said. 'I thought he'd be back by now.' She took out a pastry and bit into it. It tasted as delicious as it smelled. 'I saw your mother a little while ago.'

Molly's face became hard and closed – a strangely old look on her still-young face. 'Oh,' was all she said, and then she turned away and picked up Dodger's currying combs.

Ivy finished two pastries and a generous piece of cheese before forcing herself to stop – Richard would probably be hungry as well, when he returned. It seemed odd that he'd been gone so long, but after their quarrel, she could hardly blame him for wanting to sleep elsewhere. She still resented some of the things he'd said to her, but she hadn't exactly been fair to him either, and she hoped he'd come back soon so they could both apologise and move on.

'The food was very good,' she said to Molly. 'I appreciate it.'

Molly paused in her combing, and her set expression relaxed. 'You're welcome,' she said, and went back to brushing the horse again. There was a long silence while Ivy wondered what to say next, but then Molly spoke without looking up:

'My mum didn't used to ride much. But lately she's been

taking Duchess out all the time. I asked her once if I could ride with her, but she said no, she needed time to herself.' Her voice turned acid on the last two words, and her hand clenched in Dodger's mane. 'Like she doesn't get plenty of that already. Sometimes I wonder why she even bothered to have me.'

Ivy was silent.

'Sorry.' Molly rubbed her face against her forearm. 'You don't want to hear all that human stuff. It's just…it gets hard sometimes, not having anyone to talk to. I mean, I have friends, but…'

Ivy felt an ache of sympathy. She knew all too well what it was like to wonder if her parents cared. And though she had friends in the Delve, the things she'd done and been through in the past week were more than she could expect any of them, even Jenny or Mattock, to understand. 'You don't need to apologise,' she said. 'I know what you mean.'

Molly gave her a watery smile. Ivy smiled back – and suddenly felt happier than she had in a long time. It was good to feel that she'd brought the human girl a little comfort, however small.

Yet she couldn't stay here much longer, even for Molly's sake. 'I'm going to look for Richard,' Ivy said. 'I'll be back.' Then she changed to swift-form and flashed out the open door.

The yard dropped away beneath her, the low rectangles

of the barn and cottage receding with it. She shot westward, passing over hedge-bordered fields and patches of woodland, bare ridges and grassy valleys, clusters of human dwellings and dark ribbons of paved road. Other birds flapped or flitted across her path, some much larger than she was and others smaller, but nowhere did she see a bird with Richard's distinctive markings. Where could he have gone?

Ivy circled to the east, rising higher as her sharp eyes searched the air. Perhaps he was already on his way back to the barn, and she'd just missed him. Surely there was no reason to worry...

And yet she did. Because deep inside her, an instinct as sure as her sense of direction told Ivy that Richard ought to have returned a long time ago. And that if she didn't find him there when she returned, then he wasn't coming back at all.

eleven

Ivy paced the barn floor, her emotions an agonising spiral of impatience, confusion, and worry. What could have happened to Richard? Had he been captured? Hurt? Perhaps even killed?

'I don't think he's the sort to take risks unless he has to,' said Molly, when Ivy voiced her fears. 'If you'd heard the way he talked the first time he was here, especially when he was ill...he doesn't fancy himself as a hero.' She stroked Dodger's nose as the brown horse lipped the last fragments of apple from her palm. 'I think he might just have decided it was time to go.'

But he promised my mother, Ivy protested silently. *He said he'd bring me to her if he could.*

And yet, surely Richard had done far more than Marigold had expected of him already? He'd risked his life, and nearly lost it, delivering her message. He'd done the near-impossible, by teaching her wingless daughter to fly.

And if that weren't enough, he'd saved Ivy's life twice over, just to bring her this far.

No wonder he'd been so frustrated by Ivy's stubbornness last night, her seeming ingratitude. No wonder he'd flown off to cool his temper – and if he'd decided in the end that it wasn't worth coming back, who could blame him?

'You're probably right,' Ivy replied, though there was a knot in the middle of her chest that wouldn't go away. Perhaps Richard considered himself well rid of her, but she wished she'd had the chance to say goodbye.

'Well, anyway,' said Molly, wiping her hands and tossing the rag aside, 'my mum's gone to the grocer's and she won't be back for a while. Why don't you come inside and get cleaned up, and I'll make you some tea?'

Ivy ran a hand through her filthy hair. She longed to accept Molly's invitation, but part of her feared to take the risk. If Molly's mother returned unexpectedly and found an oddly dressed stranger in the house, there was no telling what might happen.

Yet Ivy could hardly go to Truro covered in dirt and bloodstains, either. And if Richard didn't show up in the next hour or so, going on without him was exactly what Ivy would have to do.

'Yes, please,' Ivy said. 'I'd like that very much.'

Such a strange place to live, thought Ivy as she followed Molly into the cottage. The tunnels and caverns of the Delve had rounded ceilings and gently bowed-out walls, but everything here was sharp angles, like the inside of a box. Instead of displaying the beauty and solidity of the surrounding stones, the humans had covered them with plaster and paint. And there were windows everywhere she turned, which made her feel exposed and self-conscious.

'Here you are,' said Molly, leading her to a white-tiled room crowded with unfamiliar shapes. 'Leave your clothes outside the door, and I'll—'

'Wait,' said Ivy. 'Where do I bathe?' She could see no water-channel where she could splash her face and hands, or a pool she could pump full and step into. There was a little bit of standing water in one basin, but she couldn't imagine trying to get clean with it.

Molly broke into a grin. 'You really don't know, do you?' she said, and Ivy would have been embarrassed, except that the other girl looked so delighted by her ignorance. 'Well, if you want to have a proper soak you can use the tub, right here. First you put in the plug, and then you turn the taps like this. And you can use this towel to dry off after.' She started the water running, poured in some liquid that made it froth and bubble, then waved cheerfully to Ivy and shut the door.

There was one alarming moment when Ivy couldn't figure out how to make the water stop, but she managed to solve the mystery just in time. Soon she was blessedly clean, and shaking out her damp curls as she dressed in the clothes

Molly had left for her. First came a turquoise blouse with short sleeves and a softly gathered neckline, then a pair of dark blue breeches that came halfway to her knee – both of them too wide for Ivy's slight frame, but once she'd pulled the belt tight they fitted well enough. She hung up the towel, drained the bath, and went out.

She found Molly in the kitchen, pouring tea into two flower-painted cups. The other girl had set out a plate of split buns with butter, strawberry preserves and clotted cream, and as soon as Ivy came in she pulled out a chair for her. 'I could cut up some cheese as well, if you like,' she said. 'Or make watercress sandwiches.'

'This is lovely,' said Ivy, reaching for the butter-knife. She had loaded up one of the splits and taken a bite – they were as good as anything Mattock could make – when Molly spoke again:

'So how are you going to find your relative, if Richard doesn't come back? Have you been to Truro before?'

The food caught in Ivy's throat, and she had to take a sip of tea to ease it down. 'No,' she said. 'But I'm sure I'll find her somehow.' Though since she had no idea where the dance school was or what it looked like, it might take a while.

'Oh,' said Molly. 'And when will you be leaving?'

Ivy's hands tightened around her teacup, seeking its comforting warmth. There was a hollow feeling inside her, and she realised that she'd given up hoping that Richard would return. 'As soon as I'm done here,' she said.

'And this relative of yours…' began Molly, then stopped and gave an apologetic smile. 'Sorry, I'm asking too many questions again, aren't I?'

Guilt stirred in Ivy. This girl had been so kind to her, and asked for so little in return. Was it really fair to leave her in the dark?

'It's my mother,' she said. 'She disappeared five years ago, and I never knew what had happened to her. Until I met Richard, and he told me she was alive, and wanted to see me.'

'And she's been in Truro all this time?' Molly frowned. 'That's a bit odd, isn't it? If she wanted to see you, why didn't she come and find you herself?'

She was right, of course. No matter how hard Ivy tried to rationalise it, that was the one thing about her mother's story that had never made sense. 'I'm not sure,' she replied. 'Perhaps there's a reason, but I won't know until I see her. The problem is—'

She was about to tell her about Cicely, but a crackling noise from the front of the cottage interrupted her. 'That's my mum's car!' Molly exclaimed, snatching Ivy's teacup out of her hand. 'Quick – hide in my bedroom. Third door on the right.'

There had to be a better plan, but Ivy didn't have time to think of one. She ran down the corridor to the room Molly had indicated, darted inside and shoved the door closed behind her. Heart drumming, she pressed her ear to the wood and waited.

'Mum!' exclaimed Molly brightly from the kitchen. 'I was just making lunch. Would you like some?'

'It looks more like tea to me,' the woman replied, disapproval in her tone. 'What a mess you've made! But I suppose. Go and get the other bags from the boot for me, please.'

'Right,' Molly said, and the front door banged in her wake. Ivy kept her ear to the wood, afraid to move. What if Molly's mother guessed that her daughter had not been here alone? What if she came looking for the intruder? But no footsteps sounded in the corridor, and at last Ivy relaxed. She let her hands slide from the door, turned – and her lips parted in amazement.

Molly's bedroom was full of faeries.

Printed on the coverlet and the draperies, etched on ornaments dangling from the ceiling, framed in wood or casually stuck to the wall, pictures of the Small People were everywhere. Faery dolls of all sizes formed a teetering pile in the corner, and the shelf beside the window was cluttered with little statues of them, from a glass-winged faery in pewter to a pottery piskey with a look as mischievous as Keeve's...

Wait. The *window*. If Ivy opened it, she could change to swift-form and fly out. Dodging past the shelf, Ivy took hold of the right-hand pane and pulled. It creaked, but didn't budge.

'What's that?' came a sharp voice from the corridor, and Ivy's mouth went dry. She looked about for a hiding place, but she could already hear footsteps clicking towards her, and there was no time. She dropped to a crouch and turned herself invisible as the door swung open, and Molly's mother strode into the room.

She had changed out of her riding clothes into a floral dress that emphasised her willowy shape, and her hair fell in a smooth bell to her shoulders. She was pretty in a fine-boned way – though Betony would have said she looked unhealthy – but the hard, suspicious look on her face made Ivy shiver. Her eyes swept the room, searching…

'Mum?' asked Molly from the corridor. 'What's wrong?'

She sounded so innocent, as though she hadn't a fear in the world. No wonder Richard had encouraged her to become an actress.

'Never mind,' said the woman, her gaze flickering past Ivy one last time. 'It must have been the wind.' She kicked a prop into place to hold the door open, then walked away.

Molly waited a few seconds before stepping into the room. 'Ivy?' she mouthed.

'I'm here,' Ivy whispered back. 'Open the window for me, please?'

The girl hesitated, a line forming between her brows. For a moment Ivy wondered why she looked unhappy – then she realised, and felt a stir of pity. 'It's all right,' she said.

'I'm not going to run away without saying goodbye. I'll meet you in the barn.'

Molly's face relaxed. She hurried to the window and slid the pane open, then flashed Ivy a grateful smile and slipped away.

'I've got your clothes,' said Molly when she came into the barn a little while later. 'I had to work fast to keep my mum from seeing them, but I don't think she suspects anything. Still…phew!' She wiped her brow dramatically, and thrust a cloth sack at Ivy. 'They're still damp, though. Keep my clothes on for now.'

Ivy slung the bag over her shoulder. 'I'm grateful for all your help,' she said. 'I wish I knew how to repay you.'

'I'll tell you how,' replied Molly. 'You're going to let me come with you and help you find your mother. And don't say I can't,' she went on before Ivy could protest, 'because I looked up dance schools in Truro and there was only one that did dance *and* theatre, so I know exactly which one it is. If we get on the next bus, we can be there in less than an hour. And my mum already said I could go, so there's no good reason for you not to let me.'

'But what if Richard comes back, and you're not here to—'

'He's not coming back,' Molly interrupted. 'I know he's not. Because he did the same thing to me, last time.' Her mouth twisted into an unhappy shape as she said it, but then she raised her chin again. 'Are we going or not? Because the next bus will be here in ten minutes.'

Until now, Ivy had thought she'd be better off alone. But though flying to Truro might be quicker at first, it would be useless if she ended up lost the moment she got there. She needed someone who not only knew the city, but also understood the ways of the human world, to show her where to go and what to do.

And perhaps that was what Richard had intended all along, by bringing her and Molly together. Not only so that Ivy could get the help she needed, but so that Molly would get what she wanted, too.

'All right,' Ivy said. 'It's a bargain.'

By the time the two girls had run up the hill to the bus stop Ivy was flushed and short of breath, but not nearly as winded as usual. Perhaps the sunlight and fresh air was doing her some good. 'Do I look human enough?' Ivy asked Molly as the bus rumbled towards them. 'You don't think anyone will notice that I'm not?'

'I'm sure they won't,' Molly said. 'You're the right size for a human, and you're wearing my clothes.' She pulled a handful of coins out of her pocket and began counting them. 'I don't even know why I made such a fuss when my mum came up the drive. I could have just introduced you as a friend from school, and she'd never have known the difference.'

The bus slowed to a stop, its door hissing open. Molly galloped up the steps and Ivy followed, trying to imitate her confidence. They dropped into their seats and the bus started off again, bumping along the hedge-lined road.

At first they passed only scattered cottages and the occasional abandoned mine, but soon after the houses grew taller and closer together, and bigger buildings crept in among them. The lane broadened to a roadway teeming with vehicles, and for a time Ivy was mesmerised by all the different shapes and colours speeding past. Then they circled into a turn and the route narrowed again, buildings of stone and plaster closing in on both sides. Some of them bore large signs with names that Ivy was still trying to decipher – what was an *Optician*, for instance? – when Molly said triumphantly, 'See, we're nearly there. Told you it wouldn't take long.'

Ivy's hand curled tight around the metal bar beside her. Soon she would look into her mother's face for the first time in five years. Would she see the gentle, loving woman she remembered, or a cold-eyed stranger? Had Marigold summoned Ivy to apologise for the hurt she'd caused, or only to justify herself?

She still hoped that everything would make sense to her, once she'd heard what her mother had to say. But though Richard had said it was no dark secret, Ivy still couldn't imagine what Marigold would be doing at a dance school. Perhaps she was tidying up the place by night in exchange for food and lodging, as piskeys of old times had done for humans who showed them courtesy. But that didn't explain why she'd left the Delve in the first place, or stayed away so long without a single word...

'Here we are,' announced Molly, jumping up as the bus jolted to a stop. Breathing deeply to calm her jittering nerves, Ivy pulled herself to her feet and followed. They stepped off into an open, stone-paved area surrounded by buildings, where humans sat on benches or strolled past carrying brightly coloured bags. In the near distance three tall, pointed towers rose above the rooftops, grey against the cloud-feathered sky. Some sort of fortress, perhaps?

'This way,' said Molly. 'Come on.' She set off at a brisk pace, and Ivy hurried after her. At any other time she would have paused to gaze at all the new things around her – this was her first visit to a human city, after all. But right now her every step whispered *Mother, Mother, Mother*, and she could think of nothing else.

They turned left at the first corner they came to, onto a street lined with handsome grey stone buildings and vehicles parked along both sides. They walked along the gently rising pavement for some time before they reached another corner. Molly led her across the road to a doorway tucked between two shops, with a sign above it that read RISING STAR DANCE & THEATRE ACADEMY. Music floated down from the windows on the upper floor –

a fast, pounding tune that made Ivy's feet itch to dance. She pushed the door open, and Molly followed her in.

They walked into a narrow entry room papered in cream and purple, with a desk taking up most of the right side and a staircase rising steeply to the left. The woman at the desk looked up and smiled. 'Hello, girls,' she said. 'What can I do for you today?'

Ivy stood paralysed, unable to think of an answer. How could she explain that she was here to look for a missing piskey who might or might not call herself Marigold? But Molly stepped in quickly to rescue her. 'We're interested in your dance classes,' she said. 'Could we go upstairs and have a look?'

The woman hesitated, her eyes flicking past Ivy and Molly as though searching for a parent behind them. But when Molly clasped her hands beneath her chin and gave her an imploring look, her expression softened. 'Go on, then,' she said. 'As long as you don't disturb the class. And if you've got any questions, come and talk to me.'

Ivy's legs felt shaky and her pulse beat raggedly in her throat, but she couldn't wait any longer. Eyes on the staircase, she stepped past Molly and began to climb. Three, four, five steps she rose, and with every one the music became louder. Soon she could hear the thumps and creaks as the students moved across the floor.

'Five, six, seven, eight!' called a clear voice. 'Kick, and *turn* – well done, Meg, you've got it now!'

On the fifteenth step the staircase ended, opening onto a room lined with mirrors on one side and windows on the other. Music boomed from a pair of boxes set high into each corner, and in the middle of the floor a group of girls were dancing. But Ivy had only an instant to take it all in before her gaze fell on the woman leading the class, and her mind emptied with shock.

It was her mother.

Marigold wore fitted black clothing and soft slippers, with her brown-gold hair knotted atop her head. Her wings had vanished – hidden by glamour maybe, or perhaps they had simply disappeared when she grew to human size. She was still slender, but now there was a strength to her body and a rosy glow to her skin that Ivy had never seen before. And though five years had passed, she looked younger than ever – no older than Molly's mother in fact, though Ivy knew enough of Marigold's history to guess that she must be at least fifty. How could that be?

'Go on, Ivy,' Molly whispered, poking her in the back. 'You're blocking the way. Ivy!'

The music was so loud, it seemed impossible that anyone could have heard. But Marigold stopped dancing, turned – and froze, her wide eyes fixed on Ivy. For a timeless moment the two of them stared at each other, as one by one the students began to falter and glance around in confusion. Then Marigold blinked as though waking from a dream, stepped quickly to the oldest of the girls, and whispered a few words in her ear. The girl moved to the front of the class, calling her fellow students to attention – and as the others went back to dancing, Marigold hurried over and seized Ivy's hand.

'Come,' she whispered. 'This way.'

Blood pounding in her ears, Ivy obeyed. She was only dimly aware of Molly giving her a grinning thumbs-up as Marigold led her into an adjoining room. She shut the door, turned swiftly – and then at last Ivy was where she had longed to be, in her mother's arms.

'Oh, my brave, beautiful girl,' Marigold murmured, stroking her hair. 'I can't believe you're here. What you must have gone through, to come all this way…and how big you've grown!'

Ivy pressed her face against her mother's shoulder, breathing in the scent of her skin. She had always smelled sweet, like the sachets of dried herbs and petals she scattered among her clothes. But now the fragrance was richer and more subtle, like a living plant instead of a dead one. 'I thought the spriggans had taken you,' Ivy said, her voice thick with emotion. 'I thought I'd never see you again.'

'I know you did,' said Marigold, clasping her tighter, as though afraid Ivy would vanish if she let go. 'And I am so sorry, my darling.'

The old grief ached in Ivy's chest, and she pulled back. 'Then why did you do it?' Ivy asked, searching her mother's face. 'How could you run away, leave us all thinking you were dead, for…this?'

'You think I left the Delve so I could teach human girls how to dance?' Marigold's brow creased in dismay. 'Oh, no, no, dearest. I would never have done that to you. I only came here because I had nowhere else to go.'

'How could that be?' asked Ivy. 'You had the Delve. You had us.'

Marigold sighed. She drew up a chair for Ivy, then sat down across from her. 'I was very ill when I lived in the Delve,' she said. 'More ill than I ever allowed you or anyone else to see. So I couldn't have stayed with you much longer, even if—' She swallowed, touching her throat as though it hurt her. 'Even if other things hadn't happened.'

Ivy could guess what those *other things* might be, but it didn't make her feel any better about it. 'You mean the fight between you and Dad,' she said flatly.

Marigold recoiled. 'How do you know about that? You should never—' Then she stopped and went on in a calmer tone, 'Flint told you about it, I suppose.'

'Mica overheard it,' said Ivy. 'He told me you wanted to take me and Cicely with you, but Dad said no.'

The tension went out of Marigold's face. 'Ah,' she said softly. 'I should have guessed. Poor Mica.' She bowed her head and went on, 'Yes, your father and I fought, and we parted on unhappy terms. I couldn't convince him to leave the Delve with me, and he wouldn't let any of you children go either. But he knew that I had to leave, and that there was nothing he could do to save me.'

'Why? If you were sick, then Yarrow could have—'

'I was dying,' Marigold interrupted. 'I was coughing up blood, and Yarrow had done as much as she could for me already.' She closed her eyes. 'I was terrified of being caught by the spriggans, and I knew nothing about the outside world. But I had to get out of the Delve.'

'Why?' Ivy asked, baffled. 'What was so bad about the Delve?'

'So many things,' Marigold murmured. 'More than I ever realised, until it was too late. I'd seen Betony's only child die stillborn, and it took so long for me to have children at all… I think part of me knew all along that something wasn't right. But when you were born without wings, so weak and tiny, and I saw you struggling to breathe…I couldn't deny the truth any more.'

She still wasn't making sense to Ivy. 'You mean there's a curse on the mine, or on our people? Something the spriggans did?'

'Not magic,' Marigold said soberly. 'Poison.'

Ivy caught her breath. 'But where? Who would—'

'It could be in the air, or the water, or perhaps in the rock itself; I don't know enough about such things to tell, and I never had the chance to search it out. But every piskey in the Delve is dying of it, whether they realise it or not.' Her lips thinned. 'I tried to warn them – your father first, and then Betony. But they refused to believe.'

Poison. Ivy could hardly fathom it, and yet she couldn't deny the possibility. It would explain why Richard had found it so difficult to heal her, and why she felt stronger now than she ever had living underground. And when she remembered her father's coughing, his yellowed teeth and shaking hands – surely that was no ordinary sickness.

Yet she could understand why Aunt Betony had been sceptical, too. There were parts of Marigold's story that didn't seem to add up. 'But why would you be sicker than anyone else?' Ivy asked. 'Why not the knockers, who work in the mine every day?'

'The knockers have some immunity,' Marigold replied, 'built up from centuries of working underground. And they and the hunters can go outside whenever they please, which helps to strengthen their resistance. But the women are more susceptible. Especially the faery-born ones…like me.'

Ivy's stomach turned cold. Her mother, a faery? 'That's not possible,' she said faintly. 'You were born in the Delve – you've lived there all your life—'

Marigold gave her a sad smile. 'I know. I found it hard to believe at first, too.' Her eyes became distant as she went on, 'My mother died giving birth to me, and I never knew her. I only knew that the other children in the Delve were brown and sturdy, where I was pale and fragile-looking and often found it hard to breathe. Aster, the healer before Yarrow, made me potions to help me grow stronger, and I learned to use glamour to make my thin, glassy wings look more like a piskey's should. But I never understood why I was different, until I left the Delve and began meeting others of my kind.'

She took Ivy's hand, folding it between her own. 'One of the first strangers to show me kindness was a faery who had escaped the destruction of Thistledown Wyld, my ancestral home. She had seen my father killed in battle, and my mother taken prisoner with the rest of the women. Her captors didn't realise that she was already expecting a child.'

'The spriggans, you mean,' said Ivy a little wildly. Surely only spriggans would do such a terrible thing. 'They attacked your village, and then our people rescued you—'

'Spriggans!' Marigold gave a bitter laugh. 'There haven't been spriggans in Kernow for decades, or at least not enough of them to matter.' She shook her head. 'No, Ivy. It was piskeys who destroyed my home and took my mother captive. And if they hadn't gone underground where no one could reach them...' Her expression turned hard. 'Then my people – my *true* people – would have wiped them out long ago.'

twelve

'No!' Ivy pulled away from her mother and scrambled to her feet. 'That's a lie! Our ancestors fought against the faeries, but only to stop them invading our land. If we went around attacking peaceful folk and stealing their wives and daughters – if we were no better than the spriggans – how could we live with ourselves? How could we forget something as horrible as that?'

'I don't know,' said Marigold, and now she sounded weary. 'Like you, I only know the legends as they are, not how they came to be. But I know I was not the only faery woman to be captured and brought to the Delve. Just one of the few who lived long enough to marry and bear children.' She looked down at her pale, ringless fingers. 'There are many kinds of deception, Ivy. Sometimes the most powerful lies are the ones we tell ourselves, because the truth is too ugly to bear.'

Ivy covered her face with her hands. She wanted to deny

what her mother was saying, but how could she? If Mica was right, she'd done the same thing herself. In the grief and horror of losing her mother, she'd blocked out the memory of her parents' fight so completely that she couldn't recall it even now.

'No wonder you never came back to the Delve,' she said hollowly. 'Why are you even telling me this? Why did you ask me to come, if you don't want anything to do with us any more?'

'Oh, my darling, *no*,' said Marigold, getting up swiftly and gripping Ivy's shoulders. 'Discovering that I was a faery changed many things, but it never changed my love for you. That's why I sent for you, so we could be together—'

'What about Mica and Cicely? They're your children too!'

'Yes, of course,' said Marigold soothingly. 'But they take after their father, and his knocker blood makes them strong. They may live a hundred years in the Delve and never guess that they could have, *should* have, lived longer. But you...' She tucked a loose curl tenderly behind Ivy's ear. 'You are more faery than either of them, and you have been dying since the day you were born. How could I abandon you?'

'And yet you did,' Ivy said, twisting away from her and backing up against the wall. 'You left me there for five years, never knowing if you were dead or alive. Where were you all that time? Why didn't you send us a message? *Why didn't you come back?*'

Marigold sighed. 'For many reasons,' she said. 'But the worst mistake was mine. I trusted someone I should not have trusted. And because of that, I was captured and dragged off to London, where I spent the next four years as a slave.'

London. Ivy had heard the name once or twice in the droll-teller's stories – the greatest city in England, unimaginably huge and far away. 'Whose slave?' she asked, hushed with disbelief.

'She called herself the Empress,' said Marigold. 'She was old, but very powerful, and her ambition was to conquer the whole faery realm before she died. I managed to escape her once, but her lieutenants captured me before I even reached the border of Kernow. And the horrors I witnessed after that, when she sent me and her other servants into battle…' She passed a hand over her brow, as though to wipe away the memory. 'I longed to send you a message, but I feared even to try in case it was intercepted. If the Empress knew about the Delve, she would surely have tried to conquer it as well.'

'But you got away from her in the end,' said Ivy, 'or you wouldn't be here. So why didn't you send us a message then?' It was a struggle to pull her turbulent thoughts together, but she had to know the truth. If her mother was a faery and not a piskey, if she'd been the pawn of someone evil, could Ivy trust her any more?

'I wanted to,' said Marigold. 'But even once the war

ended and the Empress was dead, it was some time before I was free to return to Kernow. And even then, there were…obstacles. I had to wait for the right opportunity, and a messenger I could trust.' She glanced towards the door, as though remembering for the first time that Ivy had not come alone. 'Where is Iago? I must tell him how grateful I am for bringing you to me.'

She must be talking about Richard. How many different names could one faery have? 'He left,' Ivy said. 'I don't know where he went.'

'Ah.' Marigold sounded wistful, but not surprised. 'Well, at least he kept his word.'

'Is that really his name? Iago?'

'He had another name once, when we were both slaves of the Empress. But I also know why he prefers not to use it.' Marigold gave a rueful smile. 'He has made some powerful enemies, and I took a great risk in protecting him. But I also knew it would put him in my debt, and that he would do anything to be rid of that burden.'

So that was all Ivy had been to Richard – a burden. It wasn't really a surprise, but it was surprising how much it hurt.

'Do you understand now?' asked Marigold softly, reaching out to touch her face. 'I know I've hurt you. I know I've made mistakes. But now we're together, and I want to make things right. Can you forgive me? Can we start again?'

Ivy hesitated. All her emotions pulled towards her mother, yearning for her approval and love. Only the part of her that feared to make herself vulnerable, that dreaded the thought of being tricked or betrayed, warned her not to trust too quickly. But she'd listened to her suspicions with Richard, and what had that gained her?

Besides, this wasn't just about Ivy's feelings any more, or even her mother's. There was something far more important at stake – and it was time Marigold knew it as well.

'I want to,' she said at last. 'I'm willing to try. But first, I need your help.' She took a deep breath. 'Cicely's gone missing.'

Marigold looked shocked, then increasingly distressed as Ivy told how she and Mica had discovered Cicely's absence. Soon her eyes were brimming with tears, and Ivy no longer doubted that her mother cared about Cicely's fate.

But Ivy didn't tell her everything. She wasn't sure what her mother would think of her shape-changing, and she couldn't bring herself to admit that Cicely's disappearance was her fault. All she said was that Cicely had vanished, like Keeve before her, and that the search parties from the Delve hadn't been able to locate either of them.

'I thought she'd been taken by the spriggans,' Ivy said, lowering her voice as the music from the adjoining room stopped. 'Especially after Gem and Feldspar saw that stranger by the Engine House. But if there aren't any spriggans, then—'

'Mrs Flint?' The door opened, and a girl with long brown hair leaned inside. 'We've finished the lesson.'

'Excellent, Claire. I'll be right with you.' Marigold wiped her eyes hastily with her fingers, then touched Ivy's arm and whispered, 'Don't worry. We'll find her,' before following the human girl out.

When she had gone, Ivy blew out a long breath and leaned her head against the wall. Difficult as it had been to tell her mother of her sister's loss, it was a huge relief to know that she would no longer have to continue the search alone. But as she listened to Marigold apologising to her students for her absence and praising their hard work, Ivy felt a stir of misgiving. Her mother sounded so human now, so at ease in this strange new world. Even if they did find Cicely together, it seemed that Marigold had no intention of returning to the Delve—so how could they ever be a whole family again?

Chattering voices filled the dance studio, followed shortly afterwards by the sounds of multiple feet galloping down the stairs. The commotion in the other room had barely subsided when Marigold opened the door and said to Ivy in a puzzled tone, 'There's someone here to see you.'

'Ivy!' exclaimed Molly, popping up behind Marigold and waving a handful of papers. 'I had a brilliant talk with the receptionist downstairs. She says I might be able to get into one of their advanced classes, if I can talk my mum into letting me audition.'

'That's wonderful,' said Ivy, and turned to her mother. 'Mum, this is Molly – she's a friend of Richard's. She was the one who brought me here today.'

'It's all right,' Molly said in a confiding tone, before Marigold could speak. 'I know you and Ivy are faeries. But I won't tell anyone.'

She'd said *faeries* and not *piskeys*, but Marigold didn't correct her, even for Ivy's sake. 'How extraordinary,' she said faintly. 'And you're interested in our school?'

'Oh, yes,' said Molly. 'I want to be an actress more than anything.'

Oddly, that seemed to put Marigold at ease. The colour returned to her face, and she smiled. 'Now I see where Richard comes in. I didn't realise he had a protégée. Well, I'm not involved in the theatre part of our programme, but I'd be glad to put in a good word for you with Trix, our drama teacher. I can't tell you how grateful I am to you for bringing Ivy to me.'

Molly blushed. 'It was really nothing,' she said. She folded up the papers and stuffed them into her pocket, then turned to Ivy with a shy smile. 'Thanks for letting me come with you.'

And there was that *thanks* again, so casual it was almost meaningless. But Molly obviously meant well by it, so Ivy smiled back. 'I won't forget your kindness,' she said. 'I hope we'll see each other again.'

'Me, too,' said Molly. She looked from Ivy to Marigold, her expression wistful and a little envious. 'Good luck.' She scampered down the stairs and went out.

Marigold laid a hand on Ivy's shoulder. 'I know a spell that may help us find Cicely,' she said. 'But we can't do it here. Let me look after a few things, and then I'll take you home.'

When Ivy and her mother left the dance school, the air was misty with rain. As they walked down the hill Marigold spoke to her in an undertone, drawing her attention to all the new things around them and comparing them to more familiar sights and concepts Ivy would know from the Delve. She pointed out shops and restaurants, galleries and museums, and showed Ivy how and where to cross the street.

'I was terrified when I first came to Truro,' she said, tucking her arm into Ivy's as they reached the other side. 'I don't want you to feel that way. It's a lovely city, and now that we're together there's nothing to fear.'

Before long they had made their way back to the open, cobble-paved area where Ivy and Molly had climbed off the bus. But now they were facing the opposite direction, and Ivy was surprised to see that half the square was filled with cloth-draped booths, much like the Market Cavern at home. The smells of hot food wafted towards her, savoury and sweet, and beads clattered as a merchant woman rearranged the necklaces in her stall. Nearby a boy in short trousers was juggling four balls at once, while a crowder with pink hair played a lively jig on her fiddle. They passed a booth draped with scarves in a jewel-box of colours, another full of wooden puppets that danced on strings, and a third selling animals knitted out of woolly yarn. They were coming to the end of the row when a brightly painted sign caught Ivy's eye. It read: CORNISH PISKEYS – FOR GOOD LUCK! And beneath, in smaller lettering, *Handcrafted in Kernow by local artisans.*

Beneath the sign stood a table crowded with brown clay figures. They were the right height for piskeys, but their bodies were squat and their features comically grotesque. Was this really how humans imagined her people? Ivy picked one up, surprised at its lightness, and turned it over. The inside was hollow.

'Like those, do you?' said the seller, a weathered human with wild grey hair. 'They're special, those little piskeys are. Make a nice gift, or a souvenir.'

They looked crude and hideous to Ivy, but she didn't want to insult him by saying so. 'Do you make them?' Ivy asked, but the man shook his head.

'I just sell 'em, lass. Eight pounds each. Or ten for Joan the Wad, she's the luckiest of all, see?' He lifted up a figure of a bristle-haired piskey hugging her knees, but Ivy had never seen anything that looked less like Betony, or anything she was less anxious to own. She lowered the statue she was holding, about to excuse herself and walk away.

But she couldn't put the thing down. It stuck to her hands, as though magnetised. A buzzing sensation spread through Ivy's palms, and she looked up at the seller in alarm. But he only beamed at her and said, 'Good choice. I'm fond of that little fellow myself. Want me to box him up for you?'

Ivy shook her head in desperation. 'Mum!' she cried out, and immediately Marigold hurried over. She seized the piskey in both hands and twisted it out of Ivy's grip. 'Not today,' she said to the man, and set it on the table.

Ivy's hands stung and her legs felt shaky, but she couldn't help glancing back as Marigold pulled her away. The last thing she saw was the old piskey-seller waving cheerfully at her, before he retreated into the shadows and disappeared.

'I've never felt anything like that,' said Ivy, taking the teacup her mother handed her. They were sitting in the kitchen of the place where Marigold lived – she called it a *flat* for some reason, even though they'd had to climb a flight of stairs to get there. 'It was like some kind of spell, but…humans can't use magic, can they?'

Marigold poured her own cup and sat down across from her. The rain was falling hard now, pattering against the glass like tiny fists knocking to be let in. 'No,' she said. 'But there are old powers in the earth of Kernow, and not all of those powers are good ones. The piskeys and the faeries fought some terrible battles here, and the spells they used against each other still linger in the soil…and beneath it.'

'Do you think he knew that? The man who was selling them?'

'I doubt it,' said Marigold. 'But I'd stay away from those statues, if you see them again. I've learned to be cautious of things made from Cornish earth.'

'But you touched it, when you were helping me,' said Ivy. 'Didn't it pull at you too?'

Marigold shook her head. 'I could never sense things in the rock and soil, not the way your father and the other piskeys could. But then, faeries were not made to live underground. I had no idea how weak my magic was, or how much stronger it could be, until I came out of the Delve.'

She reached for Ivy's hand. 'You'll see for yourself, when you've been here a little longer. There is so much faery in you, and you've been trapped in the earth so long…you've barely even begun to come into your power.'

Her tone was soothing, but the words made Ivy more uneasy than ever. She felt sure her mother was right about the Delve being poisoned – why else would Ivy feel so much better outside of the mine than she ever had living in it? Yet she didn't like the eager, almost hungry way her mother looked at her when she spoke about power. Or the way she'd said *when you've been here a little longer*, as though she felt sure that Ivy would never leave Truro again.

'What about Cicely?' Ivy asked. 'You said you had a spell that would help us find her.'

'Yes,' said Marigold, taking Ivy's other hand. 'A faery spell for searching, stronger than the one Betony tried back in the Delve. Close your eyes, and I'll show you.'

The searching charm Marigold taught Ivy was meant to locate any faeries within fifty miles' distance, or so she said. Since Cicely was half-faery, it ought to be able to find her – and it would show her where to find them, as well. Ivy concentrated as her mother told her, linking her power with Marigold's as they searched for the telltale flare of her sister's magic. But though she pushed her magical strength to the limit, she felt not even a single answering spark.

'It's not working,' she said at last, letting go and knuckling her eyes in frustration. Was her magic too weak? Was her sister too far away?

Or had the worst happened, and Cicely was already dead?

Marigold touched her cheek tenderly. 'You're tired,' she said, 'and so am I. Don't lose hope. We'll try again tomorrow.' She rose and began putting away the dishes.

Ivy didn't want to wait. She wanted to keep searching for Cicely, even if it took all night. But Marigold's magic was clearly more powerful than hers, and if they couldn't locate

Cicely together, what hope did Ivy have of finding her alone?

She slumped in her chair, picking at the too-soft wood with a fingernail, and looked around. Her mother's flat was a good deal smaller than the cavern she had left behind, and painfully bare of decoration. The furnishings looked flimsy, all wood and cloth without a trace of stone or metal to be seen, and the white walls and gauzy blue curtains gave the place a washed-out, ghostly feeling. Even her mother no longer wore the rosy topaz pendant and earrings that Ivy's father had given her at their wedding, only a thin twist of hemp with a few glass beads and shells strung upon it. How could she be happy living in such meagre surroundings, all alone?

'What if we could get rid of the poison in the mine?' Ivy asked. 'Would you come back then?'

'It's not as easy as that,' said Marigold, her eyes on the dishtowel she was folding. 'Betony never thought I was good enough to marry her brother. And she hated me even more for having children, since she and Gossan never could. When I told her about the poison in the Delve—' She put a hand to her throat as though the words choked her, and for a long moment she was silent. Then she said, 'I can't go back, even if I wanted to. I have a life here. And I can't leave Serita.'

Ivy frowned. 'Who is Serita?'

'She started the Rising Star Academy with Trix, five

years ago. When I came to Truro for the first time, weak and sick and not knowing where to turn, she was kind to me. She invited me to one of her performances, and when I watched her dance...' Her eyes grew faraway. 'I'd never seen anything so wonderful, or so free.'

'But there was plenty of dancing in the Delve,' Ivy said.

'Not like this,' said Marigold, with a shake of her head. 'In the Delve it was always the same steps, the same dances, over and over. Never anything new.' She pulled out her chair and sat down across from Ivy again, her gaze eager and intent. 'Don't you understand, Ivy? There's a price we pay for our magic, faeries and piskeys alike. We can do many things that humans can't, but they have something we lack – creativity. That's why we need them, even more than they need us.'

'That doesn't make sense,' Ivy said, a little resentfully. 'Most of the women in the Delve have never seen a human, but they still create all kinds of things.'

'Perhaps,' Marigold said, 'but the methods they use to make them haven't changed since the day they went underground. Now and then you might see a piskey-woman with a new clothing pattern or a new recipe, if her husband or son brought it back from the surface. But that doesn't happen often – you know how men are.' Her tone became scornful. 'As long as their beds are warm and their bellies full, they hardly notice what we women do.'

There was some truth to that, Ivy had to admit: she'd

been annoyed by Mica's selfishness too many times to think otherwise. But she also couldn't forget how shattered Flint had been by his wife's disappearance, the emptiness she'd left inside him that no amount of good food, or even the love of his children, could fill.

And Marigold hadn't even asked how he was doing.

'But when magical folk and humans work together,' Ivy's mother continued more brightly, 'everyone benefits. We gain new ideas and skills from our human friends, and at the same time, our presence makes their creativity stronger. And the more time a faery spends with a human, the greater their shared creativity becomes. That was what happened with me and Serita.' She gave a reminiscent smile. 'Once I got up the courage to try the new dances she showed me, it wasn't long before I could do them as well as she could.'

'Did she know you were a…a faery?' asked Ivy. It was still hard to get used to the idea that her mother had no piskey blood in her at all.

'No,' said Marigold. 'And when I was captured by the Empress, I thought Serita would never forgive me. I'd left without even saying goodbye. But when I returned to Truro she welcomed me, even though I couldn't tell her where I'd been. Then she told me she was ill, and that she wouldn't be able to teach for several months. She asked if I would take her place at the school until she was better again.'

Which explained why Marigold had sent Richard to

deliver her message, instead of coming herself. She'd made a promise to Serita, and like a true faery she was determined to keep it. But the revelation brought no comfort to Ivy. She could understand her mother not wanting to come back to the Delve as long as the poison remained. She could even understand her being afraid of Betony. But she'd made it sound as though Serita was more important to her than her own husband and children.

'Yet I never forgot about you,' said Marigold softly, no doubt reading Ivy's thoughts in her face. 'I missed you every day. And I'm so glad you came to me. I feared you'd choose to stay in the Delve, and I couldn't have borne it if—'

She plucked a white cloth from the box on the table and dabbed at her eyes. Then she went on in a firmer tone, 'But you're safe now, and that's all that matters. Once we find Cicely, we'll send a message to your father and brother, and tell them what's happened. Then everything will be all right.'

Ivy slept fitfully that night, and woke with the first rays of dawn. It wasn't that she'd been uncomfortable on the sofa – Marigold had offered her the bed and she'd declined it, knowing she'd feel more secure with a wall at her back. But she couldn't stop thinking about Cicely.

When her mother emerged from her tiny bedroom, Ivy got up at once. 'Could we cast that searching spell again now?' she asked.

'Yes, of course,' said her mother, taking both Ivy's hands in her own.

They stood together with eyes closed and heads bent, their shared magic rippling out across the city and into the countryside beyond. Marigold had been right in urging her to rest, thought Ivy; her mind felt clearer, her power stronger than before. Hope rose inside her, and she concentrated with all her might. Surely they'd find Cicely now.

But though they sent out one call after another, there was no answer – not even the tiniest flash of light. 'I'm sorry,' said Marigold heavily at last, letting go of Ivy's hands. 'It's no good.'

'But we can't give up,' said Ivy. 'We have to keep trying!'

'We can cast the spell again tonight,' her mother said. 'But I don't know what else to do. I fear...' She turned away, then looked back sharply. 'Where are you going?'

'Out,' said Ivy hoarsely. 'I need to—' Then her eyes started to burn, and she couldn't speak any more. She hurtled out of the flat and down the stairs, slamming the door behind her.

Ivy returned to the flat late that evening, weak with exhaustion and misery. She'd flown across Cornwall from one end to the other, stopping every few miles to cast the searching spell. But only once did she sense the glow of another faery's magic, and as soon as she did it vanished, as though whoever it was didn't want to be found. It might have been Richard, but it certainly wasn't Cicely.

When Marigold opened the door, she didn't ask Ivy what had happened. She threw her arms around her, and Ivy closed her eyes and stood motionless until she could breathe again. Then she came inside and ate the dinner her mother had saved for her.

Yet later that night, when the flat was dark and quiet, Ivy's grief welled up again. She wept into her pillow until she had no tears left and then fell into exhausted sleep, her dreams haunted by the truth she could no longer deny.

Her sister was dead, and it was her fault. Her mother was a faery, who'd left the Delve by her own choice and had no intention of ever returning. Ivy had destroyed her family and betrayed her people, all for nothing.

And now she could never go home.

thirteen

Over the next few days Ivy gradually became accustomed to life in Truro, though she still felt restless and discontented. Marigold bought her new clothes and a proper bed and introduced Ivy to her human friends – including the ailing Serita and Trix, the academy's drama teacher. But she didn't offer to cast the searching spell again, and Ivy didn't ask her to.

Ivy had been in the city for nearly a week, and had lost hope of ever seeing anyone from her past life again, when she made a discovery that changed everything. She was walking the streets around the cathedral one afternoon when she felt an itch at the back of her mind – a nagging sensation as though she had forgotten something important, or as though some soundless voice were calling her name.

It was impossible to ignore that feeling, even if she'd wanted to. Ivy followed it along the pavement, step by step, until she found herself in front of a shop that sold books and art supplies – and her gaze fell to the grinning piskey sitting in the window.

Not again, she thought in disgust, and tried to walk away. But the tug inside her was too strong, and before she could stop herself she'd reversed direction, put her hand on the latch, and pushed the creaking door open. A bell jangled, and the shopkeeper sang out, 'Be with you in a moment!'

'It's all right,' Ivy called back to him – she'd learned a few things from shopping with her mother. 'I'm only looking.'

'Right then,' came the reply, and Ivy was left alone with a line of bookcases stretching away on both sides, and the window display in front of her. The piskey sat with its back to her, just within reach.

Ivy's hands were tingling now, blood rushing to the surface of her skin. She didn't want to touch the figure, and yet she felt as though she needed to – as though it were some missing part of her own body, and without it she'd never be whole again. She fought the compulsion one last time, shutting her eyes and backing away. But her head and her heart throbbed in unified protest, and the piskey's call was too urgent to ignore. With a last nervous glance over her shoulder, she bent and lifted the piskey statue from its place.

It was as ugly as all the others she had seen, a little man in a pointed cap and short jacket. But this one didn't stick to her hands, and it felt oddly heavy compared to the one she'd held before. She turned it over, wondering what made it different – and nearly dropped the statue in shock.

For an instant, so quick she might have missed it if she'd blinked, its eyes had glowed silver.

Ivy gripped the piskey convulsively. *What are you?* she thought, and at the same instant a voice echoed in her mind: *Help…me.*

But not just any voice. A voice she had heard before.

It was Richard.

'How much for this?' Ivy asked, brandishing the statue at the startled owner. Whether Richard was trapped inside the pottery figure or whether he'd only been using it as a vessel to speak to her, Ivy didn't know. But either way, she wasn't leaving the shop without it.

'It's not for sale,' the man said, looking baffled. 'It's just for show—'

'I'll pay you twice what it's worth,' said Ivy, reaching into her bag. 'Where did you get it? And when?'

'A couple of days ago, in the Pannier Market,' he said. 'But look, if you want it that badly, I won't cheat you. Nine pounds'll do it. Want it boxed up?'

Ivy cradled the statue against her side. 'No, that's all right,' she said. 'I'll carry it with me.'

'…And that's when I heard Richard's voice,' Ivy explained to her mother as they sat at the kitchen table with the clay

220

piskey between them. 'But I've been trying for hours to get it – him – to talk again, and nothing seems to work.'

Marigold rubbed her forehead, as though the news pained her. She'd just returned to the flat after teaching her last class and she looked tired and dishevelled, her hair wind-blown and her clothes spattered dark with rain. 'Ivy, are you sure? It might simply have been an echo. A shadow, a memory, of some piskey or faery who died calling for help a long time ago.'

'It was Richard,' Ivy insisted. 'I know it was. We have to help him.'

Reluctantly Marigold took the statue in her hands. But after a moment she set it down again. 'I can't feel anything,' she said. 'I don't see how he could be in there, Ivy.'

Ivy looked into the clay figure's dull brown eyes. It definitely felt heavier than the other statues she had handled, and the base was solid, not hollow. Did she dare to smash it, and see if Richard was trapped inside? But what if he was part of the statue now, and she ended up killing him?

'I don't like this,' said Marigold. 'We should get rid of it.' She reached for the figure, but Ivy pulled it away.

'I owe Richard my life,' she said. 'I can't give up on him like that.'

Her mother's lips thinned, and she gave the statue a resentful look. But she must have known it was fruitless to argue with Ivy, because after a moment she sighed and sat back.

'Molly rang the school today,' she said, unwinding the knot of her hair and running her fingers through it. 'She's going to audition for Trix tomorrow.'

And just like that, Ivy's mother was changing the subject. Did she really not believe that Richard was in danger? Was she so wrapped up in her own concerns that she didn't care? Or was there something else going on that Ivy didn't know about – something her mother didn't want to tell her?

Either way, the message was clear enough. If Ivy wanted to help Richard, she'd have to do it on her own.

Ivy remained sitting by the window long after her mother had gone to bed, waiting for the clouds to part and the moon to rise so she could try some spells on the piskey statue by moonlight. But the sky remained closed, and the rain refused to stop falling. At last, discouraged, Ivy set the clay figure on the tea-table and lay down on the sofa beside it.

'I'm sorry, Richard,' she mumbled, her fingers tracing the statue's homely features – so unlike the sharp, fine-boned face she remembered. 'I wish I knew what to do.'

The statue didn't answer, or give any sign that it heard. But there was something forlorn about it despite its comic grin, and it felt wrong to leave it sitting there all alone. What if Marigold got up and took it away in the night? Ivy picked it up and tucked it in beside her – and immediately felt better, as though that was what she should have done all along.

'Good night,' she whispered, and closed her eyes.

Ivy hadn't dreamed in a long time, at least not that she could remember. But that night her mind was full of images, each more vivid and strange than the next. She flew over the rooftops of a great city she'd never seen before, where buildings of glass and steel rose like armoured giants against the sky. She held a pebble that turned into a knife, its silver blade sharp enough to kill. She looked into the faces of people she'd never seen before – an older human with blunt grey hair and a wry expression, a cheerful-looking man who winked at her before disappearing behind a curtain, and a faery with blonde curls and a sweetly vicious smile. One moment she was in the midst of a group of skinny boys all fighting like wild animals; the next she was sprinting across a darkened lawn with smoke billowing all around her and light exploding on every side. But none of the dreams seemed to connect to each other, or make any sense.

Then everything went black, and for a dreadful moment Ivy could see nothing at all. She might have thought herself dead, if not for the searing pain around her ankle. But when the darkness greyed into an eerie twilight and a girl with tousled black hair dropped to the ground before her, Ivy realised with a shock that she was looking at herself.

These weren't dreams; they were memories. *Richard's* memories.

Where are you? she cried out to him silently. *Who did this to you? How can I set you free?*

At first the answer came only in images, as disjointed as the ones that had come before. A wounded swift spiralling towards the ground. Molly looking startled, then furious. Marigold rising from a crouch, eyes narrowed and one hand blazing with magical light. But just as Ivy began to despair that she would ever make sense of it all, she heard Richard's voice:

Don't trust... The words were weak and fragmented. *Mother...*

Ivy's heart gave a hard thump. Did he mean that the way it sounded?

Trapped me...Keeve is...Cicely...

Cicely! Was he saying she and Keeve were still alive? Could they be trapped inside the piskey statues too?

Find them... Richard whispered, and then even more faintly, *Molly...your blood...save...*

She was losing him, and she couldn't bear it. Not when she understood so little of what he'd been trying to say. *I want to save you!* Ivy shouted. *And Cicely too, but you have to tell me how! Richard!*

There was no answer. Then a shadow loomed up behind her, and Ivy knew something terrible was about to happen. She tried to run, but her feet were locked in place, and suddenly she couldn't move, couldn't speak, couldn't even breathe—

With a strangled cry, Ivy bolted awake. She was lying on the sofa with the blankets tangled around her legs, and around the edges of the nearby window the first light of dawn was glowing. Next to her the piskey statue beamed its foolish grin, its gaze as vacant as ever.

Yet it hadn't been just a nightmare; she was certain of that. Richard had spoken to her. Ivy stared across the room, sickness burning her throat. She had to remember everything he'd said to her, before—

'Ivy?' Marigold appeared in the doorway of her bedroom, clutching a robe about her. 'Are you all right?'

Her expression was anxious, and in that moment she looked exactly like the woman who had tucked Ivy into bed when she was ten years old. And yet Ivy couldn't forget how she'd appeared in Richard's memory, with remorseless eyes and power crackling around her fingertips.

Don't trust... Mother...

Ivy pushed the piskey statue under the covers. 'I had a bad dream,' she said. 'But it's over now.'

The Pannier Market was a busy place, full of shops and booths selling every kind of merchandise. Ivy made her way past lighted cabinets full of fresh meats and cheeses, shelves of china and antique silver, and a gorgeous display of cut flowers, until she found the stall she was looking for.

'Well, good morning,' said the grey-haired vendor, folding his newspaper and getting up to greet her. 'Thought I might see you again. Looking for these?' He gestured to the clay piskeys lined up at one side of the table, next to a set of porcelain faeries holding flowers in their outstretched palms. 'Only got six at the moment, but I'll be getting more soon. Collect the lot!'

Ivy shifted the weight of the bag on her shoulder, conscious of Richard's weight inside. 'Where do they come from?' she asked.

The man scratched his ear. 'Well, now…d'you know, I can't quite remember. Can't be far, though, or I couldn't sell them as local. St Austell, maybe?' He squinted as though trying to bring back the memory, then shook his head. 'Sorry. Mind's not what it used to be. It's all a bit—' He waved his hand vaguely.

An unpleasant suspicion was creeping into Ivy's mind, though she didn't want to believe it, not yet. 'Then tell me everything you know, please,' she said, pushing a little magic into the request. She couldn't afford to waste time on half-truths and evasions, not when there were lives at stake. 'Who brought them to you the first time? And when?'

'It was about a fortnight ago, I know that much. But…' The merchant frowned, his expression troubled. 'Can't recall what she looked like, or even how old she was. Isn't that odd.'

She. Ivy clutched her bag tighter, dreading what was to come.

'Anyway, she gave me one of these piskeys, said she made them herself. Told me to keep it in my stall for the weekend, and see if it didn't bring me good luck.' His face softened. 'And didn't it! Got a head full of ideas all of a sudden, and knew just how to show off my merchandise. Never sold so much in two days in all my life. I was sorry to see that little fellow go, I can tell you, but she said she'd bring me more when they were ready...and she did.' He picked up one of the piskeys and contemplated it. 'Can't say these ones seem as lucky, though. Not sure why.'

Ivy knew the answer – she could see from where she stood that the statue was hollow, with no living piskey or faery inside it. And it wasn't hard to guess that the *little fellow* he was talking about, the one who'd brought him such good fortune, had been Keeve.

So the piskey-maker was a woman – a woman who knew that Cornish clay had strange powers, and that contact with magical folk enhanced human creativity. She despised piskeys enough to make a mockery of them, and sell them in the market as slaves. And as if that weren't proof enough, she'd erased the man's memories so he wouldn't be able to identify her...

The same way she'd erased Ivy's memory, the night before she ran away.

What if Marigold no longer cared about the piskeys of the Delve, not even her own husband and son? What if she'd come to hate them for having destroyed her home, killed her father, and taken her mother underground to die? What if she'd decided that a slow death by poison wasn't good enough, and come up with a more fitting revenge –

a scheme to capture any piskeys who ventured outside the mine, and trap them inside clay statues for the rest of their lives? Keeve could have been her first victim, and then – if only by accident – Cicely. And then Richard had found out the truth and confronted her, and she'd had to get rid of him too…

Ivy had missed her mother so much, these past five years. She'd been willing to take any risk, brave any danger, to see her again. But she was no longer the woman Ivy remembered. She might still care about Ivy – *you are more faery than any of them*, she'd said. But anyone else with piskey blood would find her a ruthless and implacable enemy.

And now she had a plan to destroy the Delve.

A plan that Ivy had to stop.

For the rest of the morning Ivy wandered the streets of Truro, brain working feverishly as she tried to decide what to do next. But with every road she crossed and every corner she turned, she found herself more at a loss than before.

Her first thought was to confront Marigold, and demand that she release the piskeys she had taken prisoner. But even though Ivy's magic was growing stronger by the day, she was still no match for Marigold's faery powers. If she acted hastily, she might end up as a statue herself.

Then she thought of flying to the Delve, and warning Betony of the danger. But how could she prove to her aunt that that her suspicion was true, let alone tell her what to do about it? She hadn't found Cicely or Keeve yet, and she had no proof that Marigold was behind their disappearances. All she had was a foolish-looking statue, and the person trapped inside it wasn't even a piskey.

Obviously she had to find out more about the spell her mother was using, and whether there was any way to break it. Maybe then she'd be able to figure out a way to stop Marigold before any more piskeys disappeared...

'Ivy!'

Startled, she turned as Molly bounded up to her, a shopping bag in each hand. 'You look so... I mean, you look great!' the human girl exclaimed. 'Are you having a good time with your mum?'

She looked so delighted to see Ivy, so full of health and life and innocence, that Ivy couldn't bear to discourage her. 'I'm glad to see you, too,' she said. That much, at least, was true. 'Are you here by yourself?'

'Oh, no,' Molly said. 'My mum's in there, trying on clothes.' She pointed to a shop up the road. 'But she's coming to my audition this afternoon, and—' She bit her lip. 'I'm really nervous.'

Ivy had forgotten about Molly's audition; she'd been too wrapped up in her own worries. But she'd seen Molly in Richard's dream-message, and heard him say her name. What if the human girl was more important than Ivy had guessed?

'I tried about twenty different speeches,' Molly went on fretfully, 'and my mum helped me pick the best one, but I don't know.' She toed the cobbles. 'I wish Richard was here.'

He was, if only Molly had known it. But if Ivy showed her the statue and told her what had happened, she'd probably be too upset to audition at all.

Yet theatre was Richard's passion, as dance had become Marigold's. Surely he'd want to help Molly do her best, even if he couldn't see it. 'Would it help if we – if I came with you?' Ivy asked.

'*Would* you?' The doleful expression vanished, and Molly's eyes shone again. 'That would be brilliant. I think it would help a lot.'

The only problem was that Marigold would be working in the adjoining office, but Ivy had to face her mother sometime. 'What about your mum, though?' Ivy asked. 'Do you think she'll mind me being there?'

Molly waved this aside. 'Oh, I've told her all about you. I mean, not *everything*, obviously – but when I showed her the pamphlets from Rising Star, I told her that I had a friend whose mum was a teacher at the school. I was afraid she'd never let me go, but that really seemed to make her feel better about the whole thing. She's looking forward to meeting you.' She swung one of her shopping bags over to the other hand, and hooked her arm into Ivy's. 'Why don't you join us for lunch?'

Until now Ivy had been too busy worrying to even think of food. But now, as she looked into Molly's eager face, she began to feel better – and hungry.

'All right,' she said. 'I will.'

Mrs Menadue looked dauntingly perfect in a sleek grey dress and sandals, her hair unruffled by the summer breeze. She smelled of the same musky perfume as before, which made Ivy's nose wrinkle. But she spoke graciously enough when Molly introduced them – and she even insisted on paying for Ivy's lunch, though she seemed preoccupied and let the two girls do most of the talking.

Once the meal was finished they all walked to the Rising Star Academy, where Trix was waiting for them. 'Well, hello!' she said warmly, clasping Mrs Menadue's hand as the three of them came in. 'You must be Gillian. I'm Beatrix Little.' She shook Molly's hand with equal warmth, then gestured to the stairs. 'Come up to the studio, and we'll have a chat. Ivy, are you looking for your mum? She's in the office.'

'I came to see Molly's audition,' Ivy said. 'But I can wait here, if you like.'

'Do that, there's a love,' said Trix. 'I'll call you when we're ready.'

Ivy sat down on the bottom stair, but even so she could hear most of the conversation taking place above. Gillian Menadue seemed concerned about how much it would cost to send Molly to the school, and Molly was insisting she could pay for some of the lessons herself, while Trix was suggesting ways they might make it easier to afford.

All of which was none of Ivy's business, so she did her best to ignore it. But it made her realise something she hadn't thought about before. Life in a human city was expensive compared to the simplicity of life in the Delve, and judging by the sparse appearance and tiny size of her flat, Marigold didn't have much money to spare. Yet she'd bought a foldaway bed and plenty of new clothes for Ivy, and they'd been eating regular meals together. Could that be why she was selling the piskey statues – to pay for all those things? The thought was revolting, and yet…

'Ivy!' Trix called down to her. 'We're finished now. Come on up.'

Tucking her bag under her arm, Ivy hurried upstairs to find Molly standing at the head of the room, fidgeting as she waited for her audition to begin. Gillian sat with folded arms, her face impassive, but Trix gave Molly an encouraging smile.

'Go ahead,' she told her. 'And don't worry too much – you're not auditioning for a role, it's just to help me decide which of our classes you belong in.'

Molly nodded. Her eyes sought out Ivy's and held them, and then she began to speak.

'*Oh, misery, misery!*' she declared. '*Again comes on me the terrible labour of true prophecy, dizzying prelude.*' Her face contorted and her voice broke with anguish as she went on: '*Do you see these who sit before the house, children, like the shapes of dreams? Children who seem to have been killed by their kinsfolk, filling their hands with meat, flesh of themselves...*'

Trix looked taken aback, but Gillian remained unmoved. Ivy clutched Richard's cloth-covered statue closer to her side, unsettled as much by Molly's haunted expression as by the gruesome words she recited. Surely she couldn't really think that this was what Trix wanted to hear? She cast a pleading look at the human girl, hoping she would stop and try a different speech instead. But Molly continued as though she hadn't noticed.

'*...For this I declare, someone is plotting vengeance,*' she finished huskily, bowing her head, and let the words hang in the air a moment. Then she bounced upright, her old self again. 'How was that?'

'Er,' said Trix, looking flustered. 'I can't say I expected a thirteen-year-old to choose that particular audition piece. But you delivered it...quite convincingly.' She turned to Mrs Menadue. 'Your daughter has talent. I think she could go far given the proper training, and I'd be glad to put her in one of our advanced classes.'

Gillian looked resigned. 'Well, I'll have to discuss it with my husband. But I suppose we might be able to work something out.'

'Oh, *thanks*, Mum!' Molly exclaimed, and threw her arms around her mother's neck. For an instant Gillian's face pinched with distaste, but then she relaxed and patted Molly on the back.

'All right,' she said. 'I should have known you were meant for the theatre, dramatic thing that you are. Just like your father.'

Just then the door to the office opened and Marigold emerged, smiling. 'I heard your speech,' she said to Molly. 'That was quite—' Then her gaze focused on Gillian and she stopped dead, the colour draining from her face.

Mrs Menadue detached herself from her daughter and stood up. 'Marigold,' she said, a note of triumph in her voice. 'So this is where you've been.'

fourteen

'What's going on?' whispered Molly, tugging Ivy's arm as their mothers stared at each other. 'Did you know my mum knew yours?'

Ivy shook her head. 'I had no idea.' But judging by the expression on Marigold's face, she wasn't nearly as glad to see Gillian as the human woman was to see her.

Trix must have sensed the tension in the air, because she turned to Mrs Menadue and said a little too brightly, 'You'll give us a ring then, when you decide what you'd like to do about the lessons? Our advanced class is quite popular, and it would be a shame if I had to put Molly on the waiting list.'

'Yes, of course,' Gillian replied. But she didn't move.

'So...' Trix tried again, turning to Ivy's mother. 'Everything all right?'

'You can go now,' Marigold told her quietly. 'I'll look after things here. Have a good night.' She watched Trix until she'd disappeared down the stairs, then swung back to

Gillian. She looked determined now and even a little angry, as she had in Richard's memory. 'What do you want?' she asked.

'Only to talk,' said Gillian. 'Is that so wrong? I've—' For the first time her voice faltered, and she sounded as young as Molly. 'I thought we were friends.'

Marigold studied her a moment. Then she said, 'Ivy, would you and Molly leave us alone for a little while?'

Molly looked at her mother uncertainly, but Gillian waved her off. 'We'll be fine here,' she said. 'Go and buy yourselves some ice cream.' She moved towards the office, and Marigold stepped aside to let her past. The door closed, and the two girls were left alone.

'Well,' said Molly, but Ivy shushed her with a gesture. She sidled across the room, moving so lightly her feet didn't make a sound, and put her ear to the office door.

'*No*, Ivy,' said Marigold from within, and Ivy knew she was beaten. She might not like the thought of leaving her mother alone with Molly's, but Gillian hadn't looked fearful when she walked into the office, and Ivy couldn't think of any reason why Marigold would do the human woman harm.

Reluctantly she turned away, and followed Molly down the stairs to the street.

'I can't figure it out,' said Molly, as the two of them walked through Lemon Quay a few minutes later. 'Your mum's a faery, and my mum's, well, my mum. How would they know each other?'

Ivy shook her head, equally at a loss. Perhaps Gillian had been one of the humans who helped Marigold after she'd first left the Delve five years ago, and they'd lost touch when Ivy's mother was captured by the Empress? But Gillian hadn't seemed shocked to see Marigold again, only disappointed at her unfriendly manner. As though the two of them had been on good terms until recently, but then Marigold had started avoiding Gillian without telling her why…

'It's not like she *knows* your mum's a faery,' Molly added, gazing into the distance. 'She doesn't believe in that kind of magical stuff. My dad's never minded me being mad about faeries, but my mum's always got so annoyed when I talked about seeing them, or wanting a faery of my own.'

Ivy tightened her grip on her bag. 'What do you mean, *of my own*?' she said.

'I mean to be a real friend, and stay with me always,' Molly said defensively, her cheeks reddening. 'Not someone who goes away with no warning at all, and won't even tell me where they…'

All at once she caught her breath, as though she'd been struck by an epiphany. 'Your mum's *a faery*,' she whispered. She whirled to face Ivy, a wild light in her eyes. 'What if my mum can see faeries too, like I can? What if she met your mum years ago and they got to be friends, like you and Mar— I mean Richard – and me?'

Ivy was startled. She'd never considered that possibility. Richard and Molly had an obvious connection in their mutual love of theatre, but Gillian wasn't a dancer, and the only human Marigold seemed to have that kind of bond with was Serita. 'I don't see how—' she began, but Molly kept talking rapidly, as though she hadn't heard.

'But then your mum went away, or stopped talking to her, or – or something. And my mum was so disappointed, just like I was.' She broke into an incredulous smile. 'Don't you see? *That's* why my mum was trying to keep me away from faeries! It wasn't because she thought I was stupid for believing in them, it was because she was trying to protect me!'

To Ivy it sounded as though Molly were making her own story into Gillian's, and telling herself what she wanted to hear. But she couldn't deny there was a chance the girl was right. Perhaps Gillian had helped Ivy's mother when she first left the Delve, and they'd become friends. But then Marigold had been captured and forced into the Empress's service…and when she came back, she'd been so wrapped up in helping Serita and carrying out her plans for revenge that she didn't have time for Gillian any more.

'It makes sense of everything,' Molly said slowly. Then a determined look came over her face and she pushed past Ivy, heading back the way they had come.

'Wait,' called Ivy. She wasn't exactly afraid of returning to the school – Marigold had no reason to suspect Ivy of turning against her, not yet. But they'd only been gone a few minutes, and she doubted that Gillian and Marigold would be pleased with Molly barging in on their conversation. 'It's too soon,' she said. 'We need to give them more time.'

But Molly didn't slow down, or even look round. Ivy had no choice but to run after her.

'Back already?' asked the woman at the school's front desk, but Molly ignored her. She sprinted up the stairs, and with an apologetic glance at the secretary, Ivy followed.

When they reached the upper level Molly started towards the office, but Ivy was quicker. She darted in front of the other girl, and put her ear to the door. Molly did likewise. There was no sound.

The two girls exchanged looks, and then Ivy eased the door open. Two chairs faced each other across the desk, and the computer spun a web of coloured light in one corner. The window stood open, curtains rippling on the breeze. But apart from that the room was empty.

'They must have gone out,' said Ivy. She backed into the main room and called to the secretary, 'Did my mum say where she was going?'

'What do you mean?' asked the woman, appearing at the foot of the stairs. 'She's in the office.'

So the secretary hadn't seen them leave. Perhaps she'd

239

merely been distracted at the time, but Ivy feared otherwise. What if Marigold had left the school by magic, and taken Gillian with her?

Yet why would she? What possible role could Molly's mother have in her plans to destroy the Delve?

'Come on,' Ivy said to Molly, silently telling herself not to panic. Nothing bad had happened yet. 'Let's go back outside, and walk about a bit. Maybe they'll turn up.'

For half an hour Ivy and Molly wandered the streets in search of Gillian and Marigold, but without success. They were on their way back to the school, and Ivy was wondering if she ought to cast a searching spell, when she smelled the cloying, familiar scent of Gillian's perfume. Relieved, she hurried towards it – and saw Molly's mother stumbling around the corner, her dress rumpled and her hair in disarray. All her poise had vanished: she was ashen and shuddering. And Marigold was nowhere to be seen.

'Mum!' exclaimed Molly, rushing to her. 'What happened to you?'

'I'm all right,' she murmured, gripping Molly's shoulder for support. 'I'm just – I've had a bit of a shock.'

'Where's my mother?' Ivy asked sharply.

Gillian blinked, as though the question puzzled her. 'We were talking,' she said. 'Something about a plan, and fixing past mistakes…' She put a hand to her forehead. 'How long was I gone?'

Queasiness rose inside Ivy. She sounded like the vendor in the Pannier Market – as though her memories had been deliberately tampered with.

'It's OK, Mum,' said Molly. She glanced at Ivy, and for once there was no warmth in her eyes. 'I know about Marigold being a faery.'

Gillian's shoulders sagged. 'I should have told you,' she said. 'But I kept hoping you'd grow out of seeing faeries, or at least you'd stop wanting to get close to them…'

'What did my mother do to you?' Ivy asked. 'What did she say?'

'She asked me to help her,' Gillian replied. 'Something to do with clay… But I said no. And then—' Her forehead furrowed, as though she were struggling to remember. 'She was angry. She raised her hand, and everything turned so bright…'

Ivy turned away, too sickened to hear any more. It had been painful when she first began to suspect her mother might be responsible for turning Keeve, Cicely and Richard into statues, but until now part of her had still clung to the hope that her theory might be wrong. After this, though, how could she doubt it any longer?

It was obvious what had happened. Marigold had tried to convince Gillian to help her carry out her revenge, but the human woman had refused, and paid the price for it. It was just a mercy that Ivy's mother hadn't turned Gillian into a statue as well…though seeing as Marigold hadn't spared her own daughter, it was hard to imagine why. Unless the spell only worked on magical folk?

'Did she hurt you, Mum?' Molly asked anxiously.

'No,' said Gillian. 'But she's gone now. And I don't think she's coming back.'

Ivy sat alone in the kitchen of Marigold's flat, staring dully at the table. Even now that she knew her mother was evil, she found it hard to believe that Marigold would abandon her. Why bother to send Richard to find Ivy and bring her to Truro, only to leave her behind?

But when she'd looked in the refrigerator and found nothing but a small bag of apples and a half-empty container of yoghurt, it was hard to conclude anything else. Perhaps her mother had just forgotten to buy more food – but more likely she'd known she'd be leaving soon, and hadn't thought shopping worth the trouble.

The worst of it was, even now that Ivy was sure of her mother's guilt, she still had no way to prove it. Marigold wasn't foolish enough to make herself conspicuous, and Ivy didn't even know what kind of spell she was using to turn the piskeys into statues. Perhaps her mother had invented some sort of trap using the magic-soaked Cornish earth she'd spoken of before, but even so her traps couldn't be easy to spot or Keeve and Cicely wouldn't have fallen into them. And she couldn't have set them in any of the obvious places either, or a lot more piskeys would have vanished by now...

Which left Ivy in the same quandary as before. She could turn herself into a swift and fly to the Delve this very minute, but what use would that be if nobody believed her when she got there?

The other problem was that Ivy had no idea where her mother had gone after she'd fled from Gillian, let alone what she was doing. She could cast a searching spell to locate her, but that would also alert Marigold that Ivy was coming her way – and in that case she might as well stay here, for all the good it would do.

Ivy dropped her face against the crook of her arm and let out a shuddering breath. She was still lying there, fighting tears of rage at her own powerlessness, when the telephone let out a trill.

It couldn't possibly be for her. But she couldn't ignore it, either. Ivy got up, picked up the receiver awkwardly in both hands, and said, 'Hello?'

'Ivy?' said the voice on the other end. 'It's Gillian Menadue.'

The last time Ivy had seen Gillian, she'd still been badly upset by her fight with Marigold. In fact Molly had urged her to see a doctor, but she'd said that all she wanted was to go home. And as the two of them got into their car and drove away, Ivy had felt a miserable certainty that neither one of them would want to see her again.

Apparently, she'd been wrong. 'Oh,' said Ivy blankly. 'Hello.'

'Has your mother returned?' Mrs Menadue asked. She sounded calm now, more like her usual self. 'Is anyone looking after you?'

'No,' Ivy said.

'I was afraid of that.' Gillian sighed. 'Well, Molly and I have been discussing it, and we don't like to think of you being left there all alone. Would you like to come and stay with us, at least for tonight? Molly's room is a bit small for two, but we can make up a bed for you in the study.'

Ivy was quiet, considering the offer. It seemed unlikely that Marigold meant to return to the flat at this point. And Ivy couldn't forget that Richard had mentioned Molly in his dream-message. Maybe it was time to tell the human girl what had happened to him, and see if she knew anything that might help. If the two of them could free Richard, maybe he'd be able to help Ivy stop her mother...

'Yes, please,' Ivy said, picking up Richard's statue and stuffing it back into her bag. 'I'd be glad to come.'

When Ivy got off the bus, Molly was waiting for her. 'I can't believe my mum invited you over,' she said as the two of them walked down the hill in the evening cool, midges swarming about the hedge beside them. 'It's like she's a different person all of a sudden.' She broke into a smile, then sobered and added, 'I'm sorry about your mum, though. I hope she's not... I mean, maybe it was just a misunderstanding.'

Soon the Menadues' cottage rose up before them, looking snug and welcoming with its softly lighted windows and open door. 'I need to finish up in the barn,' Molly said. 'Why don't you go in? My mum's got some supper for you, if you're hungry.'

Ivy would have preferred to stay with Molly, but her stomach betrayed her with a loud rumble. 'All right,' she said, and crossed the yard to the front step of the house, where Mrs Menadue was waiting. Her perfume hung heavy in the air as she led Ivy to the kitchen and sat her down with a bowl of soup and some crusty bread.

'This must be hard for you,' she said, taking the chair across from Ivy. 'I'm sorry.'

Ivy had disliked Gillian Menadue at first, but now she felt ashamed of herself for judging the woman so harshly. 'I'm sorry for what my mum did to you,' she replied.

Gillian gave a faint smile. 'It could have been worse,' she said. 'It was my mistake to think that I could reason with her, and convince her to let go of the past.' She poured herself a cup of tea and sipped it. 'I should have realised how impossible that would be, after she'd spent so long trapped in the Delve.'

Ivy nearly inhaled her soup. 'You know about the Delve?'

'Oh, yes,' said Gillian. 'Not that your mother ever told me exactly where it was. Only that she had been living in an old mine somewhere between here and Redruth.' Her gaze became faraway. 'She was so weak and ill when I found her, and so unhappy. When I recognised her as a faery and offered to help her, she seemed so grateful. I thought we'd be friends forever.'

'Did she say anything to you about her plan?' Ivy asked. 'I know you don't remember much, but—'

'I do remember some things,' Molly's mother said. 'Especially when I think back to a conversation we had in the beginning, when she discovered the truth about her past. Something about how if she wanted to avenge her family and rescue the women of the Delve, she'd have to get rid of all the men. Once the hunters and foragers were gone, the others would have no choice but to come out onto the surface.'

Ivy's heart was galloping now. 'Did she say how she planned to do it?' she asked, but Gillian shook her head.

So Marigold probably hadn't figured out the details until recently. Maybe she'd got the idea of turning the piskeys into clay statues while she was a slave of the Empress, but she'd had to wait until she was free to carry out her revenge...

The pieces were coming together in Ivy's mind now, and she could imagine how her mother had done it. It must have taken some time for Marigold to find the magical earth she needed, and longer to figure out how to use it. But as soon as her spell was ready, she'd sneaked back to the Delve and set a couple of traps on the hillside to test it out. And then she'd sent Richard to fetch Ivy, not wanting her half-faery daughter to get caught up in her revenge.

Catching Keeve would have pleased Marigold, but it must have been a nasty shock when Cicely fell into her trap. So why hadn't she released Ivy's sister right away? Perhaps she didn't know how to undo the spell, or – more likely – she'd been afraid to release Cicely in case she interfered. So she'd hidden her somewhere safe, while she used the clay-bound Keeve to win over the vendor in the Pannier Market. Then she gave the man some empty statues to keep him busy and make a little money for herself, until she had more of the real piskeys to sell.

It was hard to imagine how Richard had ended up as a statue, though. Perhaps he'd flown back to the Delve to investigate Cicely's disappearance, and caught Marigold setting another trap. He'd confronted her, and she'd cast the spell on him to keep him from talking…

Gillian touched her hand, calling her back to the present. 'Ivy,' said Molly's mother seriously, 'I know all this must be very upsetting to you. But your mother must have wanted to protect you, or she wouldn't have gone to the trouble of bringing you out of the Delve. You may see her again if you're patient, but you mustn't chase after her. You'll only get hurt if you try to interfere.'

She was right, and Ivy knew it. Yet she couldn't shake her conviction that time was running out for the piskeys of the Delve, and that if she didn't act soon it would be too late to save any of them. Marigold knew the Delve's entrances and exits as well as any piskey; in a matter of minutes she could lay her traps in front of every one. If she could find a way to lure all the males out onto the surface at once...

It was only a theory, but even the possibility was more than Ivy could bear. How could she sit idle while so many piskeys she knew and loved – her brother and Mattock, Hew and Gem and Feldspar, and even the Jack himself – were turned into statues and sold off as good-luck charms? Even Flint...her father might be safe for a few days in the depths of the mine, but once all the other men were gone and the women were crying out for food, surely he'd have to come out too.

'I know it could be dangerous,' she said to Gillian. 'But I have to do something. I just don't know what.'

Mrs Menadue sighed. She got up and put her teacup away, while Ivy stared at her soup as though she might find the answer floating in its surface. But the scattered vegetables and bits of meat refused to give her any ideas, and it seemed that Molly's mother didn't have any either.

Or did she? There must be a reason Ivy's mother had wiped Gillian's memory and then disappeared, instead of staying to carry out her plans at a more leisurely pace. Perhaps something had happened during their conversation that forced Marigold's hand, and convinced her she had to carry out her attack on the Delve right away...

And if Ivy could figure out what her mother was afraid

of, perhaps she'd know how to stop her.

'Do you remember anything else she said to you today?' she asked Mrs Menadue. 'Or what you said to her, when you were alone?'

Gillian looked exasperated. 'Enough,' she said, taking the bowl from Ivy. 'Time you went to bed – the study's the first door on the right. We can discuss it in the morning.'

And that was so maddeningly *human*, and so like a mother as well. As though Ivy were the one being unreasonable, and if she went to sleep like a good girl the problem would go away.

'But I need you to tell me now,' insisted Ivy. She didn't want to have to use magic to make the woman talk, especially since her mother had meddled with Gillian's mind already. But she'd never forgive herself if she got to the Delve too late. She reached out with her mind, and *pushed*—

Mrs Menadue gave her a stern look. 'Not in this house, you won't,' she said. 'And if you try using your magic on me again, I'll throw you out.'

Richard had told her the house was protected, but Ivy hadn't realised the charm would work that way. Shame hunched her shoulders, and she left the table without another word.

The study was dark and quiet, and the bed Mrs Menadue had made up for Ivy was as comfortable as the one at her mother's flat, if not more so. She'd said a subdued good night to Molly under Gillian's watching eye, then discreetly slipped Richard's statue out of her bag and laid it beside her, in case he found the strength to send her another dream-message. But that had been more than an hour ago – and no matter how hard Ivy tried to quiet her restless thoughts, she couldn't sleep.

If this were the Delve, she would have gone for a walk. But the air outside the cottage was fresh, and Ivy feared it was more likely to wake her up than make her sleepy. Besides, her mind was the problem, not her body.

Perhaps she should try reading. There weren't many books in the Delve, except a few dry accounts in the Joan's library; stories were the droll-teller's business, not something to be put down on paper. But Ivy knew her letters well enough, and it wouldn't hurt to try.

There was no need to turn on a lamp, not when she carried her own light with her. Glowing softly, Ivy slid out of bed and crept to the low bookcase that stood against the wall. But to her disappointment, most of the volumes seemed to be about fixing mechanical things like cars and motorcycles – subjects that would probably have fascinated Mica or even Cicely, but held little appeal for Ivy.

She had worked her way to the bottom shelf without finding anything of interest when she spotted something called a *Road Atlas*. Wondering what that might be, she pulled it out and found it was a book of maps, not only of

Cornwall but the rest of England as well. Now *that* was worth looking at. But as she turned the pages, a square of folded paper slid out. Another map?

Carefully Ivy opened the page and smoothed it out. It showed far more detail than any other map she'd seen – even individual farmsteads were marked and named, along with a great many places starting with 'Wheal' that Ivy recognised as the locations of old tin and copper mines. In fact she knew that the Delve had been called Wheal Felicity, back when humans still worked there. Could it be on the map too?

It took a little searching, but eventually she found Wheal Felicity in the top left corner, with the neighbouring wood a little to the east. But someone had pencilled an X next to it, for some reason... No, two X's, one to the north-west and another between the Delve and the wood. And now that Ivy looked more closely, she could see cross-marks beside a number of the other old mines in the vicinity as well. As though the map's owner had been visiting one location after another, and marking off their progress as they went...

Not that your mother ever told me exactly where it was, Gillian had said. *Only that she had been living in an old mine somewhere between here and Redruth.*

Ivy sat back on her heels a moment, staring at the map. Chills rippled up her body as she realised what a dreadful mistake she'd made, and how much danger she was in. Then with shaking hands she folded the map and tucked it back into its hiding place. Hurriedly she dressed in her old skin waistcoat and breeches, pushed Richard's statue back into her bag and slung it over her shoulder. Then she slipped out into the corridor, turning herself invisible as she went.

She was halfway across the living room, almost to the front door, when she remembered something. The mischievous-looking piskey she'd seen on Molly's shelf, the first time she came to the cottage…could it be?

It hadn't looked anything like Richard's statue, or any of the others she'd seen. But if there was even the slightest chance that it might be Keeve, then she couldn't run away and leave him. Steeling her courage, Ivy made herself turn back.

The curtains in Molly's room were drawn, and only a thin slice of moonlight glimmered between them. Easing herself past the bed where the human girl slept, Ivy moved to the shelf and picked up the little clay piskey.

No wonder it had reminded her of Keeve. It *was* him. Every detail of his face was perfect, though he was half the size of the crude figures the vendor in Truro was selling; in fact he could have fit inside one, and probably had.

But how had he come to Molly? Ivy looked back at the girl huddled beneath the faery-printed coverlet. Her unbraided hair snaked across the pillow, and she was drooling a little in her sleep. Did Ivy dare to wake her?

It could be a mistake – perhaps a fatal one. But she

needed to know the truth. Ivy crouched next to the bed and whispered, 'Molly.'

She held her hand ready to clap over the girl's mouth if she cried out, but Molly only rolled over. 'What?' she mumbled.

'I need to know about this piskey,' Ivy said, and held the statue of Keeve up for her to see. 'Where did you get it?'

With a groan, Molly struggled up onto her elbows. Ivy watched for any hint of fear or guilt as her eyes focused, but the girl only looked bemused. 'That? My dad gave it to me. A couple of weeks ago.'

'Your *dad*?' echoed Ivy, before remembering to lower her voice. 'But hasn't he been away?'

'Yeah, but…he buys me presents sometimes, before he leaves. And then he leaves them for me to find while he's gone, so I know he's thinking of me.'

She reached for the figure, but Ivy held it away from her. 'Are you sure it came from your father? Not your mother?'

Molly wrinkled her nose. 'Why would my mum give me a piskey statue?'

And that was all the answer Ivy needed. Molly didn't know, she'd assumed. And judging by her reaction, she had no idea that there was anything sinister about the statue, either.

'Never mind,' Ivy said, with a glance at the corridor to make sure it was still clear. 'Just one more thing. You said your mum was a teacher. What does she teach?'

Molly heaved a sigh. 'Can't we talk about this tomorrow?'

'Please,' said Ivy. 'It's important.'

'I teach a beginners' art course,' said Gillian Menadue mildly from the doorway. 'We do sketching, painting… and sculpting with clay.'

Ivy's heart collided with her ribs and dropped into her stomach. How could the human woman have crept up on her unnoticed? She backed towards the window, muscles quivering with the urge to fly. But both the glass panes were shut.

'Mum?' asked Molly. 'What's going on?'

'Nothing you need to worry about,' Gillian replied. 'Go to sleep.'

It wasn't a suggestion, it was a command. Molly blinked, and a bewildered look came over her face. She opened her mouth to protest – but then her eyes closed and she slumped against the pillow, unconscious.

Ivy turned to Gillian in shock, unable to believe that a human could wield such power. But then she caught a whiff of the woman's natural scent, a sweet herbal fragrance utterly unlike the false perfume she'd worn before…

'You're not human at all,' Ivy said, husky with disbelief. 'You're a faery.'

Gillian smiled.

fifteen

'You can't fly,' said Gillian softly as she and Ivy faced each other, the sleeping Molly between them. 'And you won't run, either. Not when I have your sister...and now your mother as well.'

She was right, but Ivy hated her for it. She stood stiffly with her back to the window, cursing herself for not seeing through Gillian's deception sooner. Until a few minutes ago she'd believed that Gillian had been lucky to escape from Marigold – now she knew that her mother had been the unfortunate one.

'Where are they?' she demanded. 'What have you done to them?'

'I can take you to them, if you like,' Gillian said. 'They're still alive, though neither one of them is particularly comfortable at the moment. But you could change that.' She motioned to the corridor. 'Why don't you come out, and we'll talk about it?'

'And be turned into a statue?' asked Ivy. 'I don't think so.'

'If I wanted to do that to you,' Molly's mother replied, 'I would have done it by now. Do you want to see your family, or don't you? Trust me, you'll never find them on your own.'

For one last moment Ivy hesitated, studying Gillian's face for any sign of treachery. Then she pushed herself away from the wall and walked to join her.

The faery woman smiled. With all the grace of a hostess she ushered Ivy to the front of the house, then out into the cobbled yard, where the moon glowed like a lantern among the pin-pricked stars.

'I'll saddle Duchess,' she said to Ivy, opening the barn door. 'We'll get there quicker on horseback.'

Ivy's brows crooked together. 'You're going to leave Molly here all alone?'

'No harm will come to her in this house,' Gillian replied airily as she walked into the barn. 'Not with all the protective charms I've laid around it. And she'll sleep peacefully enough until morning.'

As though it didn't even matter to her how Molly would feel, when she realised what her mother had done. An unpleasant suspicion surfaced in Ivy's mind, and she spoke it aloud: 'Is she even yours? Or did you kill Molly's real mother, and take her place?'

That got Gillian's attention; she stopped and turned.

'What an unpleasant idea,' she said. 'Of course Molly is my daughter. Where do you think her faery blood comes from?'

'Well,' said Ivy, 'you seem to have come up with a few unpleasant ideas of your own. Like turning piskeys into statues, for instance.' She gripped the strap of her bag, where the figures of Richard and Keeve were hidden. 'Did you turn my mother into a statue too?'

'Of course not,' Gillian replied, taking Duchess's bridle off its hook. 'The Claybane only works on those of piskey or spriggan descent, and your mother's lineage is as pure faery as my own.'

'So is Richard's,' said Ivy. 'But that didn't keep you from turning him into a statue.'

'You mean that weasel-faced creature your mother sent to find you?' Gillian looked surprised, then amused. 'So he managed to make contact with you, even while trapped in the Claybane. I wouldn't have thought that possible, unless the two of you had a *very* strong connection...' Her brows rose in mock dismay. 'Dear me. Does your mother know?'

'Yes, that's who I mean,' said Ivy, refusing to take the bait. It made sense that she and Richard had some sort of bond after all the magic he'd put into healing her, but that was none of Gillian's business. 'Why punish him? What did he ever do to you?'

'He arrived at a very inconvenient time,' said Gillian as she opened the door to Duchess's box and slipped the bridle on. The grey mare tossed her bony head and stamped, but she held the reins until the horse subsided. 'I'd almost persuaded your mother to tell me where the Delve was located, so I could go and fetch you out before you died of the poison. But when your Richard turned up, she decided to send him instead.'

So that was what the map had been about, with all the crossed-off marks. Gillian hadn't known which mine the piskeys lived in, so she'd been visiting each one in turn, leaving a trap or two at each one to see if any piskeys fell into it. But there were hundreds of abandoned mines in this part of Cornwall, so the search could have taken her months – or years.

'Though he did turn out to be useful, when I tracked him to the Delve,' Gillian continued, heaving the saddle onto Duchess's back. 'I caught my first piskey that night. And after that I no longer needed your Richard, so I left a few hints to your people about where to find him, and I thought that would be the end of it.'

No wonder Mica and Mattock had caught the so-called spriggan so easily. Richard could never have guessed he'd been followed, much less betrayed. 'But it didn't work,' Ivy said. 'He escaped. And then what? He came back to the Delve one night looking for my sister, and found you setting more of your traps?'

Gillian gave a little shrug as she crouched to pull the girth tight. 'It was remarkably poor timing,' she said. 'One might even say bad luck. But more so for him than for me, in the end.'

'So you sold him to the dealer in the Pannier Market, and left him to die.'

'Die?' Gillian straightened up, looking offended. 'Certainly not. Only the first piskey I caught died, and that was an accident.'

Ivy had already guessed that Keeve might be dead, but it still hurt to hear it. The lump of clay in her bag was all that was left of that black-eyed, mischievous boy who'd left so many bottles of cream at her door, and now he'd never milk another cow or play another prank again.

'Why are you doing this?' she asked, her voice cracking with emotion. 'Keeve had nothing to do with what happened at Thistledown Wyld – that was fifty years ago! You can't have been more than a child yourself when—'

'Cleverly guessed,' Gillian said. 'But you're only half-right.' She seized Duchess's bridle as the mare danced sideways. 'You're also half-piskey, as I recall. Do something about this beast.'

'Shhh,' said Ivy, reaching up to stroke the horse's shivering neck. 'I won't let her hurt you.' Duchess lowered her head meekly, and Ivy led her into the yard.

'Good,' said Gillian, swinging herself into the saddle and reaching a hand down to Ivy. 'Now get up behind me, and I'll take you to your mother.'

*

Ivy had longed to ride a horse ever since she was a child, learning her animals from the mosaic on the walls of the Upper Rise. She'd heard the droll-teller describe how piskeys of old used to borrow horses from their human neighbours simply for the pleasure of riding them around the countryside, and it had been a cruel disappointment to her when she realised she'd never be allowed to do the same.

Now she had her wish after all, but it brought her no pleasure. Bumping along on the back of a leather saddle while Gillian held the reins, forced to cling to the faery woman's waist for support, was far from the joyous romp Ivy had envisioned. Especially once they came down the slope into the wood below, where the branches arched thickly over the darkened path. Only the hovering light-spell Gillian had conjured kept Duchess from stumbling off course.

'The first time I saw a piskey,' Gillian said as they trotted along, 'I was six years old. They came to our wyld, armed and armoured, and demanded that we pay them tribute. But our queen refused, saying that we had lived there in peace for a hundred years, and that the land was ours as much as it was theirs. So they left, but that night they returned in force. My father was killed in the fighting, and my mother and sister taken captive. I was the only one who escaped.'

'I know about Thistledown Wyld,' said Ivy. 'My mother told me. But—'

'You don't know anything,' said Gillian curtly. 'The wyld

where Marigold's parents lived was my second home, where I found refuge after the first was destroyed. When the piskeys came to Thistledown, I was a woman, and this time it was my husband they killed.' Her hands tightened on the reins. 'I escaped again, but at bitter cost – I lost the child I was carrying, and nearly died myself. And as I lay in the ruins of my home with the bodies of my people around me, I swore on my own lifeblood that I would hunt down the men of the Delve and punish them as they deserved.'

Ivy looked away, swallowing. It nauseated her to hear that her ancestors had been so ruthless, and she would never look at some of the old uncles in the Delve the same way again. Yet Gillian's story didn't explain everything that she had done, much less justify it. 'But my people don't fight any more,' she said. 'Now they're the ones hiding, and living in fear.'

'The *women* live in fear,' Gillian retorted. 'I learned that much from your mother. Your men may be wary of other magical folk, but it doesn't keep them from hunting and foraging, and trading with the humans as they please. What kind of justice is that, after all the evil they've done?'

'It's not like—' began Ivy, but Gillian cut her off.

'Don't tell me they're risking themselves for your protection. Haven't you noticed that the men of the Delve live longer than the women, that they show fewer signs of age, that their injuries heal more easily and that they're less prone to sickness? Can't you see they're deliberately keeping you weak, so they can control you – the daughters and granddaughters and great-granddaughters of the faery women they stole from wylds like mine?'

She might have a point, but Ivy wasn't about to give in. She couldn't forget that she was talking to the woman who held Cicely prisoner.

'But the Joan is the most powerful piskey in the Delve,' she argued. 'And she's the one who decides how we should live. Why would she keep us underground if she didn't believe it was for the best?' Yet even as she said it, she was reminded that Betony could go outside any time she liked, and often did. It was her responsibility to maintain the wards and glamours that protected the Delve from intrusion, after all – and with her ability to conjure fire, no one would dare to tell the Joan it was too dangerous.

'I've never met your Joan,' Gillian replied, 'but she wouldn't be the first female to put her own interests ahead of anyone else's. Perhaps she's afraid that if she lets the other piskey women go above, one of them will grow strong enough to challenge her for the throne. Or perhaps she fears the males will overthrow her if she does anything to threaten their privilege and power.' She leaned sideways to avoid a jutting branch, then continued, 'But she can't really believe that you're safer underground, even if a thousand spriggans were waiting on the surface. Surely your mother told you about the poison in the mine? If you'd seen how ill Marigold was when she came to me, you'd agree that death itself could hardly be more cruel.'

'So that's why you decided to turn the men into clay statues,' said Ivy, 'and let the women go free?'

'Not exactly,' Gillian said. 'Even after meeting Marigold and hearing her story, I still meant to kill every male in the Delve if I could. But I was only one faery, and I knew that even if I could convince your mother to join me, we would not have enough power between us to kill more than a few. I discovered the Claybane much later, after Marigold had disappeared.'

'After you betrayed her, you mean,' Ivy said coldly. Now she knew what her mother had meant when she said, *I trusted someone I should not have trusted...*

'The Empress's servants found her without any help from me,' Gillian retorted. 'She was careless, and too unskilled at hiding. I was sorry to see her taken away, but what good would it have done to interfere? I had been living as a human for a long time while I planned my revenge, and I had no intention of throwing away my disguise to fight some fool of a so-called Empress.'

Her indifference made Ivy furious all over again. 'So that's all Molly was to you? Part of your disguise?'

'Hardly,' replied Gillian. 'Faeries may be less emotional than piskeys, but that doesn't make us heartless. Still, I was glad when I heard the news that the Empress was dead, and that I no longer needed to stay so close to my human family. By that time I had located the site of an ancient battle between the piskeys and my ancestors, and discovered a book which told of spells my people had used against their enemies – including the magical clay that would trap any piskey who touched it, but leave faeries and humans unharmed.'

She kicked Duchess into a canter as they crossed a roadway, then settled back into a walking gait on the other side. 'When Marigold returned to Truro I sought her out and apologised, hoping to rebuild our friendship. I knew she was anxious about your welfare, so I encouraged her to send a message to you, and offered to deliver it myself. But Marigold's time with the Empress had changed her, and she was no longer so quick to trust. She began to avoid me, and when I saw her talking with your Richard, I knew she had grown suspicious of my motives.'

'Why didn't you let her go, then? If you already knew she wasn't going to help you—'

'I would have,' Gillian replied, 'if not for your sister...and you. When I found Cicely trapped in the Claybane I had no idea who she was, but it troubled me. I had thought that only male piskeys and the Joan ever went out of the Delve. I wanted to talk to your mother again to make sure I hadn't misunderstood, but she was still keeping her distance. It wasn't until Molly came home with her pamphlets from the school, and I saw Marigold's name on one of them, that I found my chance to talk with her again.'

And by that time Ivy's mother had seen the clay piskeys,

and knew that Ivy believed Richard to be trapped inside one. She knew that Cicely was missing, as well – so once Gillian showed up, it wouldn't have taken Marigold long to realise that her old friend had become the piskeys' deadliest enemy.

'She fought you, didn't she?' asked Ivy. 'She wanted you to let Cicely go.'

'Yes,' said Gillian. 'At first I tried to reason with her. I offered to free Cicely if she would agree to help me – or at least promise not to interfere in my plans. But she refused to cooperate, and I was forced to restrain her.' She sighed. 'That was when I decided to approach you instead, in the hope that you would be more sensible.'

'Sensible?' asked Ivy. 'You killed a boy I grew up with. And now you're talking about turning my brother and my father and – and all the other men I care about into statues for the rest of their lives. How am I supposed to be *sensible* about that?'

'You know that the way you were forced to live in the Delve was unjust,' Gillian said. 'You know that you were deceived, or at least misled, about the dangers of going up to the surface. You know that your Joan refuses to believe that the mine is unfit to live in, even though you were born crippled and your mother nearly died. Doesn't that make you angry, Ivy? Don't you believe that something needs to change?'

'Yes, but—'

'Don't answer yet,' Gillian told her. 'Just think about it. And when we reach the place where your mother and sister are waiting, we'll talk again.'

A few minutes later, Gillian brought Duchess to a halt and nudged Ivy to dismount. Beside the path, barely visible through the shrubbery that surrounded it and the vines that netted its surface, stood a low stone building that looked as though it might once have been part of a mine.

'Here we are,' Molly's mother said, securing Duchess's reins to an overhanging branch and leaving the mare to graze. As she walked towards the entrance, she raised a hand and the plants recoiled, revealing a surprisingly stout and modern-looking door. She unlocked it with a spark from her fingertips and pushed it open. 'My workshop. Mind the step.'

Willing her skin to glow brighter, Ivy climbed cautiously over the threshold and down onto the floor below. The building consisted of a single bare room, damp and musty-smelling. She glimpsed shelves along one wall and an old plastic feed bucket in the corner, but apart from that the place seemed empty.

Ivy turned to Gillian, about to demand where she'd hidden her mother. But at the same moment, the faery woman waved her hand. The shadows parted, and now Ivy could see—

'Mum!' Ivy cried, rushing to her side. Marigold slumped

against the wall, her brown hair hanging over her face. Her chest rose and fell as she breathed, but she didn't move, even when Ivy shook her. 'What have you done to her?'

'Nothing more than it seems,' Gillian replied. 'She's asleep – but she won't wake until I allow it. As for your sister, she too is safe, and in good company.'

Ivy looked up, and her heart flipped over. The whole bottom shelf was filled with ugly grinning piskey statues, empty and waiting. And on the shelf above them stood a row of the real piskeys, frozen in mid-struggle. She saw Gem there, twisted back on himself as he tried to wrench one foot free. She recognised Feldspar, his hands uplifted and his eyes bulging in shock. And at the end of the row stood a terrified-looking piskey girl with two braids hanging over her shoulders.

'Cicely!' Ivy snatched the little figure down from the shelf and cradled it in her hands. Like the statue of Keeve in her bag it was perfect in every detail, her sister's mouth still frozen open in her last, wordless scream. No wonder Gillian had crafted those jolly-looking shells to hide her victims; what human would want to buy a statue that looked like this?

'I would have freed her, if I could,' said Gillian. 'I had no desire to harm a child, especially a girl. But the spell to release her requires not only my blood but the blood of a near relative, so there was nothing I could do for her until today.'

Ivy looked sharply at her. Richard had said something about blood, too. 'Why does it have to be a relative?'

'My ancestors created the Claybane as a method of taking hostages,' Gillian replied. 'It was designed to hold enemies captive without need for prison or guard, until someone from their tribe came to make an offer of peace. If no one came within seven days, the piskey or spriggan trapped in the Claybane would die.'

So that was what had happened to Keeve. His time had run out, and there'd been no one to save him. Ivy clutched Cicely's statue's tighter. 'Then the others will die too, if they aren't released?'

'No,' said Gillian. 'I altered the spell, once I realised my mistake. They will live indefinitely…if you can call it living.'

So there was still a chance to free Cicely. She might even be able to rescue Gem and Feldspar, if she could convince Gillian to change her mind. But there was nothing she could do for Richard. Grief knotting her chest, Ivy lowered her bag to the floor.

'You can't save the men of the Delve,' Gillian told her. 'With or without you, I will have my revenge. But you can save your sister and your mother, and make it easier on the other women as well, if you help me.'

Ivy looked down at Cicely's tiny, pleading face. How could she let her sister go on suffering when she had a chance to rescue her? It was Ivy's fault that Cicely had fallen into Gillian's trap; now it was Ivy's responsibility to bring her out of it...

'What do you want me to do?' she asked quietly.

'I know where to find the Delve,' said Gillian, 'but not any of its entrances and exits, or the paths that your hunters use. Your Joan's protective glamours are too strong.' She moved closer to Ivy. 'I could carry on setting traps here and there about the hillside, but it will be over much more quickly if you show me where to put them.'

Ivy felt as though an iron band had clamped about her chest. 'And if I don't?' she managed to ask.

'Then your sister will remain trapped,' Gillian said. 'Your mother will sleep herself to death. And you will stay here with them, a helpless prisoner, while I carry out my plan.' She walked a circle around Ivy, fingers trailing across her wingless shoulders. 'But you won't make me do that, will you, Ivy? Your father and brother may believe that their lives are worth more than yours, but surely you know better?'

Revulsion shivered up Ivy's spine, but she didn't move. All at once she found herself thinking of Mica – how arrogant and selfish he'd become in the wake of their mother's disappearance, and how little he seemed to care about anything Ivy did. How she'd been ready to share her deepest secret with him, only to be shamed into silence by his superstition and bigotry. The shattering pain she'd felt when his stone struck her in mid-flight, and nearly killed her.

And her father, too. What had Flint ever done for her, since her mother went away? How many times had she turned to him for comfort, and met nothing but stony indifference? He might as well be a statue already, for all the life that was in him now. Why should she sacrifice her own life, let alone Marigold and Cicely's, for his sake?

'Don't think of it as a betrayal,' Gillian urged softly. 'Think of it as justice for all the faeries your piskey ancestors killed – those faeries were your ancestors, too. And think of what you'll be doing for the women of the Delve. They may not understand at first, but once they learn the truth, they will hail you as their deliverer.'

Ivy gasped out a laugh. 'After I've helped to turn their husbands and sons into statues? I don't think so.'

'Of course they will. Don't you see, Ivy? Once the present Joan is gone and the women of the Delve are free, they'll need a leader who knows the ways of the upper world. They'll have no choice but to look to you for guidance, and once they discover how much stronger and healthier and happier they are living on the surface, they'll realise how foolish they were to trust someone like Betony.'

The moonlight slanted through the open door behind Gillian as she spoke, haloing her auburn hair and limning her body with silver. For a moment she was as beautiful as the faeries of legend, and Ivy could almost see the world she was describing. A world in which the women of the Delve were free to walk in the sunshine or gaze at the stars whenever they pleased. A world where sickness was rare instead of commonplace, and piskeys could live three hundred years without growing wrinkled or feeble, or losing their wits with age. A world where her people could live in peace with faeries as well as humans, and creativity could blossom freely among them.

Yet when she looked into Gillian's avid, expectant face, the vision died away. She had seen that expression on the faces of her fellow piskeys right before they pulled off a prank, and it reminded her that Gillian cared far less about saving the women of the Delve than about taking revenge on the men she hated. It also reminded her that Molly had to have got her theatrical gift from somewhere, and it might not have been from her father's side...

For this I declare, whispered Molly in her memory, *someone is plotting vengeance.*

Ivy raised her head defiantly. 'No. I'm not helping you. If you want to destroy the Delve, you're going to have to do it by yourself.'

Fury twisted Gillian's features, but it only took her an instant to regain composure. 'So you would rather I left you here with your mother and sister to die?'

'I'd rather take my chances with them than trust you,' said Ivy. 'I don't know if you can lie or not, but even if you can't, I know you're hiding something. I'm not going anywhere.'

There was a long, cold silence. Then Gillian took a little pouch out of her pocket. 'You are as stubborn as your mother,' she said. 'I only hope your sister can forgive you for it.' And before Ivy could react, she flicked a pinch of sparkling dust on the ground at Ivy's feet.

Ivy tried to shape-change, but it was already too late. The dirt beneath her had turned to a slimy puddle of clay, gluing her feet to the floor. She threw her weight from one foot to the other, trying to break free – but she was already paralysed to mid-calf, and the muck was spiralling higher up her legs every second.

'I'm sorry it had to come to this,' Gillian said, plucking Cicely's statue from Ivy's grip. 'I would have preferred not to use a child – they can be so unreliable. However...' She took out a pocket knife, flicked it open and pricked Marigold's finger with it. 'I've waited too many years for this to be patient any longer.'

The clay had crept up past Ivy's hips now, and her whole lower body was numb. Ivy fought against it, hurling all her magic into the effort, but still the spell kept rising.

Yet surely there must be hope if it hadn't engulfed her already? Cicely had only screamed once before she was trapped, and the others looked as though they hadn't had time to cry out at all...

If Gillian noticed the Claybane's slowness as well, it didn't appear to trouble her. She held Marigold's hand over Cicely's head and squeezed a drop of blood onto the clay; then she pierced her own finger and smeared it across the figure's feet.

Crackling fissures spread over the statue, thin at first but rapidly growing wider. A second later the clay crumbled into dust and Ivy's little sister staggered out, tiny but alive.

'Cicely!' Ivy shouted, as the Claybane slithered over her waist. 'Don't listen to her! Don't do anything she says!' But Cicely was still stumbling around in circles, too dazed and disoriented to respond.

Gillian stooped and lifted Cicely from the ground. 'Don't worry,' she said, cradling the piskey girl in her hands. 'I'll tell her everything she needs to know. Perhaps she'll prove more reasonable than you and your mother. In fact I would hope so, if I were you.'

Then she walked out, and the door swung shut behind her.

'Cicely!' Ivy screamed, but there was no answer. Alone in the growing darkness, she thrashed from side to side, teeth grinding with the effort of trying to break free of the Claybane. She had to save her little sister – had to warn Betony and the other piskeys about Gillian's plan—

But as the clay inched up over her ribs, Ivy knew it was no use. Her mother was asleep, Richard trapped inside his statue, and no one but Gillian even knew that Ivy was here, let alone had the power to free her.

She had risked everything to save the mother and sister she loved. But she had failed them both...and now Ivy could not even save herself.

sixteen

By the time the clay reached Ivy's shoulders, she no longer had the strength to fight it any more. Hoarsely she shouted, 'Mum! Marigold! Wake up!'

But her mother did not stir. The only sound was a scraping of branches against the door, and a distant whinny that must have been Duchess, protesting as Gillian rode her away.

Ivy drew a sobbing breath. 'No,' she begged, not even knowing with whom she was pleading. 'It can't end like this. It's not – please. Please, if there's anyone who can hear…' Then she threw her head back and screamed with all her might, 'HELP ME!'

The words dropped like stones into the silence, and for a few heartbeats all was still. Then the door cracked open, and she heard the last voice she had ever expected to hear:

'Ivy?'

If she hadn't been encased in stiff clay up to her neck, Ivy would have collapsed with the shock. 'Molly?'

The girl stooped through the doorway, electric torch in hand. The beam fell on Ivy, and she exclaimed aloud. 'What happened to you?'

'No time,' Ivy wheezed as the Claybane crept along her jaw. In a few seconds, she wouldn't be able to speak at all. 'Only blood can break the spell – my mother's on my head, your mother's on my feet – has to be a relative—'

She'd barely gasped out the last word when the clay covered Ivy's mouth, cutting off her breath. Her eyes rolled wildly as the slime crawled across her cheeks, and then everything went black.

No sight, no sound, no feeling. Utter darkness surrounded her, unrelieved by even the tiniest pinprick of light. Her lungs refused to fill, and even her heart had stopped beating. Ivy knew she ought to be dead…and yet in some way that only magic could explain, she wasn't. She was alive, and worse, she was *aware*.

And yet there was nothing to do or see, no reason to go on existing. She felt no pain, but as the minutes dragged on her numbness became an agony in itself. She would have welcomed the stinging slash of a knife or an arrow piercing into her side, if only it meant she could feel anything at all.

Now she knew how Richard must have felt when he woke from the beating Mica and Mattock had given him, and found himself chained up in a cavern silent and black as death. No wonder he'd been half-crazed by the time Ivy met him; no wonder he'd taken to reciting Shakespeare to break the intolerable silence. She'd tortured him without even realising it, giving him a taste of the light he longed for and then taking it away. It had scarcely occurred to her to care how he must feel. Why should she? He was only a spriggan...

Just as to Gillian Menadue, Ivy was only a piskey.

Despair rolled over Ivy, crushing her spirit. She was never going to get out of here. Even if Molly begged her mother to show Ivy mercy, even if Cicely betrayed the whole Delve in exchange for her freedom, Gillian would never let her go. She'd spend the rest of her life in this horrible nothingness, knowing all the while that Richard, and Mica, and Mattock, and so many others were suffering the same fate – and that it was her failure that had put them there.

Ivy wanted to scream, to weep, to pound her fists against the darkness until it shattered and let her go. But she couldn't. She could only stand there helpless for one interminable second after another – and the worst of it all was knowing that she still had a lifetime of imprisonment ahead.

But just as Ivy was certain that she could endure it no longer, that she would go mad with the sheer pointlessness of her existence, *something* happened. The tiniest feather-touch on her forehead, so light that at first she thought she'd imagined it. But then a tickle ran across her scalp, as though some buzzing insect had landed in her hair – and the itch kept growing, spidering over her forehead and across her brows until she was half-wild with the need to scratch it.

Then suddenly – oh, glory – the shell over her face cracked apart, and she could breathe again. Ivy let out a moan, and opened her eyes.

'It's OK, don't be scared, I'm here,' blurted Molly, sounding nearly as frantic as Ivy felt. She was scratching at the Claybane that covered Ivy's neck and shoulders, tearing off fragments as fast as she could go. 'I couldn't find my mum so I tried my blood and your mum's instead, and I didn't think it was going to work at first but then it did, and I'm going to get you out of there—'

Ivy's mouth was dry, and her tongue felt thick and heavy. In a slurred whisper she asked, 'How...find me? Thought...sleeping.'

'No, I wasn't,' said Molly, pulling a chunk of Claybane off Ivy's upper arm and flinging it away. 'I was only pretending. I got dressed as soon as you and Mum left the house, and when I saw the two of you ride off on Duchess I followed you. But I didn't want to get too close in case she spotted me, and then I lost the trail for a bit, so by the time I got here – *oh!*'

And with that the spell broke, and the last of the clay dissolved into powder. Ivy's knees buckled, and she almost keeled over before Molly caught her, lowering her to the dusty floor. 'Are you all right?' she asked anxiously, dropping down beside her. 'You look like you're going to be sick.'

Ivy waved a hand in what she hoped was a reassuring gesture. It was like a gift to feel her chest expand and contract with each breath, and her heartbeat with a steady, reassuring rhythm that she'd never take for granted again. But her wits, like her muscles, were still weak with shock. 'Molly,' she said when she could speak, fumbling for the other girl's blood-smeared hand. 'You saved me. I owe you my life.'

Molly squeezed back, but Ivy could feel her fingers tremble. 'My mum…she's a faery. And that makes me…'

'Half-faery,' said Ivy. 'That's how you broke her spells.'

'But I've lived with her my whole life. How could I never have noticed – never even guessed…?'

Ivy tried to get up, but her legs were too shaky to hold her. She sighed and leaned against the wall. 'She fooled a lot of people, Molly. Other faeries, even. Don't blame yourself.'

'But why did my mum put you in that clay stuff? What is she trying to do?'

Ivy explained the situation to Molly as briefly as she could. Then she finished, 'I have to stop her, Molly. She's got my sister. And if I don't get to the Delve right away, she'll turn my father and brother into clay piskeys and sell them in the market, like she did to Richard.'

'Richard!' Molly sat up, her eyes wide. 'You found him? Where is he?'

Ivy pulled her bag across the floor and opened it up to show Molly the statue. 'He's trapped in this,' she said. 'Your mother turned him small, and sealed him inside.'

Molly picked up the fat, smiling piskey and stared at it, her face wrinkling in revulsion. 'Can we...is there any way to get him out? Without hurting him?'

'The outer shell's hollow,' said Ivy. 'We could break off the head, I suppose, but—'

Without waiting for her to finish the sentence, Molly whipped around and slammed its pointed cap against the wall. The head shattered, and as Molly wrenched what was left of the shell apart, a tiny figure dropped out. She caught it with both hands and raised it to the light.

Even in the half-darkness the despair on Richard's face was clearly visible, and Ivy's insides twisted with shame. How could she have misjudged him so badly? He hadn't flown off and abandoned her, as she'd assumed – he'd been trying to help her find Cicely, and this had been his reward.

'It's no use,' she said miserably. 'Even if your blood does work as a substitute for your mother's, we can't free him without finding one of his relatives as well.'

'I don't care,' retorted Molly. 'I'm going to try it anyway.' She squeezed her cut thumb until the blood welled up again, and smeared a scarlet line across Richard's feet before setting him firmly on the ground between them. 'Your turn.'

'Molly, there's no point—'

'I don't care!' Molly was shouting now, her eyes brimming with tears. 'I thought he flew away because he didn't care, but he was stuck in that stupid ugly statue all the time, and it wasn't his fault, and we're all he's got!' She snatched up one of the pottery fragments littered across the floor and thrust it at Ivy. 'We have to try! We owe him that!'

She was right. Ivy set her teeth, stabbed the shard into her thumb, and wiped a streak of blood across the statue's brow.

'Please,' whispered Molly, clasping her hands together and rocking back and forth. 'Please let it work.'

But though the two girls watched and waited, not a single crack appeared in the figure's surface. 'I'm sorry,' Ivy said quietly. 'There's nothing we can do.'

Molly picked up the statue and bowed over it, her shoulders shaking. Ivy reached to comfort her – and found that she could move easily again. She let her hand rest on Molly's shoulder a moment, then pushed herself to her feet.

'Look after him,' she told Molly softly as she limped towards the door. 'And my mother, too. I'll be back soon – I hope.'

Then she flung herself into swift-form, and flashed away.

Ivy had never flown so hard or so fast, not even when the other swifts were chasing her. She didn't know how far she was from the Delve, but her instincts told her unerringly which direction to go, and she was determined to get there before Gillian could carry out her plan.

She zoomed over hills and valleys, rocky ridges and thin strips of woodland, the open-pit scar of a modern mine and the greenery-smothered ruins of several old ones. Once she glimpsed a falcon – perhaps even a hobby – wheeling overhead. But Ivy had no time for any fears but one, and she kept flying.

Soon she began to spot landmarks she had noticed from previous flights, and knew she must be nearing the Delve. Yet she'd seen no sign of Gillian and Duchess, let alone Cicely, anywhere. Perhaps the faery woman had turned them all invisible, so they could ride right up to the Delve without being noticed?

Or more likely, Ivy realised belatedly, she hadn't bothered bringing the mare at all, and simply transported herself and Cicely to the Delve by magic instead. In which case, Cicely could be showing Gillian the Delve's hidden entrances at this very minute, and Ivy might already be too late…

A few seconds later the familiar broken chimney and slanting walls of the Engine House rose up before her, black against the night sky. Ivy circled around the capped entrance to the Great Shaft, then dived straight between the bars, plunging into the darkness below.

But in bird-form her skin didn't glow, as it did when she

was in piskey-shape. The blackness inside the shaft was too dense for even a swift's night vision to penetrate, and panic leaped up in Ivy as she realised she was flying blind. Fluttering wildly to slow her descent, she scrabbled with her short feet until her claws found an outcropping and then hung there, breathing fast.

Now what? She still had to get down to the adjoining tunnel somehow. But if she changed back to piskey-shape here, she could lose her grip and fall straight to the bottom of the shaft. And if the drop didn't kill her the landing would, because the flooded part of the shaft went down for fathoms and she had no idea how to swim.

Yet she couldn't cling here forever, either. Her swift's heart drumming, Ivy dug her claws deeper into the crack and willed her body to change.

As her form shifted, so did her balance. Her fingers slipped, and for one awful moment she felt herself start to fall – but then her piskey skin leaped into brightness, illuminating every feature of the surrounding rock, and she jammed her hands into a bigger crack just in time. Hanging by her fingertips, she slid her feet from one side to the other until she found a toehold. Then she inched her way over the rock to the tunnel entrance, swung herself past the iron railing, and dropped to the ground below.

She had made it. She was inside the Delve.

Dawn was coming, and soon the younger men would be heading outside – right into Gillian's traps. Should

Ivy warn Mica and Mattock and the other hunters herself? Or should she go to the Joan first? Ivy wavered, but only for an instant. By the time she convinced Betony to listen to her, it might be too late. She sprinted down the tunnel, heading for her home cavern.

As she skidded around the corner Mattock stepped out of the doorway just ahead, yawning and scratching sleepily at his ear. But he was fully clothed, with his hunter's knife at his side, and Ivy knew where he must be heading.

'Matt!' she called to him. 'Don't go!'

He turned towards her, his face blank with astonishment. Urgently she went on, 'You can't go out of the Delve. It's not—' But she never got the chance to finish the sentence, because Mattock sprinted to her and snatched her up off the ground, whirling her around in an exuberant embrace. 'Ivy! You're alive!'

Crushed against him, Ivy could hardly breathe. Yet it was so good to see Mattock's broad honest face that she couldn't help hugging him back.

'I missed you too,' she said, but then she wriggled out of his hold and backed away. 'Mattock, you have to listen to me. There's a powerful faery up above who wants to capture all the men in the Delve, and if you go out you'll fall right into her trap.'

Mattock didn't even question her, let alone argue. He kept his mouth shut – he'd always been good at that, unlike Mica – and gave Ivy all the time she needed to explain. And by the time she'd finished telling him about Gillian and the Claybane, his expression was so bleak that Ivy knew he'd believed every word.

'You tell the Joan,' he said. 'I'll get up to the Earthenbore and stop anyone who tries to come through.'

She'd meant to warn Mica and the other hunters herself, but having Mattock do it would be even better. Especially since she wouldn't have to waste any more time on explanations. She squeezed his arm. 'I won't forget this, Matt. You'll be a hero to the whole Delve, when all this is done.'

'I'll settle for being yours,' he said, and covered her hand with his own. Then, before Ivy could even think of a reply, he flashed her a lopsided smile and dashed away.

'...And she's up there with Cicely this very moment,' Ivy said, pacing around the Joan's stateroom. It had driven her nearly wild to have to wait until her aunt was dressed and ready to receive her, and now she was determined to make up for lost time. 'Soon she'll have sprinkled Claybane around all the exits, and if anyone so much as touches it they'll be trapped. You have to tell the hunters to stay inside, or—'

'Do not presume,' Betony interrupted, 'to tell me what I have to do.' She slammed her palms down on the arms of the chair and pushed herself to her feet, wings stiff with irritation. 'For a hundred years the Delve has been our refuge and our pride. I will not allow some upstart faery to turn it into a prison.' She turned to her consort. 'Gossan, how long will it take your knockers to open a passage to Wheal Diligence?'

That was the nearest mine to the Delve, its shafts and adits far enough away that Gillian probably wouldn't waste her time trapping them, even if she guessed that they were there. A grudging admiration roused in Ivy at her aunt's foresight, and she began to think that perhaps they'd be able to stop Molly's mother after all.

But Gossan shook his head. 'It's below the waterline,' he said. 'Even with all the knockers working together, it'd take days to pump it out and clear away the debris.'

'No chance of sending up a war party and taking her by surprise, then.' Betony tapped a finger against her lips, eyes narrowed with thought. 'Very well, there's only one thing to do. I shall have to fly out and confront this Gillian myself.'

'But that's exactly what she wants you to do!' Ivy protested, as Betony strode forward. 'The Claybane doesn't only work on males, it works on *any* piskey who steps into it. If you—'

'I said *fly*,' retorted Betony. 'I understand why such a solution would not have occurred to you, but a trap on the ground is no threat to someone who can hover in midair.' She turned to add, 'Gossan, set the knockers to work on a new passage to the surface, and warn the other males to remain underground until I give the word. Nettle, send a runner to tell the women and children to remain in their caverns for the time being. I will call a meeting in the Market Cavern when I return.'

'My sister's still out there,' said Ivy. 'I'm coming with you.'

'Cicely has already suffered enough because of your foolishness,' Betony replied icily. 'As have your father and brother. You are far too reckless to be any use to me, even if I thought I could trust you. You will stay here.'

Ivy turned a pleading gaze to Gossan, hoping he would intervene. But he didn't even look at her. He walked to the doorway where Betony stood, and took his wife's face in his hands. 'Be careful, my love,' he said, and kissed her. Then he slipped out.

Betony tightened her belt and smoothed back her hair, a high colour in her cheeks. 'I will return,' she announced, 'with this so-called Gillian Menadue as my prisoner. She will regret that she ever dared to threaten my Delve.' And she too walked out, slamming the door behind her.

'Don't take it to heart,' said Nettle to Ivy. 'She's worried, and that always makes her sharpish.' She reached for the cord of the message bell by the door and gave it a tug, sending a metallic jangle echoing down the corridor. 'But never you fear. Our Joan's more than a match for that Gillyflower.'

'Gillian,' said Ivy dully. She sank into the chair by the fire, wondering why she felt so cheated. Surely she ought to be grateful that Betony had taken over? Surely she didn't imagine that she, a mere piskey-girl with no authority and no great share of magic, could protect the Delve better than the powerful Joan the Wad herself...

Yet Ivy couldn't shake the feeling that she'd missed something important, and that stopping Gillian couldn't possibly be that easy. Yes, they had the advantage of surprise: the faery woman couldn't have anticipated that Molly would resist her sleeping spell, much less rescue Ivy from the Claybane. But even so, Ivy feared Gillian had more than one plan in mind, and that if her first assault on the Delve failed, it wouldn't take her long to launch another.

Either way, Ivy couldn't just sit idle – not when Cicely was still in danger. She had to do something to help her sister, or at least find out what had happened to her. But how could she get away from Nettle without the old woman getting suspicious?

Her thoughts were interrupted by a rap on the knocker. 'Reporting for duty,' chirped a boy's voice as Nettle opened the door. 'What's the message?'

It was Quartz, Jenny's little brother and the fastest runner in the Delve. And just like that, Ivy knew how to get out of the Joan's stateroom, and back to where she wanted to be. She got up quickly and laid a hand on Nettle's shoulder. 'There's no time to lose,' she said. 'I'll go with him, and tell him everything he needs to know.'

The old woman gave her a sidelong look, and for a moment Ivy feared she would refuse. But then she nodded.

Ivy grabbed Quartz's arm and pulled him into the Silverlode. 'Come on,' she said, and they ran down the corridor together.

As they headed towards the main staircase, Ivy explained to Quartz that there was a dangerous threat outside the Delve, the Joan had gone out to deal with it, and the exits were off-limits to all piskeys until further notice. At first the boy could only gape at her, so astonished to see Ivy again that he barely seemed to hear the message. But Ivy kept repeating it until she was sure he understood, and then urged him to run off and spread the word.

'And don't waste time telling them about me,' she said. 'Just pass on the Joan's orders and keep moving. My story can wait.'

Quartz looked ready to explode with curiosity, but his runner's training won out; he saluted her with a fist against his heart and sprinted off, already trilling the high-pitched call that would bring the other piskeys out to hear his message. Ivy headed in the opposite direction, resolutely ignoring her weariness as she darted up a side tunnel and took the stairs two at a time. She'd have to climb up the Great Shaft before she could turn into a swift again, but—

'Mattock? Matt! Hey, you down there – have you seen Mattock?'

Ivy stiffened, her hand tightening convulsively on the rail. Of all the bad luck, it was Mica. He must have wakened on his own, and wondered why Mattock hadn't come to fetch him. And he'd already seen Ivy's glow, so it was too late to make herself invisible, or run away.

'He's up by the Earthenbore,' Ivy called, dimming her light and trying to sound raspy and old so he wouldn't recognise her.

'No, he isn't. I looked there a few minutes ago.' His voice hardened with suspicion. 'Who's that?'

She couldn't deal with Mica, not right now. First he'd get angry and demand to know where she'd been, and then he'd try to keep her from leaving the Delve. And if Mattock wasn't in the Earthenbore after all, then something was badly wrong – she had to get up there right away. Ivy took a step backwards, then whirled and dashed back the way she had come.

'Hey!' Mica pounded down the stairs after her. 'Stop!'

This was a disaster. She couldn't let him chase her all over the Delve; she was still tired from battling the Claybane, and she needed to save her strength. But he was too close for her to get away with turning herself invisible, and there was nowhere to hide…

'Ivy?' asked Mica, faint with disbelief, and then louder, 'Ivy! It *is* you!'

She spun to face him. 'I don't have time to explain, Mica! The Delve's in danger and there's nobody to keep the hunters from going out! Cicely's alive but I still have to rescue her, so whatever you want from me, it's going to have to wait!'

He stopped and gazed at her, his eyes deep-set and haunted. Ivy readied herself to flee – but then her brother said quietly, 'All right. What can I do?'

'Mattock told me he was going to guard the Earthenbore,' Ivy panted at Mica as they raced through the tunnels together. 'Are you certain he isn't still up there? Did you go and look?'

'I went halfway up the Hunter's Stair and yelled his name,' said Mica. 'There's no way he wouldn't have heard me.'

A shiver ran over Ivy's skin. Something was wrong, badly wrong. Mattock would never have been foolish enough to go outside, not after she'd warned him of the danger – and especially not when he knew she was counting on him. She put on another burst of speed as they turned into the Narrows, shouting, 'Mattock!'

'I told you,' Mica said irritably from behind her, 'he's not up there.'

Ivy didn't bother to argue. She dodged down the corridor and up the steps, made a sharp turn – and stopped, grabbing the wall for support. In the middle of the Earthenbore, only a few paces from the top of the stair, stood the clay-covered form of Mattock.

'What the—' Mica caught Ivy as she stumbled back. 'What *is* that?'

'Something terrible,' whispered Ivy. Her legs were

shaking, but she pulled herself upright and rounded on Mica. 'Aunt Betony. Did you see her, when you were looking for Matt? Where was she going?'

'I – yes. She was heading for the Great Shaft. But—'

He hadn't even got the last word out before Ivy was off and running. Every footstep sent a jolt of terror through her body – for all she knew, she might run into another patch of Claybane at any moment. Yet she and Mica had already covered this ground, so she had to trust that the path was still safe, at least for now.

'Keep your distance!' she shouted to Mica as he ran after her. 'Stay back!' Then she hit the junction, turned into the tunnel that led to the Great Shaft…

And her foot skidded out from under her.

It was too late to catch herself, impossible to stop. Ivy gasped, flailed, and sat down hard, right in the middle of a newly laid patch of Claybane.

And she wasn't the only one. Right ahead of her, frozen in mid-stride, was a perfectly formed statue of Betony.

seventeen

Mica started forward to help her, but Ivy flung up her clay-smeared hands in warning. 'Don't!' she cried. 'Stay where you are!' She could barely speak, her throat was so choked with terror. Any second now the Claybane would come slithering up her body and she'd be trapped again, this time with no hope of ever getting out. 'Find Gossan. Tell him…'

And then words failed her, because what could she say? Even if Mica managed to warn the Jack that the enemy was inside the Delve, there was nothing he could do about it. With Cicely to guide her the whole Delve was open to Gillian, so her traps might be anywhere – and everywhere. And the Claybane dust was so fine it would be practically impossible to see until the spell took effect, so Ivy couldn't even tell her fellow piskeys what to watch for…

'Tell him what?' asked Mica in a puzzled tone. 'Why don't you get up?'

Was he really that stupid, that he couldn't see what was

happening to her? 'Because I'm stuck in the Claybane!' Ivy shouted. 'And any minute now I'm going to end up like—'

But then it dawned on her that she *hadn't* ended up like Mattock and Betony, after all. Her hands and legs were wet with slime, but the Claybane hadn't crawled any higher, even though she ought to have been half covered in it by now. Disbelieving, Ivy pushed herself up onto hands and knees, then clambered to her feet. There was no resistance.

'It's not working,' she murmured, staring at her muddy palms. 'But why?'

'Why indeed?' asked a cool voice from the darkness. 'And how did you manage to escape my Claybane the first time, for that matter? Apparently the faery part of you is a great deal stronger than I'd thought. How irksome. I can see I'll have to deal with you some other way.'

Ivy whirled as the far end of the tunnel lit up and Gillian Menadue stepped out of the shadows, no longer invisible. She'd made herself piskey size when she came into the Delve, and for the first time Ivy saw her wings, translucent and brittle-looking as a wasp's. Yet there was nothing delicate about the way Gillian held them. They were raised at a menacing angle, like blades that might come slashing down at any moment.

'Mica,' said Ivy, not taking her eyes off the faery woman, 'get out of here.'

'But you—'

'I can look after myself!' Ivy shouted. 'Just *go!*'

And for a wonder, he did. As his hurried footsteps faded, Gillian tipped her head to one side and gave Ivy a curious smile. 'Was that your brother? Handsome boy. But he'll never make it, you know. There must be Claybane traps all over the Delve by now.'

'Enough,' said Ivy tightly. 'What have you done with my sister?'

'Cicely? Oh, she's well enough.' Gillian waved a hand at the statue of Betony, and it shrank to the same tiny size as the figures Ivy had seen in the workshop. She nudged it aside with her foot. 'She's just a little busy at the moment. I told her that unless she carried out my instructions, everyone in her family would die. And since then she's proved quite useful…for a child.'

'So you sent her to sprinkle Claybane around the tunnels for you, while you waited here for the Joan,' Ivy said, suppressing her fury at the revelation. Cicely must have been terrified, to obey Gillian with so little resistance. 'That's why you came down here, wasn't it? To make sure Betony didn't escape.'

'I was prepared to fight her, if she proved difficult. But she walked straight into my trap.' Her smile broadened, lips parting over her white teeth. 'I knew you piskeys had grown weak and careless living underground, but I never guessed destroying you would be *this* easy.'

She sounded confident. Yet if Gillian was so certain of her success, why was she still here? There must be something she had left to do, or she would have gone back to the surface…

So maybe it wasn't too late to stop her.

'And when Cicely's done your work for you,' Ivy asked, 'what then? Are you planning to sit here and wait for everyone else to turn into statues? That could take a while.'

'Oh, I have an idea of how to speed things up,' said Gillian. 'A little something I was working on before I met your mother. But it may not be necessary, once the panic spreads. We'll see.'

Ivy glanced behind her. Did she dare to turn herself into a swift, and make a break for the exit? But there were no day-lamps in the tunnels, and she wouldn't get far without light. She could make herself invisible and try to creep out, but that wouldn't hide her from an enemy as powerful as Gillian, especially in an enclosed space. Her best hope was to keep the conversation going, until she could distract the faery woman and escape.

'I warned the others about the Claybane,' Ivy said. Though half the people she'd told were already trapped – but Gillian didn't need to know that. 'They know how it works.'

'Of course you did,' said Gillian mildly. 'But as I'm sure you've noticed, it's hard to avoid a trap you can't even see. The only way to get safely out of the Delve now is to fly, and only females can do that. Or at least,' she added with a patronising smile, '*most* females.'

Once Ivy would have bristled at the taunt, but now she ignored it. Let Gillian go on thinking her wingless and weak – she'd find out how wrong she'd been about that soon enough. She sneaked a glance at the glow-spell Gillian had conjured, still floating close to the roof of the tunnel. Could she knock it out somehow, and extinguish her own light at the same time? Maybe – but she'd have to wait for exactly the right moment to do it, to make the most of the distraction.

'We'll find our way out,' Ivy told her, with more boldness than she felt. 'My people may not have the same kind of magic you do, but we know the earth and we're stronger than you think. And even if you do manage to capture all the men, what makes you think that the women won't come after you instead?'

'I doubt that, considering how ignorant they are of life outside the Delve,' Gillian replied. 'I suspect they'll be far too busy trying to find food and shelter to think about revenge. On the other hand...' She gave a little shrug. 'I haven't been particularly impressed with the piskey women I've met so far, faery blood or not. Perhaps I'll leave you all to the Claybane, and save myself the trouble.'

Inwardly Ivy cursed herself; that wasn't the conclusion she'd wanted Gillian to come to at all. But there was no taking the words back now. 'How is that any different from the way my ancestors thought about faeries?' she demanded. 'That one is as good – or bad – as another?

You're no better than they were, for all your talk about justice.'

Gillian looked at her nails, feigning indifference. But Ivy went on with rising passion, 'Can't you see how backward this revenge of yours has become? You've spent your whole life brooding over faeries who are long dead, and hating piskeys who don't even remember that you exist. What about Molly and her father? They're the ones that are alive, the ones that know and care about you. And you treat them like they're worthless.'

That struck a nerve. Gillian held up a warning finger, power crackling around its tip. 'Hold your tongue,' she said, 'or I'll burn it out. You know nothing about my family, or me.'

'I know Molly,' Ivy replied, moving closer. The crystals of an idea were beginning to form themselves in her mind. 'She's kind and bright and talented, and she deserves a mother who cares about her, not just about her own selfish plans. How are you going to look her in the face, when she confronts you with what you've done?'

'Molly knows nothing of this.' Gillian's voice was flat. 'She's asleep.'

'No, she's not,' said Ivy. 'She's back in your workshop, crying because of what you did to Richard. Her faery godfather.'

'Impossible,' Gillian said. But for the first time a note of uncertainty crept into her voice, and silently Ivy exulted. It was working! If she could just keep her distracted a little longer…

'All her life Molly's longed to get close to faeries,' Ivy went on as she walked past Gillian, towards the edge of the Great Shaft. 'No wonder, since she's half-faery herself. But you kept her away from that part of her heritage, refused even to admit that faeries existed – all so you could carry out this twisted revenge of yours. Do you really think she's going to forgive you for that? Especially now that she knows what you did to Richard, and to me?'

As Ivy spoke, she laid a hand on the railing. An icy tingle ran up her arm, but she made herself hold steady, as though it didn't bother her at all. If Gillian didn't realise that Ivy could touch iron, then maybe…

'Ivy?' said a small voice, trembling with emotion, and Ivy's breath caught. She turned to see Cicely standing at the entrance of the tunnel, an empty sack of Claybane dangling from her hand.

She would have run to Cicely, but Gillian was quicker. She stepped out between them, holding out her hands as though in benediction – but the glance she gave Ivy warned that bad things would happen if she dared to interfere.

'Well done,' she said to Cicely. 'You have saved your family, and earned their freedom. Come and join us.'

But Cicely backed away. 'You lied to me,' she said. 'You said Ivy was trapped, just like I was – that you were the only one who could release her. But she's here. And you made me—' She gave a little sob of rage, and flung the Claybane sack onto the floor. 'You *lied*!'

Gillian's face hardened, and Ivy knew the faery woman was about to do something terrible. 'Cicely, run!' she shouted, but Gillian's gaze had already locked onto her sister's, and it was too late. Cicely's shoulders went slack, hands dropping to her sides, and her face turned blank as a doll's.

'Walk,' commanded Gillian, and without hesitation Ivy's sister stepped forward – right into the patch of Claybane.

'No!' Ivy shouted, but the echo of her cry died away as Cicely continued straight through the puddle without stopping. Gillian looked startled, but she was quick to recover. She seized Cicely's wrist and pulled her to her side.

'Well,' she said. 'It appears the Claybane only works on a piskey once, so now you're both immune. Which means I can't let either one of you out of my sight.'

By now muffled shouts and screams were reverberating up the Shaft from the lower tunnels, piskeys panicking as the Claybane did its work. In the corridors doors opened and slammed again, footsteps pounded and were suddenly cut short, and a child wailed in wordless terror.

'Listen to that,' said Ivy, slapping the rail so hard the iron shuddered. 'You hate my people for what they did to you and your family. Do you really think the children of the Delve aren't going to hate you just as much for what you've done here today? Your own daughter already does!'

Gillian's hands came down hard on Cicely's shoulders. 'Never,' she said. 'Molly is *mine*.'

'She was, until you started treating her like a nuisance,' Ivy retorted. 'Not to mention deceiving her, and hurting her friends, and using magic on her against her will. But she broke your spell, and she got me out of the Claybane, too. She'll never trust you again.'

The faery woman stood immobile with Cicely in her grip. Deep lines had formed about her eyes and mouth, and for a moment she looked almost as old as Nettle. But then she shook herself, and straightened up again. 'It makes no difference,' she said. 'It's done now. And I'm about to—'

A thunderous *crack* shook the tunnel, and a shower of debris roared down. Ivy leaped back against the wall, flinging her arms over her head, and Cicely let out a scream. But when the dust cleared, the faery woman still stood with Cicely beside her, both of them encased in a shimmering bubble of magic. Rocks had fallen all around them, but none had broken through.

Still, if it was Mica swinging that thunder-axe, he hadn't struck in vain. In the confusion Cicely had broken free of Gillian's mental hold, and now she was struggling like a wild thing. Gillian held tight to her wrist, trying to twist her into submission – but the piskey girl lunged forward and bit her captor's arm.

With a shriek Gillian let go, and as Cicely hurtled away from her Ivy knew her opportunity had come. She extinguished her light, willed herself into swift-form, and flung herself straight at Gillian's face.

Nothing happened.

Arms still outspread in a futile mockery of wings, Ivy crashed to the floor of the tunnel. The breath whooshed out of her lungs, and her chin hit the ground so hard she tasted blood. She rolled over, gasping, and clutched at the rail for support. But the iron stung her hands, and she had to snatch them away.

What a fool she'd been! How could she have forgotten what had happened in Molly's barn, when that loose nail had cancelled her invisibility spell? Maybe being away from the Delve had strengthened the faery part of her nature, or maybe Richard's healing had brought it to the fore. But either way, Ivy was no longer immune to the effects of iron. She'd hoped to trick Gillian into touching the rail – but instead she'd only crippled herself.

The ceiling cracked again, more rocks cascading down. But the cave-in was going to kill Ivy long before it hurt Gillian, whose magical shield clung to her like a second, impenetrable skin. She fired off a spell that sent Cicely tumbling, then stooped over Ivy and seized her by the back of the neck.

'Try to attack me, will you?' she spat. 'Little savage. You're not fit to lead your people – you're not even fit to live.' She picked Ivy up as though she were weightless, and flung her against the railing.

The metal groaned as Ivy slammed into it, and she heard something inside her crack. For a sickening moment she hung over the rail, with the black abyss yawning below her. Then with a desperate effort she shoved herself backwards, and collapsed to the rock-strewn floor.

She'd failed, utterly and completely. Her whole plan had relied on being able to transform into a swift – her secret triumph, her greatest pride – but now even that was denied her. With a groan Ivy clutched at her injured ribs, and waited for Gillian to deliver the killing blow.

But it never came. Gillian stared down at Ivy, then at her own hands. For the first time she appeared shaken, even a little frightened. Could she be realising she'd gone too far?

'Stop this,' Ivy croaked at her. Every breath felt like someone was knifing her in the side, but she managed to struggle to her feet. 'It's not too late. You can still make it right. Molly will—'

But Gillian shook her head. 'Molly has betrayed me,' she said harshly. 'There's nothing for me to go back to. It's over – and so are you.'

She pressed her hands together, then pulled them slowly apart. A swirling ball of smoke coalesced between her palms, growing steadily until it was the size of Ivy's head. Balancing it on her fingertips, Gillian walked to the railing – but to Ivy's disappointment, she didn't touch it. She reached out over the Great Shaft, and let the spell drop.

A few seconds went by in silence. Then came a muffled explosion from below. 'What...' Ivy gasped. 'What have you done?'

Gillian gave a short laugh. 'You'll find out soon enough,' she said. 'Goodbye, Ivy.' She took a step back, her form shredding into mist...

But an instant later, her body solidified again. The spell had failed.

Disbelief flashed across the faery woman's face, and she gathered herself for another attempt. But the second time was no better. For some reason – whether it was the presence of the iron railing, or something in the rock and ore of the Delve itself – Gillian couldn't transport herself away.

For one vindictive moment, Ivy was glad. Gillian was trapped now, like the rest of them. And whatever nasty surprise she'd just dropped down the shaft, she'd have to suffer it too. But Gillian only shrugged. 'Well,' she said, 'I said it myself, didn't I? There's only one way out of the Delve now.' And with that her wings began to beat, lifting her lightly into the air.

Ivy flinched as another fissure spread across the ceiling, rocks and grit showering down. Any minute now the tunnel would collapse, and she and Cicely would be crushed to death. Gillian would escape, leaving Marigold to die alone, and the piskeys of the Delve would be trapped in clay forever.

No, thought Ivy. She couldn't let that happen. If she died trying to stop Gillian, so be it...but for the sake of the people she loved, she had to try.

Pain shot through Ivy's chest as she sucked in her breath. Then as Gillian glided past her she leaped into the air, and snatched at the faery woman's leg.

At first she thought she'd missed. But she caught her enemy's ankle at the last second, fingers skittering over the soft fabric of her trousers, then clamping tight around flesh and bone. Dragged through the air by Gillian's fast-beating wings, Ivy hurtled towards the railing once more – but this time when it hit her, she was ready. She hooked her feet between the bars, and hung on with all her might.

Gillian kicked out, and Ivy's head snapped sideways as the faery woman's heel smashed into her cheekbone. Stars filled her vision, and she felt as though her body were being ripped apart. Yet she refused to let go.

The railing creaked, and a shower of dust and gravel fell from the bolts that anchored it to the wall. Still Gillian fought to free herself from Ivy's grip, wings buzzing madly as she fired off one spell after another – but Ivy was right behind her, too small a target to easily hit. And as Ivy held onto her, leaning all her weight into the effort, she was dimly surprised at her own strength. Perhaps being half-faery was good for something after all.

But she couldn't hang on forever – she had to end this quickly, or Gillian would escape. For Cicely's sake and

Marigold's, for Mica's and Flint's, for Mattock and Jenny and all the others, Ivy had to give everything she had. Though all her muscles shrieked with agony, she grabbed Gillian's other ankle, tightened her grip, and yanked as hard as she could.

Even Gillian's wings couldn't counteract that sudden jerk. With a cry she shot backwards, Ivy's weight dragging her down. Her flailing hand brushed the rail – and the iron lit up in a sizzling flash. She screamed again and collapsed, the weight of her body crashing onto the railing as her wings went limp.

Weak with relief, Ivy let go of her ankle. But a second later the bolts that anchored the railing broke free of the crumbling stone around them, and the whole construction began to topple. *Molly*, thought Ivy wildly, and flung out a hand, but too late: the railing dropped, taking the unconscious woman with it. Bouncing off the shaft walls with one hideous clang after another, the railing and its passenger tumbled into the fathomless dark below. There was a distant splash, and then silence.

Ivy bowed her head to the stone floor, sick with horror. She'd only meant to stop Gillian, not to kill her. But another ominous rumble shook the rocks around her, and she had no time to spare for regret. Ivy heaved herself upright, staggered back down the tunnel, and dragged her unconscious sister to safety in the corridor beyond.

She was lowering Cicely to the floor, ready to collapse

beside her, when she remembered the statue of Betony. Ivy hurled herself back into the tunnel, snatched it up, and leaped to safety – just as a great slab of the ceiling smashed down, and the entrance to the Great Shaft disappeared behind a heap of fallen granite.

For a moment Ivy could only crouch there coughing, as clouds of stone dust rolled over her. Then she heard the clomp of boots, and rough but gentle hands helped her to her feet. She turned to her rescuer – and realised with dim astonishment that it wasn't Mica, after all.

It was her father.

Of course. Only a skilled knocker would have known how to wield his thunder-axe so effectively, or how to collapse a single tunnel without bringing the whole upper Delve down. He'd taken an enormous risk and he could have killed both his daughters in the process, but he'd been trying to save them – and that meant he cared. Ivy seized him by the shoulders and kissed him on both cheeks.

'How did you know we were here?' she asked. 'Did Mica tell you?'

Flint nodded. He looked more grey and weary than ever, but as he stroked Ivy's hair there was a tenderness in his eyes she hadn't seen since she was a child. 'I'm sorry,' he rasped.

There was so much Ivy wanted to tell him, so many questions she wanted to ask. He'd known Marigold was leaving the Delve, heard her warning about the poison; why hadn't he gone with her, or believed her story until it was too late? When he found her shawl tangled in a gorse-bush, with the blood she'd coughed up still fresh upon it, had he truly thought the spriggans had taken her, or did it only make him realise how ill she'd been? Was it losing her that had convinced him the Delve was dangerous after all, and made him determined to find the source of the poison even if it killed him?

Ivy longed to know, but that conversation would have to wait. She still didn't know what Gillian had dropped down the shaft, and she couldn't assume the danger was past. She gave her father one last grateful squeeze and said, 'Stay here and look after Cicely, please? I've got to find the others.'

Ivy limped through the corridors, clutching her aching side. Her cheekbone throbbed where Gillian had kicked her, and all her bones felt out of joint. If only Richard were here to heal her – but no, she couldn't let herself think about him right now, any more than she could stop to mourn for the other piskeys who stood mute and frozen along the way. Not only males either, but wild-eyed matrons, a child caught in mid-wail, and then the skinny form of Quartz, who'd barely made it halfway up Tinners' Row with his message.

By the time Ivy reached Silverlode Passage, her vision was so clouded with tears that she could hardly see. Impatient with herself, she tried to rub the blurriness away, but it only swirled in front of her eyes like smoke – because,

Ivy realised with a shock, that was exactly what it was. And now she could smell it, too: an acrid, nose-wrinkling stench like old urine on straw.

It must be from the spell that Gillian had dropped into the shaft. How dangerous was it? It couldn't be potent enough to kill anyone who breathed it, or Gillian wouldn't have bothered creating the Claybane. But it certainly *smelled* poisonous, and the further she went down the passage the more unbearably thick and pungent it became. Soon Ivy was coughing with both hands wrapped around her ribcage, and her lungs felt as though they were on fire.

Her fellow piskeys would never be able to endure this. As soon as the smoke reached the upper levels and started coming into their caverns, they'd panic and run for the exits – exactly as Gillian had planned. Somehow, Ivy had to get them safely out of the Delve.

'Gossan!' she shouted, glancing in all directions. She paused to look into the Market Cavern, but it was empty. 'My lord Jack! Where are you?'

At the end of the corridor, the door to the Joan's stateroom opened. Nettle stood there alone, looking smaller and more wizened than ever in the flickering torchlight. 'He's gone,' she said heavily. 'Just like my lady. And neither one of them's come back.'

Which meant that Gossan too must be a statue, trapped in some side corridor. But if so there was no point searching for him. Statues didn't breathe, and Ivy and Nettle did –

though it was getting more difficult by the moment. Willing herself not to panic, Ivy slipped out of her shoes and kicked them aside. With bare feet she'd be better able to feel the Claybane when she stepped into it, and tell Nettle when it was time to leap, or fly.

'Come with me,' she said. 'We've got to get the others out of here.'

By the time Ivy and Nettle reached the upper levels, there was a small crowd of frightened piskeys shuffling after them. No one had collapsed yet, but Ivy's head was beginning to reel, and she feared it might only be a matter of time.

'There's a patch here,' she shouted, as they came up to a statue of two piskey-boys clutching each other. One of the women sobbed and reached towards it, but her companions pulled her back. Ivy sidled across the Claybane-coated floor, toes groping for dry rock. 'All right,' she said, 'it's safe on this side.'

At once all the females spread their wings and began ferrying the men and boys over the trap. The first few attempts had been awkward, and they'd lost one stout knocker when the two women who were carrying him let go a little too soon. But they were getting better at it now, and soon all of them were safe on the other side.

Still, it was slow progress, especially with more piskeys joining them at every door they passed. The journey up to the Earthenbore seemed impossibly long, and Ivy wished there could be a faster way – but since both the upper and lower entrances to the Great Shaft were blocked up with rubble and the shaft itself was full of choking fumes, she couldn't think of one.

Fortunately, Ivy's people knew how to work together. Soon two of the younger hunters had stationed themselves at the back of the group and cast a shielding charm to keep back the worst of the smoke, while others gathered rolled-up mats and blankets to drop over each patch of Claybane they passed, so that they'd know where the traps were when they returned. That showed more foresight and creativity than Ivy had expected, and she wasn't surprised to find that the hunters who'd thought of it were also the ones who'd had recent contact with humans.

When they climbed the stairs to the second level, Cicely was waiting for them, with Flint behind her. Her face was dirty and there was a bloody scrape across her forehead, but her eyes were clear.

'I want to help,' she told Ivy. 'What can I do?'

Ivy explained about the spell Gillian had dropped down the Great Shaft, and the need to get all the piskeys up to fresh air. 'Can you collect everyone from this level?' she asked. 'Tell them to bring plenty of rugs to mark the patches of Claybane once you've found them – they can't stop the traps working, but they'll keep people from walking into them by accident. Then use the women to fly the men across – that's what we've been doing.'

Cicely nodded. 'I'll tell Mica.' And she dashed off so fast her feet scarcely touched the ground. Flint shouldered his thunder-axe and moved to the rear of Ivy's group, his eyes meeting hers in a long searching look as he passed. But Ivy couldn't pause to ask her father what was on his mind; the smoke was getting thicker every moment. 'Come on,' she said to the others. 'We've got to hurry.'

They'd made it as far as Long Way, and Ivy was feeling out the dimensions of a particularly large patch of Claybane, when someone behind her gasped. She turned back to see that Nettle had stumbled, and Jenny and Hyacinth were helping the old woman up again – but the dark smear of mud across Nettle's hand and cheek made plain that it was already too late.

'Move aside, everyone,' Ivy said. She hated to leave Nettle without company in her last moments, but she couldn't risk any of the others getting caught in the Claybane's spell. 'You'll have to go around her. Nettle, I'm sorry. We'll come back for you when the air's cleared.'

'Aye,' said Nettle in a tremulous voice, shuffling to the edge of the tunnel. 'I'll be well enough.'

They all glided past her, many with sorrowful looks and murmurs of sympathy, but Nettle didn't move. She looked so small and drab that she might have been made of clay already. Ivy was about to call the rest of the crowd to move on when the old woman called out:

'Eh then, young Flint, where are you off to?'

Startled, Ivy turned. Nettle was still standing to one side of the tunnel, looking back into the hazy darkness – and to Ivy's astonishment, the Claybane didn't seem to have affected her in the least.

'Wait,' Ivy told the others, and ran to join her. 'Are you a faery?' she asked Nettle in a low voice. 'No piskey blood at all?'

'Aye, but what of it?' retorted the other woman. 'Your father's just decided to run off and play the hero – or the fool. What good's he going to do going back into that mess?'

Alarm stabbed into Ivy. Surely Flint didn't think he could destroy Gillian's spell with nothing more than his thunder-axe? She ran a few steps into the darkness and made her skin glow as brightly as she could, calling his name. But the light only reflected off the thickening haze, and her father did not reply.

'Ivy!' Jenny shouted to her. 'My mum's fainting – we have to go!'

For a final moment Ivy wavered, torn between grief and duty. Then she wiped her eyes, took Nettle by the arm, and hurried to rejoin the others.

Minutes later, they had made it safely up the Hunter's Stair and were turning into the Earthenbore when a tremor shook the tunnel behind them. Ivy looked back to see Cicely and Mica sprinting up the Narrows with their own crowd of piskeys in tow, the combined glow of their skins lighting up the tunnel like noonday – but they too stopped short as the rumbling grew louder.

'What is that?' Cicely shouted up to her, but Ivy shook her head.

'Don't stop!' she called. 'Keep coming!'

The women who could still fly seized the men at the front of the crowd and began carrying them along, not even waiting for Ivy to tell them where the Claybane ended and the solid ground began. Ivy ducked past them and ran along the Earthenbore. 'We're almost out!' she yelled as she turned up a side tunnel. 'Follow me!'

She dashed through a final patch of Claybane, then turned to snatch a rolled-up rug from Hew's hands and fling it down. 'Go!' she commanded, and the piskeys flew, leaped, or scrambled across the walls to avoid the trap, then hurtled out the exit to freedom.

'That's the lot,' Mica panted, dropping down from the roots he'd been using to swing himself along the ceiling. 'Let's—'

A billow of grey-green smoke blasted up the tunnel towards them. 'Go!' he shouted, shoving Ivy out onto the hillside. Clenching her jaw against the pain, Ivy seized his arm, pulling him after her, and the two of them tumbled into the heather – just as Gillian's spell exploded out of all the exits of the Delve at once.

For a moment the whole hillside was covered in a blanket

of foul smog, and all the piskeys pressed their faces to the ground. But soon the vapours dissipated, and when Ivy raised her head there was nothing left but a few wisps of smoke. The sky was the colour of tin, a gentle rain pattering on the leaves. And to the east the sun glowed softly through the clouds, like a promise that all would be well.

'It's all right,' Ivy called down to the others, wincing as she climbed to her feet. 'We're safe now.'

eighteen

It took hours for the smoke in the Delve to clear. The piskeys made camp in the valley, hidden by the strongest glamours the women among them could cast – but it was a wet and uncomfortable spot, and when Ivy came up from her exploration of the upper tunnels and announced that the air was fit to breathe again, no one complained about having to leave it. Still, she caught Jenny looking wistfully over her shoulder as they all filed underground, and knew that it would be a long time before the women of the Delve forgot their brief time in the sunlight.

Nettle gathered a small group of the oldest and most magically talented piskeys to investigate the Claybane, and soon they'd worked up a spell to turn it to harmless dust. But that did nothing to free the ones who were already trapped. It was a grim business finding all the statues scattered around the Delve and carrying them down to the Market Cavern, and only the news that Gillian's body had been found gave Ivy any confidence that the effort would not be wasted.

It was an even darker moment when the knockers clambered out of the rubble-strewn passage that had once led to Richard's cell, carrying two bodies on stretchers. First came Flint, his hands crossed over his chest and his face peaceful as a sleeping child's. Then a dripping form with a blanket draped over it, which only Nettle dared to lift as the carriers lowered the stretcher to the floor.

'Oh, little sister,' she whispered, a tear sliding down her wizened cheek. 'My poor Gillyflower. Who was the prisoner then, you or me?'

She'd called her *Gillyflower* before, Ivy remembered with a pang. She'd even mentioned that she'd had a sister by that name, right after Cicely disappeared. But Ivy had never thought to connect Nettle to Gillian until now.

'Why didn't you say anything?' she asked, as she moved to Nettle's side. 'You must have known who she was, when I came to warn Betony and Gossan.'

Nettle wiped her eyes on her sleeve. 'I couldn't let her see me like this, all old and wrinkled and grey. I knew she'd never understand.'

'Understand what?' asked Ivy.

'That I loved the Delve, and I didn't want to leave it,' Nettle said. 'Oh, I was frightened at first, but I married a good knocker, and he was kind to me. And the Joan – the old Joan, before Betony – she treated me like a daughter, after my own mother died.' She draped the blanket gently over Gillian's bruised face. 'I might've been born a faery, but I'm a piskey now. And what's good enough for the others is good enough for me.'

There didn't seem to be much Ivy could say to that. She touched Nettle's shoulder in silent sympathy, then backed away.

'Ivy?' whispered Cicely, creeping under her elbow. 'Is Dad...is he really...gone?'

Yarrow had bandaged Ivy's ribs and dosed her with willow bark, but the thought of Flint made her chest hurt all over again. He'd given his life for the mine he loved, sacrificing himself to destroy Gillian's smoke-spell with one last, mighty blow of his thunder-axe. But the poison that was killing the piskeys of the Delve, weakening their magic and ageing them long before their time, was still there. Her father would be honoured as a hero, and yet he hadn't really saved any of them in the end.

'I'm afraid so,' she said, leaning her head against her sister's. 'But Mum's still alive, and maybe she'll wake up soon.' Yet even as she spoke the words, Ivy knew it was too much to hope for. If Gillian's death hadn't undone the Claybane, why should it undo any of the other spells she'd cast?

Mica came and stood on Ivy's other side, watching in silence as the knockers carried their father's body away. He hadn't spoken to Ivy since she'd told him that she'd left the

Delve to look for Cicely and find their mother; he hadn't even reacted to the news Marigold was alive. For a time they'd worked together as a team, and he'd even seemed willing to listen; but now that the crisis that had united them was over, he'd gone back to his old stubborn ways again. Did he blame her for Flint's death? Or was there some other grudge he was holding against her?

Ivy didn't know, and she was too tired to think about it. So when Mica stalked away without even looking at her, Ivy let him go.

Gillian's stretcher lay to one side of the tunnel. Yarrow was stooping over the body with bowl and knife in hand, ready to collect the blood which would set the trapped piskeys free. Cicely started forward, but Ivy held her back.

'You don't want to see this,' she said. 'Go and find Jenny in the Market Cavern. I'll come in a minute.'

With obvious reluctance, Cicely obeyed. When she was gone, Ivy moved to the healer and watched as she worked, her heart leaden with sorrow. She'd never meant Gillian to die, especially not by her hand. But how could she explain that to Molly?

At last Yarrow straightened up, holding out the bowl. 'There isn't much,' she said. 'We'd better try it here first and make sure it works. Did you bring the Joan?'

Ivy walked to the tunnel entrance, and returned with the tiny statue of Betony. She bit open the cut on her forefinger and squeezed a drop onto the figure's head, then held it out to the healer, who dipped a rag into the bowl and wiped Gillian's blood across its feet. Ivy held her breath, waiting...

But though they waited for seconds and then minutes, not a single crack appeared. 'I was afraid of that,' said Yarrow heavily. 'The spell needs the blood of the living, not the dead.'

Ivy nodded soberly. There was only one hope left for the piskeys now. But when Molly found out what had happened to her mother, would she be willing to help them?

In all the misery and confusion, with most of the piskeys still gathered in the Market Cavern, it wasn't difficult for Ivy to steal away. Moving gingerly to spare her bandaged ribs, she hurried up the stairs and slipped through the twisting passages, up, out, into the afternoon light. Then she changed shape – it was easy now the effects of the iron had worn off, though she still felt bruised all over – and flapped away.

Like most piskeys Ivy had an excellent sense of direction, but in bird-form it was keener than ever. Soon she spotted Gillian's workshop, and angled down to land before the door on her own piskey feet. It was probably too much to expect that Molly would still be waiting for her, but at least she could see her mother one last time.

Yet when Ivy tore aside the covering vines and pushed the door open, she found the building deserted. Gem and Feldspar's statues still stood forlornly upon the shelf, but there was no sign of Marigold – or Richard. Nothing but an overturned container that had once held Claybane dust, and a scattering of broken pottery on the ground.

Troubled, Ivy took to the air again and wheeled eastward, towards Molly's cottage. She landed in the yard, changed to human size and ran up the steps to hammer upon the door. 'Molly! Are you all right? Are you there?'

For an awful moment no answer came. Then a soft voice said, 'Ivy?' Locks clicked, and latches rattled. The door flew open – and with a laugh like a sob, Ivy fell into her mother's arms.

'She woke up after I yelled at her and shook her a few more times,' Molly said proudly, when Marigold had stopped embracing Ivy long enough to lead her inside. The sunlight lay in golden wedges on the carpet, the curtains danced on the breeze, and the sitting room looked as warm and bright as Molly herself. 'I guess it was like when I got you out of the Claybane – being only half-faery I didn't have enough power to break my mum's spell right away, but it worked out in the end.' She peered into Ivy's bruised face. 'You look awful. What happened?'

This was the moment Ivy had dreaded. 'Molly,' she said in a low voice, 'your mum's dead.'

Molly's cheeks turned ashen. She backed up until her legs bumped the armchair, and then sat down hard. 'How?' she asked in a whisper. 'How did she die?'

'She fell down the Great Shaft,' Ivy said. 'She was trying

to get away, and I was trying to stop her, and the railing broke.' She covered her face with her hands. 'I'm so sorry, Molly.'

For several seconds Molly didn't move. Then she leaped up and ran from the room. Her door slammed, but even from the other end of the corridor Ivy could hear the human girl weeping. She stood there numbly, certain that she'd just ruined any chance that Molly would ever help the piskeys of the Delve, until she felt Marigold's arm about her shoulders.

'Come and sit down,' her mother said. 'Tell me everything.'

It took a long time for Ivy to explain all that had happened in the past twelve hours, and by the time she'd finished her throat was raw and her chest ached with unshed tears. 'I couldn't stop Dad from going down there,' she said. 'It was like he *wanted* to die, and it was such a waste – I never even got to tell him you were alive...'

Marigold touched the place above her heart where her wedding pendant had once rested, the lines around her mouth deepening with sorrow. 'Oh, my love,' she whispered, as though Flint could hear her. 'We made so many mistakes, you and I.'

'I made a lot of mistakes too,' said Ivy. 'When I talked to the man in the market and found out that someone had erased his memory the way you did mine, I thought...' She faltered at her mother's sharp intake of breath, and raised pleading eyes to hers. 'I know. It wasn't you selling the piskeys, it was Gillian. But…I was right about what you did to me, wasn't I?'

Marigold closed her eyes. 'I didn't know what else to do,' she said. 'When I came out from the bedroom that night and you asked me why I was crying, I couldn't lie to you. I thought perhaps if I told you a little of the truth it would be all right, and you'd understand why I had to go. But you guessed too much – things too dangerous for you to know—'

'What things?' asked Ivy, but Marigold shook her head.

'I can't tell you that,' she said. 'But…when you realised what was happening, you wanted to come with me. I told you that the surface world wasn't safe, that there were spriggans and faeries and all kinds of things up there, and that I didn't even know if I would survive. But you said you'd follow me anyway. And I – I couldn't let you do that.' Tears glimmered in her lashes. 'I'm sorry. Please forgive me.'

Ivy's thoughts were full of turmoil, and she didn't know what to say. But when Marigold reached out to her, she didn't resist. They clung to each other for a long time, and when Ivy raised her head Molly was standing in front of them, her eyes swollen but no longer wet. How long had she been listening? Had she heard the whole story? Ivy was afraid to ask, but then Molly spoke:

'I'm sorry about your dad,' she said. 'And I'm sorry about what my mum did to yours, too.' Her lips quivered, but she pressed them together and then went on in a rush, 'If you think my blood can help the other piskeys, the way it helped you – then I'll come.'

Gratitude warmed Ivy's chest. Awkwardly she rose and hugged Molly as hard as her bandaged ribs would allow. 'Thank you,' she whispered, knowing what she said and meaning it – that her debt to the human girl was greater than she could ever repay. 'Thank you, Molly.'

Molly had never been to the Delve before, so Marigold couldn't transport the two girls there by magic – and none of them knew how to drive Gillian's car, either. But Molly had ridden Duchess back from the workshop that morning, and now that Dodger's leg had healed there was no reason they couldn't take him along as well. It seemed that Ivy would get a proper ride of her own after all, especially since they still had to pick up Gem and Feldspar on the way – though with all her aches and pains, she feared she wouldn't get much pleasure out of it.

'Come with us,' said Ivy to Marigold, as Molly led the newly saddled horses into the yard. 'Please.'

But Marigold only gave a sad smile. 'I'm afraid not,' she said. 'Tell Mica and Cicely that I love them, and that if they can find it in their hearts to forgive me, my door will always be open. But I can never return to the Delve.'

'Why not?' asked Ivy. 'Surely it's not going to kill you to come back for a few minutes? Betony's trapped in the

Claybane – she's not going to make any problems for you.'

'You don't understand. I—' She broke off and put a hand to her throat. 'I can't.'

Bitterness welled up in Ivy, and she couldn't look at her mother any more. She turned her face against Dodger's warm, quivering neck and said, 'All right.'

'But don't forget what I told you about the poison,' Marigold pleaded, as Ivy climbed stiffly onto the horse's back. 'Don't throw your life away. Please, get away from that place as soon as you can, and come to me.'

Her brown eyes were filled with anxiety, her hands clasped against her heart – the very picture of a concerned mother. Yet she wouldn't come back to the Delve even to see her own daughter and son…and she hadn't offered to heal Ivy's injuries, either. Was healing like shape-changing – something that only male faeries could usually do? Or was it a hint to Ivy, that she couldn't expect any favours unless she did what Marigold wanted?

If so, Ivy was having none of it – she was sick of faery half-truths and manipulations. She'd managed without her mother before; there was no reason she couldn't do it again.

'The Delve is my home,' Ivy said, straightening up in the saddle. 'And Cicely and Mica need someone to look after them. Maybe you couldn't convince Aunt Betony to listen to you, but I'm not going to give up until I do. Goodbye.'

Then she touched her heels to Dodger's sides and

they trotted after Molly and Duchess, leaving Marigold behind.

It had been more than a hundred years since a human set foot in the Delve, and not even the most curious miner had ever walked the tunnels the piskeys had dug for themselves. But Ivy had used her magic to turn Molly piskey size before they left the surface, and now she followed Ivy through the passages in reverent awe, once or twice lifting a hand to touch the mosaics and semi-precious stones that adorned the walls.

They reached the lower levels of the Delve unnoticed. But when the two of them walked into the Market and the piskeys caught sight of the strange girl in human clothing, shocked murmurs rose from every side. As Ivy set Gem and Feldspar down and hurried to Betony's statue, she could feel Mica's glare boring into her from the other side of the cavern. But before he could march up and demand an explanation, she held out her hand to the prick of Molly's pocket-knife, and they both stooped to wipe their blood across the trapped Joan's brow and feet.

There was a tense moment when it seemed like nothing was happening, and Ivy feared her kinship with the Joan might not be close enough after all. But finally the clay began to crack, then to crumble, and at last in a shower of dust Betony burst free, transforming at once to her proper piskey size.

'The Joan!' shouted Hew, leaping up and waving his cap in the air. 'Our Joan's come alive again!'

And with that the whole cavern erupted into chaos, as they all came running to see the miracle. Ivy nearly shouted herself hoarse before she could quiet the crowd and explain. But once the piskeys realised who Molly was and what she had come here to do, they started hushing each other and chivvying themselves into order. Soon each family had lined up beside the statues of their loved ones, while Yarrow bent over Molly's arm with a lancet.

'Molly, is it?' said Nettle, when the healer had finished the blood-letting and carried the bowl away. 'Bless your brave soul, lass. I can't tell you what Gillyflower would have said, but as your aunt, I'm that proud of you.' Then she patted Molly's cheek and limped off, leaving the human girl blinking in astonishment.

'How can she be my aunt?' she asked Ivy. 'She's a piskey. And she's *old*.'

Too old, thought Ivy sadly. She must be unusually tough to have survived even this long underground, and she probably wouldn't live many years longer. But that was more than Molly needed to know at the moment. So Ivy kept her eyes on the bandage she was tying around Molly's arm and said only, 'She was your mother's older sister. Faeries live a long time.'

By now Yarrow was hurrying about the cavern with bowl and rag in hand, touching each of the statues' feet. Gossan was the next to break free of the Claybane, and in seconds he and Betony were embracing. One by one the trapped piskeys emerged from their shells, and the great cavern echoed with shouts of joy.

'We did it,' Molly said. But her smile was wan, and so was Ivy's. They'd saved the Delve together, but at a bitter cost, and it would be a long time before either one of them felt happy again.

'Come on,' Ivy told her, holding out her hand to the girl. 'I'll take you home.'

As soon as they'd returned to the cottage, Molly rang her father and the local police to tell them that Gillian had disappeared while exploring the site of an old mine. Ivy stayed with her as long as she could – after all the noisy jubilation of the Market Cavern, the Mcnadues' house seemed almost unbearably quiet, and it would have been cruel to leave Molly there alone. But as soon as the first vehicle began turning up the lane, Ivy hugged the girl goodbye and flew back to the Delve.

As Ivy walked the tunnels, one piskey after another rushed up to embrace her or pump her hand in gratitude. Many wanted to know where she'd been for so long, and what she meant to do now – especially Mattock, who gazed down at her with an admiration that bordered on worship, and went on holding her hand long after he'd stopped shaking it. But though Ivy was glad to see all of them, she didn't like being the focus of so much attention. She ended up excusing herself, telling them she was too tired to talk about it at the moment, and hurrying on.

Ivy had never meant to be a hero, and it bothered her to find herself treated as one. Especially since she wondered whether the Delve would ever have been in danger at all, if not for her. Yes, Gillian could still have found the right mine by process of elimination – that was what the map in the Menadues' study had been about, after all. But she couldn't have set her traps half so effectively without Cicely's help. And she would never have got her hands on Cicely if not for Ivy.

Fortunately, Cicely seemed to have forgiven Ivy for her mistakes, or at least she hadn't thrown them in her face yet. But Ivy wasn't so sure about Mica. He had taken Flint's death harder than any of them, and judging by the stony look he'd given Ivy when she and Molly left the Market Cavern, he wasn't nearly as impressed with her accomplishments as Mattock…

Lost in thought, Ivy turned the corner into Long Way – and froze. The door to her family cavern was open, the day-lamps spilling light into the corridor. And standing outside the doorway, her arms folded and her broad mouth set with disapproval, was Betony.

Ivy's muscles locked up, and every instinct screamed at her to fly. But she was done with running and hiding. Mica and Cicely needed to hear the truth about Marigold's disappearance and the poison in the mine, and so did Betony, whether she chose to do anything about it or not.

Squaring her shoulders, she stepped forward. 'My Joan,' she said. 'How can I serve you?'

It was intimidating – and humiliating – to have to stand before her aunt like a criminal and give account of herself, with Cicely and Mica looking on. Especially once it became clear that Betony had already questioned Cicely at length, and learned that Ivy had been sneaking out of the Delve on a regular basis. She'd also searched the cavern and found the rope Ivy had used to climb up and down the shaft to Richard's cell.

After that, it was no use hoping that her aunt wouldn't make the connection between Ivy's night-time absences and the 'spriggan' who had so mysteriously escaped from her dungeon. And when Betony demanded to know whether Ivy was the one who had set the prisoner free, she had no choice but to admit it.

'But it was all a mistake,' Ivy insisted. 'He had nothing to do with Keeve disappearing – that was Gillian's fault. And if you'd left him in there to starve—'

'It would have been no more than he deserved,' said Betony coldly. 'Do you think I didn't recognise what he was the moment I saw him? Spriggan or not, he was a servant of the Empress, come to spy out our defences. If I had let him go, he would have returned with more of his kind, and turned us all into slaves.'

Ivy was startled. 'You know about the Empress?'

'The old Joan warned me against her, when she passed on her power to me. The Empress has been a threat to our people for decades, and part of the oath I swore when I became the Joan was that I would do my utmost to keep even one piskey from falling into her hands.' Her chin lifted proudly. 'So I made sure that Gossan taught every hunter and forager to avoid faeries at all cost, and never to travel more than a few miles from the Delve. And I encouraged the old legends about spriggans and faeries to be retold at every Lighting, so that my people would never forget how dangerous the outside world could be.'

And naturally, the women and children who'd heard those legends had assumed the spriggans to be the real danger. Even the men who knew better wouldn't be likely to correct them, since they wanted to keep their families safe just as much as the Joan did. Not a direct lie, just an omission…and done with the best of intentions, however unfortunate the result.

Still, it was high time the truth came out. 'The Empress is dead,' Ivy told her. 'We don't have to hide any longer.'

'Dead!' Betony's brows shot up, but then her eyes narrowed again. 'Is that what *he* told you? What makes you so sure he wasn't deceiving you, so as to betray you to his mistress?'

Ivy wasn't sure of anything, where Richard was concerned. He'd provoked her and bargained with her, puzzled and frustrated her, and nearly everything about his past was still a mystery, including his proper name. And when she asked Molly where his statue had gone, the human girl had seemed just as baffled and upset to find him missing as Ivy had been.

But wherever he'd come from, whoever he'd been, she owed him too much to deny him now. 'He wasn't working for the Empress, he was working for my mother,' she said, watching Betony for her reaction. 'But it doesn't matter. Gillian turned him into a statue, and we couldn't turn him back.'

If Betony was shocked to hear that Marigold was alive, she didn't show it. 'I see,' said the Joan, and the lines around her mouth relaxed. 'Then we have one less threat to worry about. So you set the prisoner free, believing he would lead you to your mother?'

'Yes,' said Ivy. 'And he did. I saw her a few days later, alive and well. That's when I found out she was a faery, and she told me about—'

Betony cut her off. 'I am not interested in what Marigold had to say. She was strange and unnatural from the first, and I should have known she wasn't a true piskey. She has no business meddling in the affairs of the Delve.'

'No business?' Ivy could barely speak for outrage. 'She has a husband and three children here!' But then she glimpsed the flicker of apprehension in Betony's eyes, and all at once she understood. 'You knew why my mother left, didn't you? You knew, because you *made* her leave. Banishing her was the only way you could stop her talking about the poison in the Delve.'

'Poison?' exclaimed Cicely, sitting upright. 'You mean the spell that Dad—'

'Not that poison,' said Ivy. 'I mean the one that's been killing our people for years.' She turned to her sister. 'Haven't you ever wondered why our people age and die so quickly, when other magical folk live far longer? Why I was born without wings, and Mum started coughing up blood, and Dad got sicker every day he worked in the diggings?' In fact that might well have been the reason Flint had started working so hard once Marigold was gone – because he'd realised that the only way to prove the mine was dangerous was to poison himself. 'We can't keep living like this. We have to change our ways, or—'

'How dare you talk as though *you* know what's best for our people!' snapped Betony. 'You're as treacherous as your mother – and if you don't hold your tongue, I'll stop it for you.'

Ivy opened her mouth to retort – and then another realisation hit her. The reason for Marigold's abrupt silences and vague explanations, her refusal to return to the Delve. The way she'd choked and touched her throat whenever she said too much ...

'You made her swear not to tell anyone what you did to her,' she said to Betony, rasping with disbelief. 'You made her promise never to go near the Delve again.'

Colour rose to Betony's cheeks, but her haughty expression didn't alter. 'She agreed to those terms in exchange for her life. And it was a fairer bargain than she deserved.'

And once again, Ivy had misjudged her mother because of someone else's deceit. Rage welled inside her, and her fingers stiffened into claws – but no, she couldn't fly at Betony now, it would ruin everything. She had to think of Cicely and Mica, too.

'Well, you can threaten me all you like,' she said defiantly, 'but I'm not my mother, and you can't frighten me into making the bargain she did. I know this mine is poisoned – I'm living proof – and I'm going to stay here until you do something about it.'

The Joan stalked up to Ivy, robes billowing. 'You know *nothing*,' she spat. 'You were born wingless because your mother's blood was weak, and for no other reason. You crave sunlight because she did – but that has nothing to do with the rest of us. The only danger in the Delve was the enemy *you* brought here by your carelessness, and the only poison that has ever threatened us was the spell your father gave his life to destroy.'

'That's not true!' Ivy shouted at her. 'How can you be so blind? The piskeys of the Delve are your responsibility, and most of them have faery as well as piskey blood, just like

I do. They need you to give them their freedom, not sit there and watch them die so you can stay in power!'

Betony slapped her across the face.

Cicely shrank back, and Mica started halfway to his feet as Ivy and her aunt stared at each other, both of them breathing hard. Then with deadly softness the Joan spoke: 'For generations we piskeys have poured our lives into this mine. We have made it a place of beauty and strength, our people's greatest pride. It protected us from the spriggans while they lived, and since then it has hidden us from the Empress and her servants. It is safe, it is secure – and most of all, it is secret. That is how our people have survived so long.

'But when this faery, this stranger, appeared in our midst, you forgot all of that. You disobeyed my order to stay away from the prisoner, and allowed him to seduce you into setting him free. What did he offer you, to make you believe you could trust him? Did he tell you he would shower you with treasure, and make you his queen?'

A spasm of nausea gripped Ivy's throat. 'No. What makes you think I would want – *no*.'

'Then what?'

She couldn't lie, much as she wanted to. 'He said he would teach me to fly.'

Betony regarded her for a few seconds in astonishment, then threw back her head and laughed. 'And you believed him?'

But horror was dawning on Mica's face, and Ivy knew he'd finally put the pieces together: their conversation about shape-changing, the swift he'd marked out as an impostor and felled with one deadly stone, the way Ivy had vanished when he and Flint needed her most.

Don't say it, Ivy begged him silently. *If you ever loved me at all, don't tell her that I can change shape.*

For one last moment Mica held her gaze. Then abruptly he got up and walked to the far side of the cavern. He braced his hands against the wall and bent his head between them, and he did not look back.

'Your brother is ashamed of you,' said Betony. 'As he should be.' She raised her voice, pronouncing each word distinctly as she went on, 'You have admitted to consorting with a servant of the Empress, and releasing him against my orders. You left the Delve on several occasions without permission, and enticed an innocent child to follow your example. You revealed your piskey nature to a human girl – whom you then brought into the Delve. Any one of those crimes would be worthy of severe punishment, but all together, there can be no question that you deserve to die.'

Cicely whimpered. Mica turned, but he didn't speak. Ivy stood unmoving, staring straight ahead as the Joan continued:

'But you are my brother's daughter, and you and Mica and Cicely are the last of our family line. For the sake of Flint's memory, and because of what you did to destroy the faery Gillian and undo her spells, I will not have you executed. But it is clear you have little respect for my authority, and that if I allow you to remain you will spread sedition among my subjects. So…' She drew herself up. 'I banish you from the Delve, now and forever. Go where you wish and call yourself what you will, but you are no longer a piskey.'

'No!' cried Cicely, leaping off the sofa and throwing her arms around Ivy. 'You can't! She didn't mean me to follow her out of the Delve, she was trying to find our mother. And she saved your life – all our lives!'

'Cicely, get away from her,' said Mica, striding over. 'Don't be a little fool.'

'No!' Cicely shouted at him. 'You can stay here and poison yourself to death if you want, but I won't!' She turned pleading eyes up to Ivy. 'Take me away with you. Please. I want to see Mum again.'

Ivy looked at the Joan, whose face might have been chiselled out of granite. 'Let me take Cicely,' Ivy said, 'and I won't fight you. We'll leave the Delve together, and you can tell everyone we went to live with Marigold.'

'Very well,' said Betony. 'But you'll go at once, without speaking to anyone. And you'll take nothing with you.' She turned to Mica. 'If you wish to prove your loyalty, son of Flint, you'll see to that.' Then she stalked out the door and slammed it behind her, the day-lamps flickering in her wake.

Cicely hid her face against Ivy and burst into tears. Mica stood awkwardly for a moment, then put out a hand and patted his little sister's hair.

'You'll look out for them, won't you?' Ivy asked him. 'Mattock and Jenny and the others.' Even if he was too disgusted with Ivy to even look at her any more, even if he was determined to stay in the Delve at any cost, he must know that their mother hadn't been lying about the poison in the mine. He was the only one who could help the piskeys now.

But Mica didn't reply. He walked to the door and held it open. 'You'd better get moving,' he said gruffly. 'You've got a long way to go.'

epilogue

Sunlight warmed the treetops, and the sky was untroubled by cloud. Ivy glided over the countryside, swift-wings outstretched on the breeze. She and Cicely had been staying with Marigold for three days now, and though Ivy hadn't minded looking after her sister and showing her the sights of Truro, she'd been longing all the while to fly again.

She hadn't told either of them about her shape-changing. Male faeries might be accustomed to transforming themselves into birds or animals, but it seemed that females had a different approach to magic, and she feared that even Marigold wouldn't be comfortable with the revelation that her daughter could become a swift.

So what was Ivy now – a piskey, or a faery, or neither? Would she ever find a place where she belonged? Ivy didn't know, and it pained her. Especially since it had already become clear that a one-bedroom flat was too small for three, and that feeding two growing daughters was straining Marigold's resources to the limit.

But Ivy was still too young to live and work on her own, even if she'd felt confident enough posing as a human to try. And she couldn't ask Molly for help, not when she and her father were still grieving...

The shadow of a crow flashed over Ivy, and with a flick of her wingtips she increased speed, leaving the bigger bird behind. It offered no threat to her, but part of her would scarcely have minded if it had. At least that would have given her a challenge to surmount, an enemy that she could defeat. At least that might have made her feel not quite so useless.

Soon another bird rose up on her left side – only a small one, but Ivy had no desire for company. She angled away, catching an updraught so she could be alone again. But the newcomer followed, easily matching her speed. She was about to put the other bird in its place with an angry shriek, when it chirruped at her, rolled over and tagged her with one outstretched foot in a very un-birdlike way. Then it dived towards the riverbank, came to a fluttering stop – and transformed into a slim, angular faery with blond hair falling into his eyes.

Ivy's heart swelled with incredulous delight. So she and Molly had been right to use their blood on him, back in Gillian's workshop – though why it had worked, she couldn't imagine. She veered through the air and skimmed to land in front of him in her own shape. 'Richard! I thought you were trapped forever!'

'So did I, for a while,' he replied. 'But it appears that all the magic I put into healing you makes us kinfolk of a sort after all. There's a precedent, but I won't embarrass you with the details.' He gave his sly smile. 'So you got my message, then?'

'What? Oh.' He must mean the dream-message he'd sent her while he was trapped. She didn't have the heart to tell him how fragmented and misleading those words had been, or how little difference they had made in the end. 'Yes. I'm sorry it took us so long to set you free.'

'I didn't think anyone could.' He was serious now, his grey eyes sober as she had ever seen them. 'It appears that I owe you my life. Again.'

'I don't think so,' said Ivy, blushing a little. 'I never repaid you properly for saving me from Mica, and you only got trapped in the Claybane because you were trying to find Cicely for me. If anything I'm in your debt, not the other way around.'

'Tell me the rest of your story, then, and we'll call it even.' He motioned to the grassy bank beside him, inviting her to sit. 'I had part of it from Molly, but she told me you'd gone back to the Delve. What brings you here?'

She sat down cross-legged by the river's edge and told him everything, her restless fingers tearing up the long grass around her until her hands were sticky with its sap. She told

Richard how she'd defeated Gillian and rescued the piskeys she'd trapped, about going with her sister into exile, and all that had happened since.

'But I don't know what to do,' she finished. 'I can't keep living with my mum – there's not enough room, and Cicely needs her more than I do. And I can't return to the Delve, not while Betony's still in control.'

With an expert flick of the wrist Richard sent a stone skipping across the water; it bounced three times before it sank. 'Why not try the other half of your ancestry?' he said. 'There must be a wyld somewhere that would take you in, if you made yourself useful.'

Ivy had considered that idea, but the thought of walking into a group of strange faeries and asking to join them, especially now that she knew what her piskey ancestors had done to their kind, made her uneasy. 'If I did,' she asked, 'would you come with me?'

'Not an option.' He picked up another stone, turning it slowly in his fingers. 'You see, I'm a fugitive from justice at the moment.'

Ivy was startled. 'What for?'

'Murder. Or actually, two murders.' With another flick, the pebble became a silver dagger; he stabbed it point-down into the grass. 'Last April I killed the Empress and her would-be successor in front of about five hundred other faeries. And I've been running ever since.'

'*You* killed the Empress? But how? I mean – why?' No,

that wasn't the right question either; both those answers were obvious already. 'What happened?'

'Ask Marigold. She saw me do it. And she was glad.'

And were you? Ivy almost asked, but she knew the answer to that question as well. If he'd taken any pleasure in killing the Empress, it hadn't lasted long. *Is there a murderer here? No. I am...*

'Are you afraid of me?' asked Richard. He spoke lightly, as though he were indifferent to the answer. Only a slight twitch in his cheek said otherwise.

Ivy considered this. 'No.'

'You might want to think a little longer about that,' he said. 'The Claybane worked on me, remember...and whoever my parents were, I very much doubt that either one of them was a piskey. I'm no good with horses, but I admit to being quite interested in treasure, and I seem to have a way of influencing air currents, not to mention probabilities...'

That startled a laugh out of Ivy. 'You mean that after all this, you really *are* a spriggan?'

'Part spriggan, anyway. I don't see what else I could be.' He pulled the dagger out of the bank, flipped it back into a pebble, and let it drop. 'I always knew I wasn't quite like other faeries, but I never knew why. Now I wonder where I came from, and if there's anything – or anyone – left to go back to.'

'We could try and find out,' said Ivy.

Richard gave her a sidelong look. 'Are you offering to come with me?'

Ivy picked a few more blades of grass and let them flutter away on the wind. At last she said, 'I want to help my people. But I don't know how, not yet. I need to learn. I need to travel. I need to find something that will make Aunt Betony listen to me – or convince the others that they ought to listen even if she won't.' She turned back to him. 'So yes, I would like to come. If that's all right.'

One corner of his mouth turned up. 'If it's what you want, I know better than to try and stop you. But it won't be comfortable. Or safe. And I can't tell you where we'll be going.'

'That's all right. I don't have anywhere particular in mind.' She gave him a tentative smile and added, 'And you can teach me more about birds on the way.'

He rose slowly, dusting off his trousers, and looked down at her a moment. Then he said, 'We can start with the house martin. That's the bird I shape most often. And it's also my name. Martin.'

'Good,' said Ivy, taking the hand he offered and letting him pull her to her feet. 'Richard didn't really suit you, anyway.'

acknowledgements

Heartfelt thanks to my smart, insightful and always encouraging editor, Sarah Lilly, and the rest of the Orchard Books team; to my ever-supportive American agent Josh Adams and my savvy and hardworking UK agent Caroline Walsh; and to illustrator Rory Kurtz, who did such a wonderful job of bringing Ivy's character to life on the cover.

I'm also grateful to Fritha Lindqvist and Jessica Smith at Orchard for their hard work and delightful company on my UK tour in early 2011 – and to all the schoolchildren, teachers and librarians who showed such a keen interest in my books and made every school visit during the tour a pleasure.

Swift would not be what it is if not for the unfailing support, shrewd insights, and generous assistance of the following individuals, who gave me feedback on the early drafts: Peter Anderson, Erin Bow, Deva Fagan, Meg Burden, Brittany Harrison, Saundra Mitchell, Kate Johnson and Nick Jessee. I also greatly appreciated the help of Brittany Landgrebe, who suggested the title two years ago and started the whole process; Thu Ya Win, whose photos and insights about Truro were invaluable in helping me develop that section of the book; and of Michelle Minniss, who graciously read over the whole manuscript to make sure I'd got various Cornish details right.

And finally, thanks to all the enthusiastic fans, faithful readers and thoughtful reviewers who've e-mailed, tweeted and contacted me on Facebook to let me know they've enjoyed my other books and were looking forward to *Swift*. Here it is at last, and may you find it worth the wait!

Read on for a thrilling
extra short story by R J Anderson…

Renegade

He'd lost track of how long he'd been flying. One day blurring feverishly into another, hour after hour of hurtling through the air without direction or destination, a flash of black and white feathers by daylight and a whisper of barn owl wings in the dark. Collapsing at last into ermine-form when he was too exhausted to fly any more, then sleeping a few fitful minutes in some abandoned burrow before dread or hunger woke him and the cycle began again.

Were the Blackwings still hunting him, or had they given up? He didn't know, but he had no intention of staying still long enough to find out.

A few weeks ago he couldn't have dreamed of living like this. He'd been idle, cynical, indifferent to anything but his own amusement – goodness knew there'd been little enough of that in the life he'd been born to. A nameless orphan with no past, restless as a young bird, sure of nothing except that he wasn't human. He'd found his magic early and used it without mercy, like his fists and his teeth and his cunning, because it was the only way he could survive.

But then *she'd* found him, the faery Empress. His voice had hardly broken when she'd plucked him from his hardscrabble life on the streets and given him his first role, the jaded courtier with the quick knife and whiplash tongue, willing to scheme and betray and kill at her command. She'd told him, laughing, that he had no heart, and he hadn't denied it. Because there was no other way he knew how to live, and he had nowhere else to go.

He'd made mistakes at first, some merely humiliating and others near-fatal, but the Empress had been patient. Within two years she'd remade every part of him, turning him from a wild thing into a sleek and pampered pet, a dirty imp with a gutter mouth to a haughty young buck who talked like the Prince of Denmark…not that he'd known anything about Shakespeare at the time, ignorant fool that he was. He'd been nothing but a performing animal, a slave to the Empress's treats and threats, and he'd quickly learned that nothing displeased her more than to hear her subjects sounding too modern, too *human*…

A black shadow passed over him and his heart fluttered, fear's cold talons gripping him once more. He'd been a fool to think he could outfly the Empress's hunters, or throw them off his trail for long. They'd cut him off any second now, trapping him in the circle of their raven wings, binding him with spells too strong for even his unruly magic to break, and then they'd drag him back to *her*.

He'd never cared much for fighting, but that didn't mean he'd forgotten how to do it. With a shriek of defiance he wheeled in mid-air, ready to hurl himself into battle—

But it was only a crow, alone and indifferent to his challenge. With a mocking caw and a few lazy wingstrokes, it flapped away.

The relief was so great he couldn't even feel embarrassed. He flitted onto an updraught, soaring high above the treetops and the flight paths of his fellow birds, so he wouldn't be caught off-guard again. But his wing muscles trembled and his head felt light with hunger, and he knew that he'd nearly reached his limit. Soon his strength would give out altogether...and the higher he flew, the further he'd have to fall.

What madness had made him believe he could escape the Empress, that she would give in and let him go? He'd followed her direction so long, played so diligently the parts she'd written for him, that he'd made himself indispensable to her schemes. She had neither time nor inclination to replace him as her court spy and sometime assassin, and her pride was too great to accept that she'd been wrong to give him that role in the first place. He must come back to her, or die.

Perhaps it would have been better if he'd never walked into that little theatre in Cardiff, never seen that first motley performance of *Hamlet*. Never known that the words of some long-dead human playwright could speak to his heart more eloquently than the Empress ever had; never taken the Bard's lines into his own mouth and felt their weight, their grandeur, their fluid shape; never guessed that he could find greater pleasure sharing in the humans' gift of theatre than he ever had in merely exploiting it.

He'd thought the humans could teach him to lie rather than merely rearranging the truth; he'd thought they could show him how to become a different person. Instead, they'd taught him the only truths he'd ever found worth having, and on their stage he'd learned, for the first time, what it meant to be himself.

But there was a cost for that self-knowledge, a higher price than he'd ever expected to pay. Because when he returned to the Empress, he'd found that nothing she said to him, nothing she offered him, seemed to matter any more. She could force his obedience, but his heart and soul were no longer hers to command.

'*I want you to infiltrate the rebels,*' the Empress had told him with cold decisiveness, a few days or a lifetime ago. '*I want you to find my wayward heir, win his trust…and kill him.*'

He'd almost done it. He'd come so close, out of habit if nothing else. But the moment he was out of her presence his mind had begun working in other directions. So many of the Empress's servants had turned against her already, including her own adopted son – would it really trouble her to lose one slave more?

The answer, as he'd learned all too quickly, was yes.

He was so tired now, he could barely flap his wings. His stomach gnawed itself with hunger, but the insects that sustained his bird-body were too scarce at this altitude for him to make a proper meal of them, even if he'd had the energy to chase them down. He had to descend, even at the risk of being spotted. He needed to slow down, take a few hours to rest and recover in his own rightful shape.

But where could he go? The hillsides and scattered woods below him were unfamiliar, and he could see no place where a fugitive might be safe. Especially not with the Empress's most skilled and ruthless hunters on his trail...

'*You are mine now*,' her voice whispered in his memory. '*By blood and bond, by debt and until death. Do you understand?*'

'No,' he gasped, but it came out as a high-pitched twitter, an alarm cry that only his fellow house martins would understand. His wingbeats faltered, his body went slack, and before he could recover he slipped off the updraught, tumbling into the wild air currents below. He fought for control, but his head reeled and he could no longer tell up from down. He was twisting, spiralling, plummeting through the sky, the earth rushing up towards him—

With the last of his strength he pulled himself out of the dive a few feet above ground-level, but he no longer had the power to hold any shape but his own. He was a dead weight, a flopping scarecrow of limbs and sinews, pale hair blinding his eyes as he collapsed onto the turf, rolled over a few times, and lay still.

It was the end: he had no doubt of that now. He would lie here, too weak to even get up, until they found him…if his ravaged body even lasted that long. He had ignored all the rules and all the warnings in his desperation, pushed his magical strength far beyond its natural bounds, and now there was nothing left to do but pay the price…

He heard a low thudding and the ground beneath him vibrated, rocks and dirt shivering against his spine. A rippling footfall, four-legged – hounds? No, it was far too heavy for that. Too drained to lift his head, he squinted down the length of his body and made out the blurred shape of a horse cantering towards him, with a small person on its back.

'Are you all right?' asked a breathless girl's voice, as she reined in her mount and leaped out of the saddle to land beside him. A round, sun-freckled face, a pert nose and wide brown eyes – she couldn't have been more than twelve, or more ridiculously human. 'Is anything broken?'

'M'fine,' he managed to mumble, though his lips were cracked with dehydration and his voice was barely more than a croak. 'Just resting.'

'I don't think so.' She gave a little laugh, half nerves and half delight. 'I saw you fall out of the sky just now. You were a bird, and then…' She caught her breath. 'You're a faery, aren't you? Don't deny it, I know you are.'

He couldn't bear this. If she was still here when the Blackwings came, it would be a disaster. They'd never let her go with her memories intact – she'd be lucky to escape with her life. 'Go 'way,' he gasped. 'Leave me 'lone.'

'Not likely,' said the girl. 'I've been wanting to meet a faery my whole life. You need help, and I'm going to give it to you.' She leaped up and seized the horse's reins, pulling the animal closer. 'Let's get you onto Dodger, and I'll take you somewhere you can rest.'

'Little fool,' he moaned. 'Don't...' But she'd already slid her arm behind his back, heaving him upright with a strength that surprised him. He'd always been lean and not over-tall, but had he really lost *that* much weight?

'Stop arguing,' she told him sternly, half-carrying and half-dragging him over the grass to the horse. It snorted disapproval and danced sideways, but she spoke a sharp 'Dodger!' and it lowered its head, meek again.

He had a vague thought of trying to change shape one last time, if only to get away. But when the girl grabbed his left foot and shoved it into the stirrup, he couldn't find the will to resist her. A mortifying few seconds followed as he tried and mostly failed to pull himself into the saddle, and she ended up behind him shoving mightily with both hands – but at last she'd draped him across the horse's back to her satisfaction, and the three of them set off.

'My mum'd have a fit if she found out about this,' said the girl cheerfully. 'Especially if she knew I thought you were a faery. So I'm going to put you in the barn with Dodger and Duchess – is that all right?'

He was too dazed to answer. Part of him was convinced that both the girl and the horse were nothing more than a dying hallucination, or some cruel trick of the Empress's. That he should be found, so quickly, by a human he'd never met before but who knew at a glance what he was – and more, that she'd be both willing and able to help him – was a piece of good luck too extraordinary for even his powers to orchestrate.

Though that assumed that it really *was* good luck, which was by no means certain yet…

He spent the next few minutes drifting in and out of consciousness, his body limp and his chin bumping the horse's side. Then the thud of hooves on grass became the clop of hooves on cobbles, and he heard the thin creak of a door opening. The barn? He lifted his head weakly to see what lay ahead, but all he glimpsed was a hazy shimmering.

For a horrible moment he thought he'd gone blind. But he could still see the girl clearly enough, even as she led him forward into the fog. Then he felt reality shift and ripple around him, and realised they'd just crossed the boundary of some kind of protective spell. Magic, in a human place? He made a feeble noise of shock, but the sound had scarcely left his lips when his vision cleared and the world solidified again. The air stilled, the sunlight faded, and a soothing coolness surrounded him as they entered the barn.

'Here we are,' said the girl, pulling the horse to a stop. She fastened the reins to a post, then came around to tug him out of the saddle. 'Just a few steps, and then you can rest.'

Did she know about the spell they'd just crossed? She couldn't have put it there herself, surely; he couldn't sense any magic in her at all. 'Ward on the door,' he mumbled. 'Protection. Who…?'

'Shush now,' the girl told him, slinging his arm around her shoulders. 'I've got you.' His legs buckled as his feet touched the floor and he felt her stagger under his weight, but she hung onto him gamely until they reached the end of the corridor. 'There's a bit of straw here,' she said as she lowered him down. 'I can get more, and some old blankets to make it more comfortable. Are you hungry? What can you eat?'

'Anything,' he gasped as he sagged against the wall. 'Everything. Just – not insects. Or mice.'

That made her giggle, though she clapped a hand to her mouth to hide it. 'OK then,' she said. 'I'll be right back.'

'Wait,' he called after her. 'Who are you? How did—?'

But she was already gone.

Left alone in the gentle darkness, he let out a long breath and allowed himself, finally, to relax. He still didn't understand how the girl had recognised him as a faery, or what had inspired her to bring him here. He doubted she even realised what a perfect refuge she'd found for him. But he could sense the ancient charm against magical intrusion that surrounded the place, even if he didn't know who had put it there, and knew that for the moment at least, he was safe.

He fell back onto his bed of straw, and in minutes was deeply and dreamlessly asleep.

no rainbows.
no pink.
no sparkles.
no ordinary fairytale.

978 1 408 30212 2 PB £5.99
978 1 408 31234 6 eBook

978 1 408 30737 3 PB £5.99
978 1 408 31264 3 eBook

978 1 408 31262 9 PB £5.99 JAN 2011
978 1 408 31370 1 eBook

R J A N D E R S O N

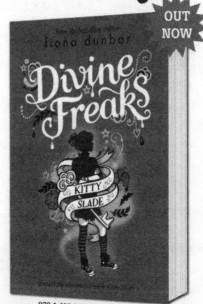